PRAISE FOR THE
***NEW YORK TIMES* BESTSELLING**
FLOWER SHOP MYSTERIES

A Root Awakening

"Kate Collins never fails to deliver a spectacular story. Abby and Marco embark on a house hunt filled with surprises and intrigue. . . . Another triumph in the well-loved Flower Shop Mystery series."

—Lorna Barrett, *New York Times* bestselling author of *Book Clubbed: A Booktown Mystery*

Throw in the Trowel

"Where most series can run out of steam around book ten, Kate Collins manages to keep each of Abby's adventures fresh and exciting, even at number fifteen. The mystery is well plotted, the characters well fleshed-out, and Abby and Marco fans will not be disappointed!" —Night Owl Reviews

"The Flower Shop Mystery series stays fresh and keeps getting better. Collins has created a small-town community that readers feel part of. The mystery in this installment keeps readers guessing all the way until the twisted end." —*RT Book Reviews*

Seed No Evil

"A great mystery. . . . Abby is one of my favorite protagonists."
—Fresh Fiction

"Kate Collins has played a major role in shaping the offshoot of the 'cozy' mystery into a growing entity of its own, the romantic mystery. I, for one, am grateful." —Once Upon a Romance

Nightshade on Elm Street

"Abby's warm and caring relationships, especially with Marco, will draw readers back as this cozy series continues to grow."
—*Publishers Weekly*

"The investigation contains entertaining red herrings and twists . . . a fun, lighthearted whodunit." —Genre Go Round Reviews

"A delightful installment. . . . I can't wait to see what awaits Abby and Marco in marriage." —Fresh Fiction

continued . . .

To Catch a Leaf

"There are twists and surprises along with the comfort of the characters we have all grown to love. . . . This story is a must read!"
—Escape with Dollycas into a Good Book

"Ms. Collins has a devious and creative mind when it comes to each new Flower Shop Mystery. Her plots are ingenious [and] Abby and Marco's chemistry is alluring." —Once Upon a Romance

Night of the Living Dandelion

"Great plotting and interesting secondary characters add depth and humor. . . . Abby and Marco's relationship strengthens and sizzles." —*RT Book Reviews*

"A heartwarming cozy. . . . Fans of the series will feel mesmerized by the plot." —Genre Go Round Reviews

Dirty Rotten Tendrils

"Each book in this series contains murder, continuous mayhem, a bit of sizzle, and one justice-seeking amateur sleuth."
—Once Upon a Romance

"Abby is an excellent heroine who finds herself in some of the most unlikely, entertaining situations." —The Mystery Reader

Sleeping with Anemone

"A nimble, well-crafted plot with forget-me-not characters."
—Laura Childs, *New York Times* bestselling author of the Tea Shop Mysteries

"A clever, fast-moving plot and distinctive characters add up to fun."
—JoAnna Carl, national bestselling author of the Chocoholic Mysteries

Evil in Carnations

"The fun, family, and romance are still fresh, and the mystery is tidily wrapped up, with just enough suspense to keep readers flipping pages." —*RT Book Reviews*

"Ms. Collins's writing remains above par with quality and consistency: fun and breezy, intriguing and suspenseful, excitement and sizzle." —Once Upon a Romance

Shoots to Kill

"Colorful characters, a sharp and funny heroine, and a sexy hunk boyfriend."

—Maggie Sefton, national bestselling author of the Knitting Mysteries

"Once again Kate Collins delivers an entertaining, amusing, and deliciously suspenseful mystery."

—Cleo Coyle, *New York Times* bestselling author of the Coffeehouse Mysteries

A Rose from the Dead

"The latest Flower Shop Mystery is an amusing graveyard amateur sleuth that will have the audience laughing." —The Best Reviews

Acts of Violets

"A delightful, lighthearted cozy." —The Best Reviews

Snipped in the Bud

"Lighthearted and fast-paced, Collins's new book is an entertaining read." —*RT Book Reviews*

Dearly Depotted

"Ms. Collins's writing style is crisp, her characters fun . . . and her stories are well thought-out and engaging." —Fresh Fiction

Slay It with Flowers

"You can't help but laugh . . . an enormously entertaining read."

—*Rendezvous*

Mum's the Word

"Abby Knight [is] rash, brash, and audacious. Move over, Stephanie Plum. Abby Knight has come to town."

—Denise Swanson, *New York Times* bestselling author of the Scumble River Mysteries

"A bountiful bouquet of clues, colorful characters, and tantalizing twists. . . . Kate Collins carefully cultivates clues, plants surprising suspects, and harvests a killer in this fresh and frolicsome new Flower Shop Mystery series."

—Ellen Byerrum, author of the Crime of Fashion Mysteries

"As fresh as a daisy, with a bouquet of irresistible characters."

—Elaine Viets, author of the Dead-End Job Mysteries

Other Flower Shop Mysteries

Mum's the Word

Slay It with Flowers

Dearly Depotted

Snipped in the Bud

Acts of Violets

A Rose from the Dead

Shoots to Kill

Evil in Carnations

Sleeping with Anemone

Dirty Rotten Tendrils

Night of the Living Dandelion

To Catch a Leaf

Nightshade on Elm Street

Seed No Evil

Throw in the Trowel

A Root Awakening

A Flower Shop Mystery

Kate Collins

OBSIDIAN
Published by the Penguin Group
Penguin Group (USA) LLC, 375 Hudson Street,
New York, New York 10014

USA | Canada | UK | Ireland | Australia | New Zealand | India | South Africa | China
penguin.com
A Penguin Random House Company

First published by Obsidian, an imprint of New American Library,
a division of Penguin Group (USA) LLC

First Printing, February 2015

ISBN 978-0-451-41551-6

Printed in the United States of America
10 9 8 7 6 5 4 3 2 1

PUBLISHER'S NOTE
This is a work of fiction. Names, characters, places, and incidents either are the product of the author's imagination or are used fictitiously, and any resemblance to actual persons, living or dead, business establishments, events, or locales is entirely coincidental.

Let us be grateful to people who make us happy; they are the charming gardeners who make our souls blossom.

—Marcel Proust

To Jason and Julie. You not only make me happy—
you make me proud.

To my beloved Jim. Our souls will be forever entwined.

Acknowledgments

"Help me, Cassius, or I sink!"

—William Shakespeare, *Julius Caesar,*
Act 1, Scene 2

What author hasn't felt her boat sinking at some point in the writing process? I am so grateful to the following people for keeping me afloat, no matter how rough the sea:

My editor, Ellen Edwards, who has guided me through sixteen books and counting, helping me make my mysteries gel and my words sparkle.

My son, Jason Eberhardt, for his fantastic plotting ability, editorial eye, and promotional skills.

My agent, Karen Solem, for her continuous support and guidance.

My beloved daughter, Julie; my family; my dear friend Barb Ferrari; and my Cozy Chick Mystery Author buddies: Ellery Adams, Deb Baker, Lorraine Bartlett, Leann Sweeney, Mary Kennedy, M. J. Maffini, and Maggie Sefton.

Chapter One

Monday

"Are my newlyweds ready to go inside for a look?" Our Realtor pressed her hands together as though praying, her smile as desperate as her enthusiastic nods, as if to say, *Of course you're ready! At that price, you'd be fools not to be. Please, please, please?*

I glanced at Marco, who was studying the dilapidated Victorian home with a shrewd and, yes, disdainful eye. Good. We were on the same page.

"No," I said, just as Marco said, "Sure."

I turned to my handsome hubby in surprise. *"Sure?"*

"No harm in looking."

"I am looking, Marco. The question is, what are you seeing?"

It was peculiar for us to be at odds because our tastes ran in remarkably similar veins. Hand us a menu and we'd pick the same entrée every time. But clearly he wasn't seeing what I was seeing today, because directly in front of us stood a narrow, wood-sided two-story with peeling paint, a porch that tilted dangerously to the right, a sharply peaked roof whose tiles had curled, dingy gray gingerbread trim, and a detached shed-turned-garage that might have held a Volkswagen Beetle—with no door handles.

The old house, built sometime in the early 1900s, swarmed with roofers and painters who'd been hired to get it ready to be put on the market. Lorelei Hays, our overly eager Realtor, had heard that the Victorian was going up for sale and wanted us to see it before the crowds beat a path to the warped brown door. As far as I was concerned, a path would have been an improvement over the cracked cement sidewalk on which we stood.

I loosened the emerald-and-navy-plaid scarf around my neck and took off my green gloves. The March sun was making a rare appearance in a week that had been rainy and cold. My little dog, Seedy, kept tugging at her leash, so I turned to see what she wanted and saw her wagging her shaggy tail, gazing up toward the roof where a painter was giving the decorative trim along the roofline above an attic window a coat of white paint. I doubted it was the worker who'd intrigued her. Seedy was a rescue dog who'd had an abusive owner, and she was still wary around most men. But I didn't see anything else that could have attracted her attention.

Studying the Victorian's shabby facade, I could only imagine what the inside was like. No, I didn't want to imagine it, because I was definitely not interested. The only positives were that it would be available in a month and it was located five blocks off the town square in my hometown of New Chapel, Indiana. And because my flower shop, Bloomers, and Marco's business, Down the

Hatch Bar and Grill, were located on the square, we could have walked to work.

Lorelei bounced on the toes of her black patent pumps. "So? Are we ready to see the interior?" She was wearing a marine blue two-piece suit trimmed in black braid, with shiny black button earrings and a black tote bag, all nicely accenting her short platinum hair.

Marco had wanted to go with a well-seasoned Realtor, but I had opted to give a newbie our business because it hadn't been that long since I'd opened Bloomers and I remembered how it felt to be the new kid on the block. In her late forties and just starting out in real estate, Lorelei fit the bill. But so far, she hadn't shown us a single house we'd liked, and we'd been looking since October.

Our landlady had been patient thus far—she didn't normally allow pets—but she'd been dropping enough hints lately that we knew we had to find something soon.

Marco was still analyzing as the roofers nimbly navigated the steep pitch. Two painters in blue coveralls stood on scaffolding on the right side of the house applying tan paint to the second story, while the third painter, the apparent object of Seedy's attention, balanced at the top of a tall extension ladder. All of the workmen wore navy baseball caps and light blue coveralls with the logo HHI—Handy Home Improvements—on them.

"Judging by the condition of the outside," I said to Marco, "this house is going to need a lot of time and money pumped into it."

"You look like do-it-yourselfers," Lorelei said. "It could be the perfect little project for you to work on together, a real bonding experience."

Or grounds for divorce.

Deep in contemplation, Marco rubbed his jaw. "I can see us working on it."

"Clearly, Marco, you've forgotten about our experience painting the bathroom at Down the Hatch over Christmas."

"That wasn't so bad," he said.

"For you."

"Sunshine, you're the one who wanted to put seven coats of paint on it."

"One application of sugar maple does not cover glossy navy blue, Marco. I can still see blue showing through—and that was three coats, by the way, not seven."

He put his arm around me. "I think the bathroom looks great. Come on, sweetheart. We should at least have a look at the inside."

I moved us off the walkway. "Between your long hours at the bar and your private investigations, when would we have time?"

"You've been looking for something to do in the evenings," he said.

"Not renovating a home—alone!"

"You wouldn't have to do it alone. I'd be there as much as possible, and I'll bet your niece and your cousin would love to lend a hand."

That, in itself, was reason to say no. Tara, my fourteen-year-old niece, would need to take a Twitter break every five minutes, while my cousin, Jillian—a spoiled pregnant diva precariously near her due date—wouldn't even paint her own fingernails, let alone someone else's walls. Besides, between running her personal shopping service and doing dry runs to the hospital, she was too busy.

"Just take one walk-through," the Realtor urged. "If you don't like its charming layout or don't see any potential, we'll cross it off your list."

We had a list? "Sorry," I said to both of them. "I really don't like it."

A cry from the roof made me turn in alarm just in time to see the extension ladder fall in an arc away from the house, the painter still clinging to the rungs. Everyone, including me, stood frozen in horror as the ladder carried the painter backward until the poor man hit the ground with a loud *thunk*, his head smacking the cement sidewalk with an audible crack. Then he lay still, the aluminum ladder on top of him.

As though someone had pressed a button, all of us sprang into action. I scooped up Seedy and ran toward the man along with Marco and Lorelei, while workmen scrambled to get to the ground. Marco was on the phone calling for an ambulance before we'd even reached the man's side.

The Realtor lifted the ladder aside as I put Seedy down and crouched beside the painter, whose coveralls read *Sergio* on the pocket. "Sergio," I called, feeling for a pulse in his neck. "Can you hear me? Can you squeeze my hand?"

His eyes were closed and he made no response, but his pulse beat steadily beneath my fingertips.

Another man in coveralls, the name *Sam* on his pocket, dropped to his knees on the other side, grabbed Sergio's face, and gave it a shake. "Sergio, buddy. Talk to me."

"Don't shake him," Marco commanded, putting away his phone. "His neck could be broken. Step back and wait for the paramedics."

The other painters joined us and within minutes the roofers were there, too, all standing in a semicircle around their fallen coworker. In the distance I heard a siren, and then another, and a minute later a squad car roared to a stop and two cops jumped out and jogged over. One of them was Marco's buddy Sergeant Sean Reilly, whom Marco had trained under during his stint on the New Chapel police force.

"What do we have?" Reilly asked Marco as he knelt beside the man.

"He's a painter." Marco turned toward the house and pointed. "When we got here, he was at the top of the ladder painting above that attic window. I heard someone cry out and looked around to see him falling backward."

Neighbors began to emerge from their houses. Then an emergency van pulled up and the two-man crew hopped out and sprinted toward us. While they began their examination of Sergio, I turned to see why Seedy was tugging on her leash and saw a short, stout woman and two children coming down the steps of the Victorian. They stopped a short distance away to watch the proceedings. I checked my watch. It was noon. What were the kids doing home from school?

The woman wore a thick brown cardigan over a white blouse and jeans, and white athletic shoes. Her long dark-brown hair hung flat against the sides of her head. She had small brown eyes and a wide nose set in a round face devoid of makeup. She was holding her children's hands as though she was afraid some danger might befall them. They must be the current occupants of this house, I thought.

The boy, who appeared to be around ten years old, had jet-black hair with a heart-shaped face and vivid blue eyes. He was wearing a quilted navy jacket, jeans, and black sneakers. The girl, whom I pegged at six years old, had wide cheekbones in a tiny face and long black hair. She wore a deep purple hooded jacket and black corduroy pants with purple-and-white sneakers. Oddly, neither child seemed interested in the accident. Instead, the boy was watching my dog, while the girl seemed more interested in me.

I was accustomed to people staring at Seedy, one of the homeliest dogs I'd ever seen. Her big pointed ears had tufts of hair on the ends, her lower teeth protruded, her muzzle was grizzly, the ridges of her spine showed, her brown, black, and tan fur was uneven, her tail was bushy, and she was missing a hind leg. But the first time I'd gazed into her loving brown eyes, I'd been captivated.

Considered unadoptable, Seedy had been at the top of the list to be euthanized when I'd found her at the animal shelter. I'd worked hard to find her a home, thinking that Marco wouldn't want to start married life with a new pet, not to mention that his landlady didn't allow them, but to no avail. In the nick of time, my intended had swept in and rescued her. Taking her had been the second best decision we'd ever made. The first, naturally, had been to marry each other.

I wasn't used to people staring at *me*, however. Maybe it was my bright red hair that drew the girl's attention.

Seedy wagged her tail and gave a little yip, tugging as

though she wanted to go see the children, so I walked her over to where they stood.

"Hi," I said, and received shy smiles from the children. Their mother was watching the paramedics work, a look of alarm on her face, so I said, "Do you know what happened?"

She shook her head. "I was in the kitchen." Her voice was like soft cotton.

"One of your painters fell from way high up."

"Is he dead?" she asked.

"He's unconscious. I can't tell how serious his condition is." I stuck out my hand. "I'm Abby Knight . . . Salvare. I own Bloomers Flower Shop."

She let go of the girl's hand to shake mine. "Sandra Jones." She put her hand on top of the boy's head. "This is Bud"—she put her other hand on the girl's head—"and this is Daisy. What do we say to Miss Abby, children?"

"Hello, Miss Abby," they replied in unison.

"Your dog has three legs," Daisy said. She pointed toward Seedy, but her vivid green eyes were still on me.

"Yes, she does, but she doesn't let that stop her," I said.

Daisy reached out to let Seedy sniff her hand, but her mother pulled her back. "You don't want to get bit, honey. Remember our rule? We never pet a strange dog."

The girl gazed at the dog with such longing that I crouched down to show her how friendly Seedy was. "My dog's name is Seedy. She likes children. She won't bite."

"Unfortunately, Daisy is allergic to dogs," Sandra said.

The child gave her mother a puzzled glance, as though that was the first time she'd heard that information.

The boy stepped forward. "I'm not allergic," he said almost defiantly, and crouched down beside me to run his hand along Seedy's back. "She has really sharp bones."

"She's a rescue dog," I said. "She was badly abused. But now she has a good home and gets lots of food and attention; don't you, Seedy?"

Seedy yipped and wagged her tail. She gave the boy's hand a lick, making him laugh.

"I had a dog," Daisy said.

"When?" Bud asked with a scoff.

She thought for a moment, then said to her mother, "I had one, didn't I?"

"Didn't I what?" Sandra asked in a schoolteacher's voice.

"Didn't I, Mommy?"

"Of course you did, honey," Sandra said, giving her an affectionate smile. She whispered to me, "Imaginary playmates."

"They're home from school early today," I said.

"They're homeschooled," Sandra said with a mixture of pride and exhaustion. "Bud, Daisy, our gingerbread cookies should be about done. We'd better go back inside and make sure they don't burn."

The boy rose with obvious reluctance.

"Say good-bye," I said to Seedy, who obliged by giving two yips and wagging her tail as the children reluctantly took their mother's hands.

"Bye, Seedy," Bud said sadly.

I heard a car door slam and turned to see a large,

balding man with a bad comb-over, wearing an XXXL shirt and battered blue jeans, climb out of a faded blue Chevy van. He paused to look at the emergency situation unfolding just yards away and then continued in our direction.

Seedy glanced around, saw the man coming, and dropped low to the ground with a whimper, her little body beginning to tremble. I scooped her up and held her close, murmuring assurances as he got closer.

"What happened?" the man asked Sandra.

"One of the painters fell," she said. "Norm, this is Abby Knight Salvare. She was here to see the house when the accident happened. Abby, this is my husband, Norm."

"We're baking gingerbread cookies, Daddy," Bud said as I shook Norm's hand.

"We were just saying good-bye to Miss Abby so we could go check on them; weren't we, children?" Sandra asked.

"I'll be in as soon as I see what the situation is," Norm said, ruffling Bud's hair. "Save me a cookie."

Norm strode toward several of the workers while Sandra hustled the kids to the front door. Daisy kept glancing back at me and paused at the door to give me a look that I didn't know how to translate, except to say that it felt as though she recognized me from somewhere.

I put Seedy down and walked toward Marco, still pondering the girl's puzzling glance. My internal radar was clanging a very distant warning, and I didn't know why.

Lorelei stood beside her black Camry talking on her cell phone, while the paramedics loaded the painter onto the stretcher and the remaining two painters carried the aluminum ladder to their van. I went to where Marco and Reilly stood, then turned to watch as Norm talked to the roofers, who were heading back to their jobs. One pointed to the peak of the roof and gestured, obviously describing the accident. I expected Norm to come talk to the cops next, but instead he went inside his house.

"Any news on the painter's condition?" I asked the men.

"He's still unconscious," Reilly said, hooking his thumbs through his thick leather belt. "His blood pressure is very low but his other vital signs are holding steady. The EMTs didn't know any more than that."

"Does anyone know why he fell?" I asked.

"One of the roofers said he's had some health problems and thought he might have suffered a heart attack," Marco said.

Seedy was tugging again, this time in the direction of a small white-and-red tube lying on the ground where the man had lain. Curious, I handed Seedy's leash to Marco and went over to investigate.

"What did you find?" Reilly asked.

"This," I said, and handed him a white Magic Marker with a red cap.

As Reilly examined it, Seedy barked and wagged her tail as though she wanted him to toss it for a game of catch. "Sorry, girl," Marco said. "Not this time."

"It must have fallen out of the painter's pocket when he fell," Reilly said. "I'll pass it along to the detectives. In the meantime, I'm going to start taking statements from everyone here, but if you need to get going, I can stop by the bar and take yours later. You don't need to stick around."

"Make sure you talk to the people in the house, Sarge," I said.

With just a hint of bemusement, Reilly said, "Anything else I should do, Captain?"

"No, seriously, Reilly," I said. "Just see if you sense anything off."

"Like what?" he asked.

"I'm not sure. There was something about the way their little girl looked at me."

"I can't question them about a look, Abby," Reilly said.

"Let's go, Sunshine," Marco said, leading me away. "See you this evening, Sean."

"I just want Reilly to be observant, Marco," I said as we walked toward his car.

"I'm sure he will."

But I wasn't. While I liked Reilly and knew him to be an honest cop with a big heart, I'd had enough dealings with him over the years to know he was a by-the-rules kind of guy. Until I could put my finger on what was bothering me, he wasn't going to pry.

"You're leaving, then?" our Realtor asked, hurrying over. "Without seeing the inside?"

"We've ruled this one out," Marco said. "Right, Abby?"

I turned to stare at the front of the Victorian, my internal radar still buzzing.

"Abby?" Marco prompted.

"On second thought," I said to Lorelei, "I'd like to see the inside after all."

Chapter Two

While Lorelei was on the porch talking with Mr. Jones, Marco studied me. "What made you change your mind?"

"It's a female's prerogative," I said, giving him my sweetest smile.

"Abby, I know you too well. You've got your snoop face on."

That was flattering.

Lorelei came toward us and she wasn't smiling. "I'm afraid we won't be able to see the house today. It's a bad time for them. We'll have to come back. What does your schedule for tomorrow look like?"

"Let's go home and think about this house some more, Abby," Marco suggested. "We'll let you know what we decide, Lorelei."

"No sense putting off the decision, Marco. We need to find a new place soon." I turned to Lorelei. "Say around eight o'clock tomorrow morning?"

Lorelei left with a smile on her face. Not so my disgruntled hubby, who scowled but didn't speak on the drive back to the flower shop. So I kept busy by pointing out various landmarks to Seedy, who lapped up every word as though she understood.

"And here comes the town square, Seedy. See the big limestone courthouse in the middle? It was built way back in the early nineteen hundreds. There's Daddy's bar across the street, and here comes Bloomers. See that bright yellow door? I chose that color because it's my favorite. And the red-and-white-striped awning? That was Lottie's idea."

"Dogs can't see red, Abby."

How about that? Silent Salvare finally spoketh. "It's not like she knows what I'm talking about anyway, Marco. Are you annoyed that I set up that appointment?"

"Not if you actually want to see the house." He cast me a skeptical glance. "Do you?"

I debated my answer. If I said yes, I'd be lying. If I said no, he'd be even more annoyed. Talk about a rock and a hard place.

When in doubt, punt. "Look, Seedy. Here's Bloomers. And there's Lottie making a new display for the bay window."

"That's what I thought," Marco said.

"You don't have to go tomorrow, Marco. I can look without you."

He glanced at me with raised brows, as though to ask, *Are you sure?*

"It's just that if you're with me, you won't have to worry about me getting myself into trouble."

This time Marco lifted one eyebrow as he glanced my way. His message was clear: *You're going to snoop, aren't you?* He might have been a man of few words, but his facial expressions could fill a tome.

"So," I said, running my fingers through Seedy's fur. "Coming with me?"

He sighed. "Do I have a choice?"

I leaned across the console and kissed him. "You made your choice when you said, 'I do.' "

Seedy yipped once and put her little paw on the window, eager to escape the car and return to her haven in my workroom.

"Are we meeting at the bar for supper?" I asked.

"Looks like it. Rafe is off tonight so I need to be there all evening."

Oh, joy. Another evening alone.

From the time Marco had bought Down the Hatch nearly two years before, he'd spent almost every evening there, so our habit was to meet for supper before I headed home for the evening. But since bringing his younger brother Rafe onto his staff, Marco had been able to cut down on his hours, giving us two nights a week and one weekend a month together, along with our usual Sundays off. However, because his private investigating business had been growing, I found myself home alone more than I liked, even when I worked the more interesting cases with him. Thank goodness for Seedy.

"Then I'll see you after five." I slid out of the car and put Seedy down on the sidewalk. I watched her hobble toward the bright yellow frame door; then I stood for a moment gazing at the three-story redbrick building that housed Bloomers.

The shop occupied the first floor, with the display room up front, a coffee and tea parlor off to one side, the workroom in the middle, and a small bathroom and kitchen across the back. A heavy fireproof door opened onto the alley and a steep staircase near the back door led to the basement. We kept larger supplies and huge flowerpots down there, along with pieces of my mom's art that we were too embarrassed to display in the shop. I tried not to go to the basement very often. It was a scary place.

I opened the door and let Seedy go in ahead of me. No matter how many times I entered, I always got a thrill from knowing Bloomers was mine. Well, okay, the bank's until the mortgage was paid off—like that was ever going to happen. Yet it was my name on the sign above the door, and I still puffed up with pride when I saw it. Little ol' me, the law school flunk-out, had her very own business.

I took a moment to gaze around the interior, inhaling the sweetly perfumed air. The flower shop had an old-world charm, with original wood floors, a high tin ceiling, and brick walls that dated back to the early 1900s. I'd worked hard to keep the same feel with the decor, using a heavy round oak table with claw feet in the center of the room to display silk arrangements, an open antique armoire, a wicker settee in the back corner shaded by a leafy ficus tree, and an oak sideboard.

There were also large potted plants on the floor around the perimeter of the room, wreaths, sconces, and decorative mirrors on the walls, silk floral arrangements in the big bay window, and assorted gift items on shelves. The only modern touches were a glass-fronted cooler on the back wall and the cash counter to the left of the door.

Through the wide doorway on the right I could see women seated at three of the white wrought-iron ice cream tables in the parlor. I'd emptied a storage room and added the parlor as a way to draw in more customers, and it had worked better than I'd ever expected. Most of its success I attributed to the woman who ran it for me, Grace Bingham, who not only brewed the best tea and gourmet coffee in town, but also baked scones every morning to sell in the shop. The flavor of the day depended on what was in season. Today it was apple.

"Hey, sweetie," my other assistant, Lottie Dombowski, said as she stepped down from the bay window. "How'd the house hunt go? See something worth a second look?"

More like some*one* worth a second look. "The outside of the house was in deplorable condition," I said, but before I could tell her the rest of the story, she put her arm around my shoulders and gave me a motherly squeeze.

"You'll find something. Don't give up the dream. The perfect house will come along when the time is right."

After months of hearing about one futile house hunt after another, Lottie should have been as disillusioned as I was. But not her. She was a fighter. As the mother of eighteen-year-old quadruplet sons, she had to be.

Born in Kentucky, the large-boned, forty-seven-year-old had brassy curls à la Shirley Temple and wore pink barrettes to keep the hair off her face. In fact, she wore pink everything except jeans, which were white. I couldn't actually have vouched for her underwear, but she swore it was also pink, and if I didn't believe her, I could ask her beloved hubby Herman.

Lottie had once owned Bloomers, but Herman had suffered such serious heart problems that the resulting surgeries and insurance expenses had nearly bankrupted them, forcing her to sell the shop. At the same time, I had been experiencing my own kind of failure. I'd been booted out of law school after my first year and subsequently dumped by my then fiancé, Pryce Osborne II. His parents, part of New Chapel's elite, hadn't wanted Pryces II through X to bear the stigma of my humiliation.

Down at heart and desperate for a job, I'd returned to the little shop where I'd worked summers during college, a haven that had called to me even back then. When I learned of Lottie's situation, I took the rest of the college money my grandfather had left me, dashed it over to the bank, signed my life away, and hired Lottie back to train me.

Grace Bingham glided out of the parlor to join us and said to me in her crisp British accent, "I heard a *but* in your comment, love."

Lottie gave her a puzzled look. "Excuse me?"

"You cut her off, Lottie, dear—not that you meant to, but there it is, isn't it? Abby, love, would you like to finish now? The house was in deplorable condition, but?"

Grace smiled serenely and waited, knowing she was right. Her fingers were interlocked in front of her, her posture as perfect as her short, stylish gray hair. An impeccable dresser, today she wore a lilac sweater set and gray skirt with gray flats.

Lottie looked at me for verification. "I cut you off? I surely didn't mean to. What else were you going to say about the house?"

"It wasn't about the house. It was what happened *at* the house. One of the painters fell off his ladder and had to be taken to the hospital. That brought the occupants out—a mom and two kids, maybe six and ten years old."

"Home at this time of day?" Grace asked.

"Homeschooled," I said. "While I was talking to the kids, Daisy, the little girl, kept looking at me strangely."

"Strangely?" Grace asked. "As in mistrustful? Frightened? Curious?"

"Maybe curious. Anyway, I've arranged to go back tomorrow morning."

"With what intention?" Grace asked. Her fingers were interlocked again.

"To see if my internal radar goes off when I see her," I said.

"Is Marco okay with this little investigation of yours?" Grace asked with a skeptical eye.

In the length of time it took me to consider my answer, the women had looked at each other and come to a decision. "He's not," they both said.

"Let's just say he's humoring me," I said.

The bell over the door jingled and two customers walked in just as a woman in the parlor signaled for more coffee.

"Tallyho," Grace said, and sailed off toward the parlor with Lottie in tow.

While they took care of the customers, I parted the curtain, stepped into my little slice of paradise, and sighed. There was nothing better than a flower shop on a chill spring day. It was always summer inside my workroom.

I inhaled the floral scents and smiled as I gazed around at my nirvana. A big slate-topped table took up the center of the room, with two walk-in coolers on the right wall, a long counter on the left wall with a built-in desk that housed my computer, fax machine, spindle for orders, and photos, and a doorway at the back that led to the tiny bathroom and small galley kitchen. Vases lined up by size and color filled shelves along two walls, and big containers below the counters held silk flowers grouped by color and type.

I glanced beneath the table and saw Seedy contentedly chewing on a rawhide toy, nestled into the pink-and-blue quilted doggy bed that Grace and Lottie had bought her. When I sat down at my desk, Seedy hobbled out and wanted to sit on my lap. With her perched on my knees, I counted the orders on the spindle, my smile spreading as the number rose. What a change from last year, when we'd gone through such an awful dry spell that I'd feared the shop would close.

I picked up a framed photo of Marco and me taken on our wedding day. "Look, Seedy. You're in the picture." The photo next to it was of my family on the same day: Mom with her peaches-and-cream English complexion and neat brown bob; Dad, freckled, redheaded, looking dapper even in his wheelchair; my brothers Jonathan and Jordan and their wives; my niece Tara holding her puppy, Seedling, who was Seedy's baby; and my glamorous cousin, Jillian, and her fussy husband, Claymore, the younger brother of the scoundrel who jilted me.

As though I had conjured her, the curtain parted and a very round stomach appeared, followed by a snakeskin tote bag, and finally my cousin. Amazingly, even though she was nearly nine months pregnant, Jillian still managed to look like a fashion plate. Today she wore an ankle-length black-and-gray-striped tube dress that was ruched in the abdominal area to allow for her expanding girth.

It was undoubtedly a designer dress—as an independent wardrobe consultant with champagne tastes, she wore little else—but with its skintight fit and stripes, she looked like a snake that had just swallowed a basketball. I dared not criticize her outfit, however, as she had already homed in on my bargain-brand khakis and button-down white shirt with a disapproving eye.

Despite the dissimilarity in our clothing styles, it was easy to tell we were related; we had the same Knight coloring—red hair and pale freckled skin—same nose (Marco had dubbed it "pert"), and same oval face. But where my hair was more of a matchstick red, Jillian's was a sheen of coppery rose. Where my skin was covered in freckles, hers had an adorable smattering of cinnamon across her nose. And those cosmetic items merely scratched the surface of our differences.

Still, Jillian Ophelia Knight Osborne would always be the younger cousin I regarded as a sister, the frail child with scoliosis I'd protected fiercely and her parents had indulged relentlessly. Surgery at the age of twelve had fixed her spine, but nothing could undo the cossetting. Then puberty hit, and the geeky, spoiled, long-limbed Jillian turned into a tall, slender beauty sought after by all the boys, reinforcing her princess status and leaving her short, freckle-faced cousin in the dust.

Seeing Jillian, Seedy immediately leaped off my lap and dove for cover under the table. She wasn't afraid of my cousin; she simply couldn't tolerate Jillian's Boston terrier, who seemed to be Jillian's counterpart—a diva dog coincidentally named Princess. The dog barked constantly, disobeyed every command, and ran in continuous loops, making everyone around her irritable. Two professional dog trainers had quit in frustration—not with Princess but with Jillian and Claymore, who treated the dog as though she were a human baby.

Fortunately, Jillian hadn't brought Princess with her today. She threw her tote bag on the worktable, scattering ivy leaves from the last arrangement, and perched on a wooden stool with a heavy sigh. "My back is *killing* me. If I *ever* think of having another baby, smother me with a pillow. So what house did you hate this time?"

"A dilapidated Victorian on Napoleon Street."

"The yucky tan and brown one? I could have saved you the bother, Abs. If you'd just let me find a house for you, I promise you'd be moving in a month."

"We have a Realtor, Jillian."

"Who hasn't found one single home that you've liked. Why won't you let me take you around town?"

"You don't have a Realtor's license, for one thing."

"Sure I do. I just have to renew it."

"You have a license? When did you ever sell houses?"

"While you were struggling in law school and didn't have the time of day for anyone but Pryce." She studied her shiny silver fingernails. "How sad that for nearly one year you forgot all about the cousin who so looked up to you."

As Jillian was a head taller, it had been a long time since she'd actually had to look up to me. But I did feel a few guilt pangs because I had indeed ignored her during those two semesters of agony. How could I refuse her simple request now, especially when it might actually find me a home?

"Okay, Jillian. If you renew your license, you can show me houses."

"Perfect! My license renewal is already in the works, thanks to your ex-fiancé."

"Do you have to constantly refer to him that way? Just say Pryce. Or call him your brother-in-law."

"Okay," she said with obvious reluctance, "but you sound less dull having an ex."

"Less dull? I own a flower shop and help solve murder cases."

"Exactly. So save tomorrow evening for me, seven o'clock. I've got the perfect house already picked out." She pushed herself off the stool and groaned as she rubbed her lower back. "I wish Baby No Name would pop out. I'm tired of being fat."

"First baby, Jill. Not gonna pop out."

"And you know this because . . . ?"

She had a point. "I thought you'd settled on a name for the baby. Rain . . . or Snow . . ."

"So last month, Abs. Try to keep up." With an over-the-shoulder wave, Jillian waddled out of the room. A moment later, Seedy peeked out from under the table as though checking to see if the coast was clear.

"She's gone," I told her.

Seedy sniffed the air, cocked her head, and waited for the bell above the door to jingle; then, after hearing it, she hobbled toward the small kitchen at the back of the building for a drink from her bowl.

* * *

A three-thirty break was the custom at Bloomers. It coincided with school letting out, providing a lull that allowed us a quick ten minutes to regroup. Right on the dot, Grace glided through the curtain bearing a tray loaded with scones, clotted cream, cups, saucers, a teapot, and napkins. Lottie followed and teatime ensued.

"It's Monday afternoon," Lottie reminded us at the end of our break. "Your mom should be making her weekly appearance any minute now."

"I wonder what project she'll bring this time," Grace said, taking a final, thoughtful sip.

Amazing how we'd grown used to Mom's strange works of art. A mention of it used to bring on shudders. Now we merely sighed. And poor Mom always thought she was helping our bottom line by letting us sell her artwork and taking the profit.

My mom, Maureen Knight, or "Mad Mo" as my brothers and I referred to her, was a great kindergarten teacher. She had the perfect temperament for it—calm, patient, loving, and able to rule a classroom without ever having to raise her voice. Mom was not a great artist, however. She came up with the oddest pieces I'd ever seen: sunglass frames covered in bits of sea glass that made the glasses a headache to wear; a tea cart that looked like a giant golf tee with a golf club handle; a six-foot-tall bowling pin painted with a human face that she designed as a hat rack; toilet seat lids covered with mirrored tiles that made a bathroom break a frightening experience—and the list went on.

She'd had a spectacular stroke of luck a few months back when two of her dog sculptures were noticed by an avant-garde artist in town who actually put on a private art show for her. But Mom soon tired of making dogs out of skateboards and shoe soles, so she'd moved on. The question was, to what?

The bell over the door jingled, followed by Mom's familiar "Yoo-hoo!"

"We won't have to wonder long now," Lottie said.

Chapter Three

"Abigail?" Mom called.

"In the workroom, Mom," I answered.

Lottie drained her cup and rose. "I'm outta here."

"Coward," I said.

"You betcha. Come on, Gracie."

"Right behind you, Lottie, dear." Grace swept up the tray and glided into the shop.

I heard the women exchange pleasantries with my mom, and then the curtain parted and Mom stuck her head in. "Any luck with the house hunt today?"

"No. Why don't you come all the way in?"

"Because you need to come outside to see what I brought you."

That old shudder was threatening to make a return visit.

I followed her through the shop and onto the sidewalk outside, where I found my dad sitting on a short, multicolored park bench placed directly beneath the big bay window. His wheelchair was beside the bench. Dad had retired from the New Chapel police force after a felon's bullet to the thigh put an end to his career. He was able to maneuver stairs with crutches but used his wheelchair for everything else.

"You made a bench?" I asked her.

"Hey, Abracadabra," Dad said, using his old nickname for me. "How's my flower girl today? Isn't this a great place to sit and watch the happenings across the street?"

I had to step back for a better look. The bench was made from what at first appeared to be glossy wooden slats painted in different primary colors. A closer look revealed that the slats were actually pairs of skis, with their curled ends on alternating sides and half lengths running in the opposite direction on the underside for support.

"Crafty use of the old stuff, isn't it?" Dad asked. "We have a whole ski theme going on here."

That was putting it mildly. The bench's arms were constructed from ski poles, and it sat on legs made from what appeared to be lengths of aspen trunks stuck in child-sized ski boots.

"Your dad is calling it the Two Skeater," Mom said. "A seat for two made from skis."

I caught a glimpse of Lottie and Grace peering through the blinds in the parlor window. I was almost certain I heard Lottie's guffaws.

Trying to keep a positive tone, I said, "So this is your new art project."

"Actually, it's your dad's project," Mom said, sitting down beside him. They squeezed hands. "He's already started a second one."

Great. Now my dad was an artist, too.

"It gives me something to do with my hands," he said. "There's only so much I can do on the computer."

And then came the question that I dreaded. "How much do you think you can sell it for, Abigail?" Mom asked.

"I'll have to do some research on it," I said. "But honestly, Mom, I'm not sure I can leave it on the sidewalk without getting permission from the town."

"You put flowerpots out in the summer," she said. "Why not a bench?"

"Abby's right, Mo," Dad said. "She might need a permit."

"Then let's find a place inside," Mom said. She thought a moment, then said, "I know. We can take out your wicker settee and put the bench in its place."

Was that my ficus tree screaming?

"Now, then," Mom said, pulling out a large tote bag from beneath the bench.

"Are you ready for *my* newest piece of art?"

No amount of preparation in the world could help me with that.

"I call it the iPot," she said, and out came a twelve-inch terra-cotta flowerpot that she'd painted neon orange. The pot might have been tolerable if she'd stopped there, but no. She'd covered it with row upon row of one-inch black-and-white stick-on eyes that jiggled when the pot moved. It was like having an audience of eye-rollers.

"So it's actually an E-Y-E pot," I said, spelling it out.

"That's my Mo," Dad said, putting his arm around her. "Always the clever one with those names."

"I've got more in the van," Mom said. "I'll bring them in as soon as we get the bench inside."

I heard screams again, but this time they were coming from inside my head.

Tuesday

Eight o'clock a.m. couldn't come soon enough for me. I'd thought about Daisy all evening and had even dreamed about her. In my dream, we were seated at a child-sized picnic table in the middle of a backyard drawing pictures. I'd made a vase full of daisies, which wasn't hard to interpret. Daisy had drawn a picture I couldn't interpret, and when I asked what it was, she said it was her puppy and it was missing not one but *two* legs. Then she'd pulled out a brown-and-white stuffed dog with the back legs ripped off.

I hadn't awakened in the best of moods. The dream had, however, cemented my desire to see Daisy again.

Marco and I met Lorelei shortly after eight o'clock in front of the old Victorian. She rang the bell and turned to smile at us. "Excited?"

"Very," I said, while Marco grunted noncommittally.

When no one came to the door, Lorelei rang the bell again and then knocked. "They might be upstairs."

When still no one answered, Marco said, "Looks like they're not home. Let's go."

I grabbed his arm as he started down the porch steps. "Give it another minute."

"Surely they didn't forget," Lorelei said, pounding now.

"Do you have a key?" I asked.

"The owner didn't provide one." She pressed the doorbell frantically.

"Let's go," Marco said, tugging on my elbow. "We're wasting time here."

Lorelei turned the old-fashioned glass doorknob and

the door opened. She pushed it wide, calling, "Hello. It's Lorelei. I'm here to show the house."

It was completely silent inside.

"Something's not right about this, Abby," Marco said quietly.

Which made it all the more intriguing. I followed Lorelei into the tiny front hall and looked around. If the exterior hadn't turned me off, the scarred wood floor, cracked plaster walls, stained ceiling, and rusty iron light fixture at the entrance would have.

"Come on," I said to my obstinate mate, who stood on the porch with his arms folded across his leather jacket, scoping out the neighborhood. "Let's have a look."

"I don't like it. Unanswered knocks, unlocked door . . . I think we should leave."

"If you want to leave, Lorelei can give me a ride back to Bloomers."

Muttering something about stubborn redheads, he followed me inside.

A few feet from the front door, an uncarpeted staircase led to the second floor, where all appeared dark. To the right of the stairs was a hallway that ran from front to back, punctuated by two arched openings along the outer wall. Through an arched doorway at the back, I could see grimy white metal kitchen cabinets.

"Hello? Mr. Jones? Mrs. Jones?" Lorelei called, heading up the hallway.

I was about to follow, but Marco put his hand on my shoulder. "Let's wait here."

I didn't like it when he got bossy, but I knew he was only concerned for my safety, so I held my tongue and watched as Lorelei glanced in each doorway.

"See? No one's home," Marco said. "Let's go."

At that moment our Realtor reached the kitchen doorway—and gasped.

That was all it took to send me darting after her. I glanced through the two doorways as I ran past, quickly taking in a dilapidated green sofa and two mismatched chairs in the first room and a round oak table and four ladder-back chairs in the second. By the time I reached the kitchen, Marco had not only caught up with me, but also had pulled out his phone and was making a call, no doubt to the police, not that I could blame him. Judging by Lorelei's shocked expression, I fully expected to see a dead body inside.

Instead, I saw absolutely nothing. No kitchen table, no chairs, no curtains, no decorations, not even a spoon rest on the stove. Some of the cheap metal cabinet doors were open, revealing bare insides. A microwave cart stood empty. There weren't even any crumbs on the old black-and-white linoleum floor.

I opened the refrigerator door to find that all of its contents were gone.

"I don't believe it," our befuddled Realtor said, taking out her phone to make a call. "They've moved out!"

Giving Lorelei a disgruntled glance, Marco put away his phone and walked through the empty kitchen to look out the back window. Seriously, had he *wanted* to find a body?

"Mr. Jones didn't say a word to me about moving when I arranged the showing," Lorelei was telling a person on the other end. "See what you can find out."

Yes, please do, I thought. *Maybe that will tell me why my radar had gone off.*

Lorelei finished her conversation and then started toward the front door, saying to me, "Let's go see the upstairs. Empty or not, you'll still get a feel for the rooms."

"I'm going up," I called to Marco, and headed after her.

The old wooden steps creaked as we climbed them, the way lit by a low-wattage yellow bulb high above us, which only made the peeling, faded gold-and-green-flocked wallpaper dingier. "Just imagine what the staircase would look like with bright sconces on the wall," Lorelei said cheerfully.

"That's a frightening thought," Marco said dryly, coming up behind me. "Abby, if you're not interested in the house, why are we doing this?"

"I'm interested in why these people fled during the night."

"First of all, we don't know that they fled. Second—"

"I don't care," I said, and stopped on the landing at the top to appraise the situation. There were four doors—one to our left and one to our right, which stood open, and two doors directly in front of us, which were closed.

"Let's see the bedroom on the left first," she said. Her cell phone rang, so she waved us on and stepped away to answer it.

My only thought as I gazed around the cramped room was, *Ugh.* It contained a beat-up maple dresser whose drawers had been emptied and a metal bed frame holding a stained mattress and sagging box springs. The mattress had been stripped of sheets and blankets, the window was devoid of a curtain, and the tiny closet was bare.

We found the same situation in the bedroom on the right—a bare closet, an emptied-out dresser, and a stripped-down mattress and box springs, this one a twin size. If there had been nightstands, they were gone now.

"Why would they move out and leave half their furniture behind?" I asked Marco.

"Some of the furniture came with the house," Lorelei said, coming up behind us. "The Joneses had until the end of the month to move. They were all paid up until then."

"The Joneses rented this house?" Marco asked.

"I must have forgotten to tell you that," Lorelei said.

"So why did they move so suddenly?" I asked.

"I'll find out," Lorelei said.

"That's okay," Marco said, discreetly tapping my arm. "It's none of our business."

Why exactly had I wanted him to come with me? I returned to the unopened doors in the hallway. "And what do you suppose is behind doors one and two?"

"One of these should be a half bath," Lorelei said. She opened one and found a tiny room containing an old pedestal sink, a toilet, and a checkered floor made from small black-and-white ceramic tiles, many of which were missing.

"No bathtub?" I asked.

"There's a full bath off the kitchen," our Realtor said. She opened the remaining door, revealing a set of narrow stairs. "This one leads to the attic."

"Let's go up," I said.

"Why do you want to see the attic?" Marco asked as Lorelei started up.

"Because I've never seen a Victorian attic."

"How about Victorian spiders?" Marco asked. "Because there's probably a bunch up there."

"Never mind, Lorelei," I called. Spiders were my Achilles' heel.

"I wish I knew why they moved out in the middle of the night," I said to Marco as we walked back to town.

"Let me remind you that we don't know they moved during the night. We were there at noon yesterday. They had all afternoon and evening to move."

"Still, Marco, don't you find the timing of their move too coincidental?"

"On the surface, yes, but let's wait until we hear back from Reilly about his interview before we decide anything. If he thinks something's off, we'll take another look. So can we forget about this house now?"

"I can forget about the house, but not the look Daisy gave me."

"Describe it," Marco said, putting his arm around my shoulders. "Was she afraid? Angry? Worried?"

"The closest I can come to describing it is *curious*."

"A curious child. Imagine that."

I had to concede the point. Marco was right. What child wasn't curious? Maybe Daisy had never seen a person with red hair before. Or maybe she'd seen me around town and couldn't remember where. I just had to put her out of my mind.

We walked along in silence until we reached Franklin Street, and then Marco said, "So our house hunt continues."

"Yep. And that reminds me—Jillian wants to show us one this evening."

"Let me know how that goes."

"Don't you want to see what she found for us?"

He gave me the *You've got to be kidding* look, so I poked him playfully. "So what you're saying is that when it comes to Jillian, you're a chicken."

"I'm saying that when it comes to Jillian, I keep my distance."

"You never know, Marco. She just might come through for us."

"If she does, I'll be happy to take a look. You can be the official scout." His cell phone rang so he pulled it out of his back pocket and checked the screen. "Reilly," he said, pressing it to his ear.

"Hey, Sean, what's happening?" He listened for a few moments, said, "I'll tell Abby. She'll be relieved," then listened some more. "Interesting. So when do they expect to hear something? And in the meantime? Sure, I'll talk to her. Make it noon."

"Tell Abby what?" I asked as he put his phone away.

"Reilly interviewed the Joneses thoroughly and found nothing suspicious about them."

Clearly Reilly's internal radar wasn't as finely tuned as mine was. "Does he know they moved?"

"It wouldn't make a difference, Sunshine. He cleared them. End of story."

Not the story in my notebook. "So even though I sense something is off, you're going to believe Reilly?"

"It's not a question of choosing one of you, Sunshine. I'm simply not interested in pursuing it unless I see some verified proof that the Joneses are doing something wrong."

I saw a challenge in that statement.

"Moving on," Marco said, "Reilly wants me to talk to the painter's wife, Rosa Marin. She's convinced that her husband's fall wasn't an accident—that someone tried to kill him."

"While we were standing there?"

"That's what she believes. And so far the preliminary medical report shows no sign of a heart attack, stroke, flu, appendicitis, or any other obvious medical condition. Toxicology results will take up to ten days. In the meantime, the detectives told Mrs. Marin that they haven't found any evidence that supports her accusation, so she informed them she would hire her own investigator. She wanted to know who the best PI in town was, so Reilly gave her my name."

"That was nice of him."

"We'll see. He said she's hot-tempered."

"Marco," I said as we stopped at the corner to wait for the light to change, "if I thought someone had tried to kill you and the detectives wouldn't listen to me, I'd be hot-tempered, too."

Marco put his arm around me and pulled me close. "Baby, you're just hot, period."

Turned out I wasn't the only one who was hot. Rosa Marin was a voluptuous, thirtysomething beauty with long legs, wavy dark-brown hair held back on either side by large silver barrettes, smooth olive skin, full lips, and expressive dark brown eyes that right now fairly sizzled with outrage. She wore a baby blue V-neck sweater that hugged her curves, a silver pendant in the shape of a lightning bolt that nestled in her cleavage, large hoop earrings, and tight black jeans with high-heeled black ankle boots.

Marco had already done some research and learned that Rosa was twenty years younger than her husband, worked as a bookkeeper for a local manufacturing company, and made a very small wage that barely covered child care costs. The Marins had one child of their own, an eight-year-old boy named Peter. In addition, Sergio also had two college-aged daughters from a previous marriage.

The three of us were seated in Marco's modern gray, silver, and black office, Marco behind his sleek black desk and Rosa and I in the black sling-back chairs facing him. He'd given me his tablet and a pen so I could take notes, which was our normal arrangement. It wasn't sexist, merely prudent. I needed to be able to read them later.

Rosa's full lips were pressed together in barely concealed anger, her arms folded beneath her breasts, one leg crossed over the other, her foot bouncing as though to release pent-up energy. Marco leaned forward in his mesh-backed swivel chair, hands folded on his desk, discreetly taking her measure, no doubt to decide whether to accept her case.

"The *estúpido* detectives refuse to believe me," Rosa said, her dark eyes snapping with ire as she glanced from Marco to me. "'Step back and let us handle the matter,' they say, as if my husband, who lies near death, is a *matter.* It was probably an accident, they tell me, but I know that's a lie! Sergio has been on ladders all his life. How would he fall backward if he wasn't pushed? And who was up there near my husband? Four men who hate him."

"What makes you believe one of them pushed him, Mrs. Marin?" Marco asked.

"Call me Rosa, please. I know one of them is responsible because of things that have been happening to Sergio lately. Bad things. A tire slashed on his truck. A dead rat left in his locker at work. Red paint splashed on his coveralls right here." She pointed to her heart. "They were *advertencias*. Warnings. Sergio told me to forget about them, that they meant nothing, but I knew better. And I was right."

"What are the names of these four men?" Marco asked.

Rosa counted them off on her fingers. "Adrian, Jericho, Clive, and Sam. I knew they were jealous but I never thought one of them would be so jealous that he would want my Sergio to die." She dug for a tissue in her oversized navy purse, dabbing the tears that rolled down her cheeks.

"Jealous for what reason?" Marco asked.

She blew her nose and put the tissue away. "Because the boss chose my husband to be the foreman."

"Are these four men painters as well?" Marco asked.

"No, they are roofers, like my Sergio. There weren't enough painters for this house, Mr. Appleruth said, and Sergio had been a painter when he was younger, so the boss had him fill in."

"What kinds of things did the men say to your husband?" Marco asked.

"They called him a bootlicker," she said, "and a brownnose, and other names I won't even say."

"This happened when Sergio was promoted?" Marco asked.

"Sí."

"What was your husband's response?" Marco asked.

She shook her head. "Not good, I'm afraid. My Sergio had a temper that he could not always control. He got into some bad fights."

"Fistfights?" Marco asked.

"No, argument fights," she said. " 'Sergio,' I would tell him, 'you cannot fight with your men. You're the boss.' And he would say, 'Rosa, they need to learn respect.' "

"Do you have the men's last names?" I asked.

"Only one, Adrian Prada," she said, nearly spitting out his name. "The boss, Mr. Appleruth, he can tell you the rest. He's a nice man. He trusted Sergio. That's why he chose him over Adrian Prada."

"When was Sergio promoted?" Marco asked.

"A month ago, maybe a little more," Rosa replied. "That's when all the bad things began happening."

"How is it that you know Adrian's last name and not the others?" Marco asked.

"Adrian and I went to the same high school," she answered, her mouth curving down in distaste. "He was a friend of my brother."

"Don't you like Adrian?" I asked.

"I cannot stand him. I called him El Diablo because he would make passes at me when Sergio wasn't around. I finally told him to leave me alone or I would tell Sergio. He stayed away after that, but who knows what he will do with Sergio laid up?"

"Where were you when Adrian made passes at you?" I asked.

"I used to work for Mr. Appleruth. That is where I met Sergio." She fingered the lightning bolt pendant, her expression turning tender. "After we were married, I took another job. I didn't want to make trouble between my husband and Adrian."

"Did Sergio know about the passes?" I asked.

"No. Sergio has a bad temper, and I was afraid of what he might do."

"Does your husband normally leave his coveralls at work?" Marco asked.

"He keeps a spare in his locker," she said. "All the men do." She turned her big, imploring gaze on Marco first and then on me. "So will you help me find this terrible person?"

"Don't you want to know how much it'll cost?" I asked.

"I don't care how much it costs," she said, her eyes sparkling with passion. "I will empty my bank account if I have to. I just want justice for my husband. I refuse to let one of *los matones* get away with this."

"What does *los matones* mean?" I asked.

With a disdainful curl of her upper lip, she replied, "The bullies."

Bullies and justice? I couldn't help but stare at her. She was the Latina version of me!

Chapter Four

"Just so you're aware," Marco said, "this is what my hourly fee is." He wrote down a figure and passed it across the desk to her.

Rosa's eyes widened; then, pressing her lips together, she pushed it back. "Just find the man who did this terrible thing to Sergio and I will find a way to pay you." She stood up. "I have to get back to work now. When will you start?"

"Right now," Marco said. "I'll contact Mr. Appleruth and take it from there."

Rosa was so happy she threw her arms around me, lifted me off the ground, and set me back down. "Thank you so much, Mrs. Salvare, Mr. Salvare," she said enthusiastically as she backed toward the door. "I feel like I can breathe again."

"Poor woman," I said after she'd gone. "If her husband dies, or even continues on in a coma, with all those medical bills piling up, what will she do?"

"Struggle," Marco said, picking up the phone on his desk. As he dialed the telephone number, he said, "I'm going to do this case pro bono."

"That's a generous gesture, Marco."

"You didn't marry a greedy man, Sunshine." He paused, then added, "Except when it comes to you." Resuming his business voice, he said, "Mr. Appleruth, please. Private detective Marco Salvare calling."

Ten minutes later, Marco had four full names and a plan.

"Mr. Appleruth said Adrian Prada will be doing some work on his building tomorrow, and we're welcome to talk to him there. Our best bet with the others is to catch them at the HHI office around five fifteen p.m. when they come back from their jobs."

Continuing to read from his notes, he said, "Clive Bishop came over from the UK about a year ago. If we don't catch him after work, we can find him at the Thrifty-Inn Motel, where he rents a room. Sam Walker lives in New Chapel and rides a motorcycle to work. And Jericho, no last name, claims to be an artist, lives alone in a trailer in an unincorporated part of the county, and likes his privacy. If we want to see some of the canvases he's done, Appleruth said to check the Art Barn, north of town. It's a collective of some kind."

"I've been to the Art Barn," I said. "My mom took watercolor lessons there one summer. The Barn displays work done by their students."

"Did Maureen sell any?"

"Yes, to my dad. That was the end of her watercolor period."

Marco put his notepad away and shut the desk drawer. "Want to visit there this evening?"

"*This* evening?"

"Did I say that in Chinese?" he quipped. "Yes, *this* evening."

"So," I said, "you're not too busy to make a trip to the Art Barn, but you are too busy to see a house with Jillian?"

He came around the desk to pull me into his arms. "If my mom claimed to have found the perfect house for us, wouldn't you want me to preview it for you?"

Marco had a valid point. I loved Francesca Salvare dearly but she did love to run the show wherever she was, which often caused us to bump heads. In fact, I was shocked that she hadn't been house hunting for us. Shocked—but grateful.

"See you later tonight, Salvare."

Bloomers was so busy that afternoon that I didn't have a chance to think about little Daisy Jones, but I did tell Lottie and Grace all about our interview with Rosa Marin and the resulting investigation. They were impressed with Marco's offer to work pro bono.

"I understand what it's like to live paycheck to paycheck," Lottie said, "not knowing if you were going to have enough left to buy food for your kids and still pay your bills. You've got yourself a winner with that man of yours, sweetie."

At that, Grace assumed her lecture pose—hands gripping the edges of her cardigan as though they were lapels, feet together, head up.

"As Kahlil Gibran once said," she began, " 'Generosity is giving more than you can, and pride is taking less than you need.' "

"Good one, Gracie," Lottie said as we both clapped.

Grace had an uncanny ability to produce exactly the right quote at a moment's notice. And she expected to be properly applauded afterward, which we always happily obliged.

Another task I didn't have time for was to call City Hall about leaving Dad's Two Skeater bench outside, but it stayed there anyway because I didn't want my lovely wicker settee to shiver in the basement. I'd found a place for two of Mom's iPots on a shelf in the antique armoire, but Lottie wasn't happy with the arrangement because she was convinced they were watching her. The other iPots that Mom had dropped off were stacked on the floor near some of our potted plants. Not one had sold. Most customers took one look, wrapped their coats tighter, and scurried past.

As busy as we were, I didn't make it to Down the Hatch until after six o'clock, which left just enough time to have a bowl of chili with Marco, drop Seedy off at our apartment, and make it to Jillian's building by seven o'clock. From there we headed to a section of new homes on the eastern border of New Chapel.

"This house is just eight months old," she said as I parked my ancient yellow Corvette on the street in front of a brown aluminum-sided ranch home. "The owners defaulted on their loan, so the bank is selling it in a short sale."

"What's a short sale?"

"A sale that is short. Duh." She rolled her eyes, then climbed out of my car with much groaning. "This is absolutely the worst possible vehicle for a pregnant woman to ride in. What is it, like, ten inches off the ground?"

"Hey, don't talk nasty about my baby. She's a 1960 vintage Corvette, Jillian. Show some respect."

"You paid two hundred bucks for a beat-up 1960 tin bucket that had been stashed away in a barn for twenty years, Abs. There are so many cracks in these leather seats, I'm surprised the farmer didn't pay you to take the car off his hands. Seriously, couldn't you have driven Marco's Prius?"

"I'm sorry. I didn't think of it."

With one hand on her lower back, Jillian climbed the porch steps and unlocked the door. "Now keep in mind that the house needs a little work. But I'm sure you'll see the potential here."

Just about what Lorelei had said about the Victorian.

The front door opened directly into the living room. It was a nice-sized room with a big picture window in the front and two double-hung windows on the outside wall. Everything in the room was beige, and the carpet still had a new smell to it.

Not a bad beginning.

Then we stepped through a doorway into the kitchen, where I gazed around in surprise. "Where are the appliances?"

"Wow. They even took the sink. But look—the walls are yellow, your favorite color."

"But look—we'd have to buy everything except the cabinets."

"But look," she retorted, "the price would be low enough that you'd have money for nice appliances—if you bid high enough and win, that is. Let's go see the bedrooms."

Following her up a hallway, I said, "I still don't understand how a short sale works."

"Ow! Ow!" Jillian leaned against the wall clutching her belly, her face turning ashen. "Ow! Oh, no. Ow!"

"What's wrong?"

Dropping to her hands and knees, she said, "I'm going into labor, Abby!"

"What? Are you sure?"

Grimacing through a contraction, she managed to grind out, "Well, we could wait around and see, but how many babies have you delivered, doctor?"

Valid argument.

"Would you just take me to the hospital?"

I helped Jillian ease into the 'Vette and managed to get the seat belt around her—no easy feat. The county hospital, which used to be just two blocks off the town square, had built a newer, larger facility north of town, turning what used to be a five-minute ride into a good fifteen-minute one. And those fifteen seemed endless right now as Jillian's complaints got louder and longer. All I could think was: a) I wasn't prepared to deliver a baby, and b) what would that do to my cracked leather seats?

"Are you trying to get a speeding ticket?" Jillian cried, in between panting and blowing air out through her mouth.

"Do you really think they'd give me a speeding ticket now? Call Claymore and tell him to meet us there."

"Ow. Ow. I can't—manage that—right now. Ow! You'll have to call."

"I can't call him and drive fast."

"This can't be happening," she moaned. "I don't have a name picked out yet."

What seemed like hours later, I followed Jillian's directions to pull up to the emergency-room door and blow the horn. When no one appeared, I said, "I think I should just take you inside."

"Right. Like you'd be able to carry me." She reached over and laid on the horn.

Finally a woman stepped outside the huge sliding glass doors to see what the commotion was about, and Jillian called through her open window, "Helen, I'm having my baby! Hurry!"

As Helen strolled toward the car, apparently in no big hurry, I asked, "You know her?"

"No, I'm psychic." How Jillian managed to roll her eyes while in such pain was a marvel only a diva could pull off. "Yes, I know her. She's a receptionist in the ER."

Helen came up to the car and leaned in. "Are we doing another dry run, Jillian?"

"No, seriously!" my cousin cried, panting and blowing. "The baby's coming!"

Helen looked dubious. "Seriously?"

"Seriously! Ow! Oh, no—is that my water breaking?"

At that, Helen ran inside, and moments later a young nurse's aid came out with a wheelchair. The two of us got Jillian into it; then I was told to park the car and come to the fourth-floor maternity ward. I did as instructed and phoned Marco as I trotted across the parking lot. "Call Claymore, Marco. I just took Jillian to the hospital. She's in labor."

"Will do. How was the house?"

"Marco, Jillian is in labor! I'll tell you about the house

later." I dropped the phone in my purse and hurried through the main doors to the elevators. On the fourth floor, I saw a nurse and said, "Where should I go? My cousin was just brought in to deliver her baby."

"You can wait in the maternity waiting room. Jillian's being examined now."

"You know Jillian?"

"Honey, everyone knows Jillian." She sized me up and added, "Yep, I can see that you two are related." Continuing on up the hallway, she looked up and muttered, "Does the world really need two of them, Lord?"

I followed signs to the waiting room, which was large and modern with tan vinyl chairs, round tables, a bank of vending machines, and a television mounted high in one corner. I had just put coins in to buy a cup of hot chocolate when I heard a familiar voice say, "I want some cocoa, too."

I spun around, and there stood Jillian, with no moans, groans, or panting whatsoever. "What are you doing out here?"

"False alarm."

"But your water broke."

She plucked my cup out of the machine and took a sip. "Actually, I was wrong about that, too. I hope you didn't call Claymore."

"No, *I* didn't call Claymore, Jillian. I had Marco do it."

"Then you'd better try to reach him so he doesn't make the trip for nothing. Shall we go back and finish seeing that cute ranch?"

"Honestly," I said to Marco when he called later that evening from the bar, "you'd think a woman would know whether her water broke."

"Not even going to comment on that. Is it safe to ask *now* how the house was?"

"Once I got over the shock of the missing appliances, the house itself wasn't bad. I just don't think we need three bedrooms yet."

"Yet?"

"Do you want to have that discussion now?"

"Right. Let's save that for another year. Were there any plusses to the yellow ranch?"

"It's a short sale. Jillian thought that was a good thing."

"If you like to gamble."

"You're a gambler. You took a gamble on me."

"Nope. You were a sure thing."

"I was a *sure* thing?"

I was trying to decide whether I should be offended when he replied, "I was sure you were the right one for me."

"Well played, Salvare."

"I could sense the tension from here. Do you want me to see this house?"

"No," I said with a sigh. "I'll keep looking. Maybe Lorelei will have something new for us tomorrow."

"How's our girl?"

"Seedy is right here on my lap. We're both bored."

"Want to learn bartending?"

"Do *you* want to learn flower arranging?"

"See you in a while."

After talking to Marco, I did a search online for homes for sale in the downtown area and came across the ad for the ramshackle Victorian that the Joneses had rented. That got me to thinking about Daisy again, so I hunted down the name of the Victorian's owner, a Mr. Theodore Mallory, through the county assessor's public database system. An Internet search produced his home address and telephone number.

I sat with the phone in my hand, debating about whether to call. Why was I pursuing this? Was it simply because I was bored?

You could find a hobby, the smart-alecky little voice in my head whispered. Scary how much that voice sounded like Jillian. Anyway, I had a hobby. It was called sleuthing.

Marco would say to let it go, that I was merely being my usual nosy self, which wasn't *untrue*. But it was much too simplistic. This was a gut feeling that something about that little girl was out of the ordinary. The more I thought about it, the more convinced I became that I wouldn't be able to let it go until I had satisfied myself that either I was right or my internal radar was off-kilter.

"Hi, Mr. Mallory? This is Abby Knight . . . Salvare. From Bloomers Flower Shop. I have a delivery for Sandra Jones, but I was just informed that she's moved. Do you have a forwarding address?"

"I'm sorry, but I don't," Mallory said.

"Well, darn," I said. "This is such a big, beautiful arrangement. I sure hate to see it go to waste."

"Yeah," he said in a bored voice. "That's a shame."

Time to try another tactic. "Sandra is an old high school friend of mine. Did she put anything on their rental application that might help me find her?"

"Hold on while I look." He sounded annoyed. After a moment, I heard papers shuffling; then he said, "I didn't know flower shops were open this late."

"I own the shop. You know how that goes."

"Not really. Okay, I can give you Sandra's previous address and the landlord's phone number."

"Great. Go ahead." I wrote down the information, then said, "Did they list any references?"

"What does that have to do with delivering flowers?"

"In case I can't find them, maybe a former neighbor would know how to reach them."

"Look, miss, I have no way of knowing whether you're on the up-and-up, so I'm not about to give other people's information to you."

"I totally understand, Mr. Mallory, but you can look me up on the Internet. Bloomers Flower Shop, New Chapel, Indiana, Abby Knight. So, does that application happen to say where Sandra's husband is employed? Maybe I can find her that way."

"Maraville School Corporation."

"Perfect. Thank you. So how were they, the Joneses?"

"What are you talking about?"

"I haven't seen Sandy in years. Does she appear to be happy? I know she has kids now. Did they all appear happy to you?"

"I met them in person once. They seemed like decent people. If you want to know more, you'll have to ask Sandra yourself."

Click.

It had been a long shot, but at least I had something to go on.

I found the Maraville School Corporation's phone number, wrote it down, tucked it in my purse, shut down the computer, and put on my pajamas. I now had a starting point for my hobby.

Chapter Five

Wednesday

At seven thirty in the morning, Marco and I arrived at the Handy Home Improvements headquarters and introduced ourselves to Mr. Appleruth, a short, sturdy, curly-haired man in his sixties. We'd already dropped Seedy off at Bloomers, where Grace was setting up her coffee machines for the day.

HHI was housed in a tan brick building on Beech Street on the southeast side of New Chapel in a chain of low-lying structures that held everything from an interior lighting store to a chiropractic clinic.

"If you want to talk to Adrian Prada, he's around back," Appleruth said.

We were standing in a sparsely outfitted outer office painted in industrial gray, where a young female secretary sat in front of a computer sucking from a straw stuck in a huge plastic cup of soda. Since Mr. Appleruth had not invited us into his inner office, I took out the notepad and pen as Marco began to question him.

"What can you tell us about Adrian Prada?" Marco asked.

"Adrian's a dependable worker, does a good job, but has something of a temper. I've had to intervene a few times to head off a fight, but that's not unusual when you have a bunch of laborers who work together sometimes for ten hours a day."

"That's a long day," I said.

"The longer the daylight hours are," he said, "the longer they work."

"Have you noticed any rivalry between Sergio and Adrian?" Marco asked.

"I don't know if I'd call it a rivalry. More like tension."

"Did that tension ever escalate into a fight?"

"No punches thrown that I know of, if that's what you mean. They just didn't seem to like each other. But it never prevented them from getting the work done."

"Were you aware that Adrian was harassing Rosa Marin while she was employed by you?" Marco asked.

Appleruth looked embarrassed as he nodded. "I spoke to Adrian about it but he swore he was only trying to be a friend to her. Ultimately, Rosa and I decided that it would be best if she worked elsewhere, so I helped find her another job."

"I'm surprised Rosa didn't file a sexual harassment suit," I said.

"That was her decision," he said.

"Why did you choose Sergio over the others as your foreman?" I asked.

"Simple. Sergio has a wife and kids to support. The others don't."

"So the only reason you chose Sergio is because he has a family?"

"He's also more experienced. I go by my gut instinct on these guys, and Sergio was the obvious choice. Otherwise, their work ethics are all about the same."

"Were you considering anyone else?" I asked.

"Seniority-wise, Adrian Prada."

"Any hard feelings there?" Marco asked.

"You'd have to ask Adrian that."

"What can you tell us about Sam Walker?" Marco asked.

"Sam used to be a wrestler but now he's into weight training, always working out. He's been with the company for about five years."

"How about Clive Bishop?" Marco asked.

"Clive has been here the shortest amount of time. He came here from the UK about this time last year, no references, no relatives, just wanting to make a fresh start. He admitted that he had been charged with petty larceny as a teenager, but he seemed dependable, so I hired him as a temp to see how he performed and eventually gave him a permanent job."

"And last is Jericho," I said, reading from my notes.

"Ah, Jericho. An interesting guy, very quiet. Keeps to himself. A little on the peculiar side, to tell you the truth. Apparently he doesn't have a last name because he had it legally changed to Jericho when he turned twenty-one. I think there were family problems."

"Do you have Jericho's original birth name?" Marco asked.

"Sorry, no."

"Any conflicts between any of the three men and Sergio?" Marco asked.

Appleruth scratched the back of his head, as though reluctant to talk. "Look, Sergio is in bad shape right now so I hate to say much, but the truth is that he wasn't well liked. He had a harsh tone and a sour disposition, and that led to some altercations. To put it simply, he could be a real bastard at times."

"Then why would you make him your foreman?" I asked.

"For the reasons I named earlier. I believe in being fair to my men. They work for me for a long time, do a good job, I reward them. It's that simple. And what foreman isn't considered a bastard to his workers?"

"What was the reaction among those three men when you announced Sergio's promotion?" Marco asked.

"There was some grumbling, but nothing else in my presence," Appleruth said. "They know good jobs are hard to come by, and I do treat my employees well. Bottom line is money. It makes up for a lot of things."

"Were you aware of several warnings Sergio received from someone in the company after he was promoted?" Marco asked.

"No. What kind of warnings?"

"Truck tires slashed, dead rat left in his locker, and red paint splashed on his spare coveralls."

"Sergio never told me," Appleruth said. "I wish he had. I would've tried to get to the bottom of it." He glanced at his watch. "Listen, I hate to cut you off, but I have to do an estimate in about ten minutes. Feel free to talk to anyone here, though. If they give you any grief, tell them I said they'd better cooperate."

Marco shook hands with him and then we headed around to the back of the building to find Adrian Prada.

He wasn't hard to locate. There was only one laborer in the back, a broad-shouldered man with coal black hair tied back in a ponytail, a square-jawed face, and a well-proportioned body. He was standing on a ladder installing new gutters, and came down when Marco called his name.

"Adrian, I'm Marco Salvare," my husband said. "This is my wife, Abby. We'd like to talk to you about Sergio Marin."

"What about Sergio?" he asked warily.

"I'm a private detective," Marco said, displaying his PI's license. "Mrs. Marin hired us to look into the cause of Sergio's fall."

Adrian pressed his fingertips against his chest, displaying a huge gold insignia ring with the letter *A* in the center of a round raised bed of glittering diamond chips. It matched the pendant on a thick gold-link chain around his neck. His dark brown eyes radiating his annoyance, he asked crossly, "And she told you to come see *me*?"

"We're interviewing everyone who was on the scene Monday morning," Marco said.

"It was an accident, *mi amigo*. If anyone caused Sergio's accident, it was Sergio."

"He caused his own accident?" I asked.

"If I had a bad heart like Sergio, I would not be eating donuts for lunch or having six beers after work—you know what I mean? You want to know why Sergio fell? Because he does not take care of himself."

"Sergio didn't have a heart attack," Marco said, "or any other apparent condition that might have caused his fall."

Adrian scowled, arms folded across his chest, clearly trying to decide what to do. "What are you saying, then? That someone here pushed him?"

"I'm saying that we're looking for the cause of his fall," Marco said, repeating his earlier statement. "So how about answering a few questions?"

"And I am telling you to stop looking my way," Adrian retorted.

"All I'm asking for is ten minutes of your time," Marco said. "Your boss told us you'd be willing to help us. Should I tell him he's wrong?"

Adrian scowled, twisting the ring on his finger back and forth as he debated what to do. Finally, he said, "What do you want to know?"

I pulled out the notepad and got ready to write.

"Does Sergio have any enemies at work?" Marco asked.

"No, not enemies," Adrian said. "It is just that everyone hates him."

"What's the difference?" I asked.

"You make war with your enemies," he replied.

"Why is Sergio hated?" Marco asked.

"Because he is a *cabrón*."

"Which means . . . ?" I said.

"Ah, it has many meanings. Let us just say a bastard. He criticized everything we did. Me, I am picky about what I do. I don't appreciate someone telling me it is no good just because he is jealous of me."

"Why would Sergio be jealous of you?" I asked.

"Look at me," Adrian said, posing like a matador—head up, shoulders back, chest thrust forward, legs together. "I am handsome, strong, and virile. Sergio is old, with wrinkles and gray hair. You really think that his beautiful wife wants to stay with him when I am right here?"

Giant ego, I wrote. Adrian was rubbing me the wrong way, and I'd only been around him for five minutes. "So," I said, "you're saying his wife would leave Sergio to be with you if she had the opportunity?"

"You look at me and decide," Adrian said, sweeping me from head to toe with a smoldering glance. "Perhaps you should ask Rosa if she slipped poison in his thermos that morning."

If I were Rosa, the poison would have gone into *this* guy's thermos.

"How well do you know Mrs. Marin?" Marco asked.

"I went to school with Rosa. She was two years younger than me, and her brother Miguel was my best friend. I would have dated her but Miguel kept me away. He said I was too much man for his little sister." Adrian laughed, clearly proud of himself.

"Did you have a problem with Sergio being promoted to foreman?" Marco asked.

"*Sí,* I had a problem with it. I would make a much better foreman than Sergio. I am smarter than he is, for one thing, and I have a lot of experience. And even more than that, as I said before, no one likes Sergio." He held out his arms. "Everyone likes Adrian Prada."

I knew two women who weren't in that category. I underlined *Giant ego* twice.

"Who was responsible for slashing Sergio's tires?" Marco asked.

"Why are you asking me?"

“Because I’m talking to you,” Marco said. “Who was responsible for the rat in his locker? Or the red paint on his coveralls?”

“When did this happen?” Adrian asked. He was doing a poor job of looking shocked.

“It happened after Sergio was made foreman,” I said. “Sounds like someone was jealous of Sergio.”

“Then it could not have been me,” Adrian said with a dimpled smile. “As I already told you, it was Sergio who was jealous of me. Now the others—I cannot speak for them. Maybe they will know more.”

“Where were you when Sergio fell?” Marco asked.

Adrian pointed skyward. “On the roof.”

“Near Sergio?”

“A few yards away. Please. You insult me. I do not like Sergio, but I would not push him. No one wants to fall to his death.”

“He’s not dead,” I said.

“Yet,” Adrian replied. “You do not survive a fall like that, *chica*, believe me.”

Chica? Later I’d have to remember to ask exactly what that meant. “I hope you’re wrong,” I replied.

Adrian shrugged, as though it would be no tragedy if Sergio died.

“If Sergio can’t come back to work for any reason, who’ll be foreman?” Marco asked.

Adrian grinned. “You want me to say I will. Sorry to disappoint you, but that is up to Mr. Appleruth. And I am finished with your questions.” He strutted away as though he’d just slain a bull.

“Let’s get out of here,” I said.

* * *

"What was your impression of Adrian?" Marco asked as we rode back to town.

"I can sum him up in four words. Giant ego, big mouth."

"Any bad vibes?"

"You bet. I dislike men who think they're God's gift to women."

"What about men who think their women are God's gift to them?"

"What?"

One side of Marco's mouth curved up in that devilish way of his. "Never mind. I couldn't resist. What else did you notice?"

"Two things stuck out. No matter how much he protested otherwise, Adrian was angry that Sergio got the promotion and he didn't. And if he had the chance, he would love to pursue Rosa. Is that enough motive to put him on our suspect list?"

"Jealousy at work and in his private life? I'd say so. We'll need to verify that Adrian was a few yards away from Sergio before the fall."

My cell phone rang so I checked the screen and saw my cousin's name. "It's Jillian," I whispered to Marco, then put the phone to my ear and said, "What's up, Jill?"

"Did you make a decision about the yellow ranch? If you want it, we need to get a bid in ASAP."

"We're not interested," I said.

"Just because it didn't have appliances? Wise up, Abs. It's so much better to be able to choose your own. Seriously, do you know how smart refrigerators are now?"

"It's not because of the appliances, Jillian. It's because we want two bedrooms, not three, and no short sale."

"Okay, fine," she said in an exasperated voice, and hung up.

I slid my phone into my purse. "What does *chica* mean?"

"Not sure, but I think it's slang for cutie."

Huh. Adrian thought I was cute.

"I'd like to interview as many of the other men as possible when they return to HHI today," Marco said. "Can you be ready to leave Bloomers at five p.m.?"

"I'm sure I can arrange that for *you*," I said, then added playfully, "Hot Pockets."

Marco glanced at me curiously. "Where did that come from?"

"Don't you remember when Tara used to call you that?"

"Yes. I meant, what brought it to mind?"

"Watching Adrian strut away. He has nothing over you, Hot Pockets."

Marco reached over to gently squeeze my hand. "Thank you. And Rosa has nothing over you, Fireball."

It was my turn for the curious look. Or maybe it was more of a glower. "Rosa? What made you think of her?"

He pretended to shudder as he pulled up in front of Bloomers. "I'm sensing that tension again. See you at five."

"We had a visit from the police," Lottie informed me as I took off my jacket and hung it on the back of my desk chair. Seedy put her paw on my leg, wanting a cuddle.

"About the bench?" I asked as I picked up my dog and let her lick my chin.

"How'd you guess? We have to submit a written request if we want to put furniture on the sidewalk."

"It's not permanent," I said. "I hope."

"Grace and I moved it into the parlor for now. It's in the back by the coffee bar. We still haven't figured out a price for it."

"If someone inquires, tell them to make us an offer. I'll have to ask Tara to do a search on eBay and see what she can find." I set Seedy on the floor, and she hobbled under the big table and curled up in her bed with a raw-hide bone.

"Look at all the orders on the spindle, sweetie," Lottie said.

"Isn't it amazing? I can't believe our good fortune these days, Lottie."

"Calls have been coming in steadily all morning. I wanted to start on the orders, but Grace has been swamped with customers in the parlor, so she couldn't cover the shop. It's too bad that Marco's mom is babysitting her grandkids now. We could really use her help."

Francesca's new babysitting gig was a good news/bad news kind of thing. When Marco and I left for our honeymoon, Francesca, a lovely, generous, yet at times overbearing woman, stepped in to help Grace and Lottie. It was supposed to last just one week, but then business really blossomed, so to speak, so we upped her to three mornings a week.

While the extra pair of hands had been useful, Francesca's presence had been something of a thorn in my side, the problem being that we both wanted to run Bloomers. As one of Grace's favorite adages went, too many chefs spoiled the broth—or, in my case, my nirvana.

Then, two weeks earlier, Marco's younger sister Gina

had gone back to work to help support her family, and Francesca decided that she should babysit her grandkids rather than put them in child care. So while she was now out of my paradise, we missed her help.

"Let's think about hiring another part-time person," Lottie said. "Even two afternoons a week would make a difference."

"It's going to be tough to find someone to work just two afternoons," I said.

"I will do it."

I turned in surprise as Rosa Marin stepped through the curtain.

"I will be happy to take that part-time job," she said. "It would be a big help with the finances right now."

Lottie and I glanced at each other in surprise as Rosa stood there in her tight turquoise scoop-necked sweater and snug platinum slacks, big silver jewelry, and gray high-heeled ankle boots, her smile revealing beautiful white teeth. "Okay?"

I glanced down at my plain white shirt and faded jeans, and all I could think of was Marco saying, *Rosa has nothing over you, Fireball.*

Chapter Six

Lottie stuck out her hand, clearly aware that I was struggling with a reply. "Hi, I'm Lottie Dombowski."

"Rosa Marisol Katarina Marin," the Latin bombshell said, turning her blazing smile on my assistant. "I am Mr. and Mrs. Salvare's new client."

"Grace Bingham," my other assistant said, stepping through the curtain. "How nice to meet you, Rosa."

There was never a need to explain anything to Grace. She eavesdropped like a spy. All three glanced at me expectantly, and Lottie gave a slight nod, as though to say, *Say something!*

Like what? That she was too sexy? "You have a full-time job," I blurted.

"I work from seven in the morning until six at night two days a week and from two in the afternoon until six the other three days. I would be happy to come here on two of those mornings. So what do you say?"

That left one argument. "I can't pay much."

"Anything would help." She threw out her arms and turned in a circle. "Where else would I find such a perfect job? I love working with customers. Everyone says I have amazing people skills. I love flowers. I was even named after the rose and the marisol."

"I've never heard of a marisol," Lottie said.

"It's a paper flower that is used for special celebrations," Rosa said. "And I will do any task you have for me."

Seedy chose that moment to hobble out from under the table and put her paw on Rosa's leg, gazing up with the same loving expression she usually reserved for me.

"Well, hello, *perrito*!" Rosa crouched down to take Seedy's shaggy little head between her hands and plant a kiss on top of her head. "What a sweet dog."

Seedy gave a happy little yip and wagged her tail, then, having accomplished her goodwill mission, returned to her bed.

"That's a first," Lottie said. "Seedy usually hides from strangers."

"Animals," Rosa said with a shrug. "They love me."

Animals, assistants . . . who was next?

She took my hand and pressed it between hers. "Please, Mrs. Salvare? Will you let me help you?"

Grace and Lottie stood behind her, nodding their approval.

What could I say? *You can work here only if you keep away from my husband*? That was tantamount to saying I didn't trust Marco, and that wasn't true at all.

Forcing a smile, I said, "I suppose we can try it. Can you start tomorrow?"

She nearly lifted me out of my chair with her hug. "I will start right now. Give me a job and I will do it. Where should I begin?"

A better question was, how would this end?

Everyone was waiting for me to say something, so I turned to Grace. “Let’s find her an apron, and then why don’t you teach her how to run the parlor?”

“An apron?” Lottie asked. We hadn’t worn the bib-style yellow aprons with *Bloomers* embroidered on the front since I took over the business.

“I was just thinking earlier that we should start wearing them again.” Like two minutes earlier. Especially since the bib part would cover Rosa’s cleavage.

Lottie pulled a stack from a cupboard and handed them out. “Here we go.”

“You have a parlor?” Rosa asked Grace as they left the workroom together.

“It’s where we serve coffee, tea, and scones, love,” I heard Grace reply.

“What are scones?”

“Oh, goodness. You must try one. I bake them myself.”

Lottie stood in front of me, arms crossed. “You look like a deer in the headlights.”

“What just happened?”

“I think our prayer was answered.”

I wasn’t so sure about that. I shook myself and plucked an order from the spindle.

“Rosa will be good for Bloomers,” Lottie said as she opened the big walk-in cooler where we kept fresh blossoms. “She’ll certainly liven things up.”

“Isn’t that what you said about Francesca?” I asked.

“You have to admit that our customers loved Francesca.”

“Let’s just hope Rosa doesn’t start bringing in food like Francesca did. We had mobs coming here to eat all those free Italian goodies and no one bought a thing. And don't forget how Francesca arranged all the tools in my drawers in alphabetical order. It took an entire morning to put everything back the way it had been."

Lottie laid her mums and roses on the table and put her hands on my shoulder. "Okay, Abby, listen to Earth Mom Lottie now. Stop anticipating problems. If you focus on things you don't want to happen, you'll draw them to you."

"Seriously?"

"You bet. Like attracts like." She pointed to the full spindle. "You think that's just a coincidence? Haven't we all been remarking how great it is to see it full? Law of attraction at work. It's in a book on quantum physics that Herman just finished reading, and whatever he reads he gives me daily reports on. Daily. Reports." She rolled her eyes. "So be positive and you'll draw all kinds of good energy."

I thought about that as I gathered supplies for a twenty-fifth anniversary arrangement. If I focused on having creamy skin, would my freckles disappear?

After choosing a combination of hybrid tea roses, grandifloras, and poly pompon roses in three shades of pink, with a few lilies in white for contrast, I prepped a silver-colored container shaped like a giant martini glass and began putting the arrangement together. I hummed as I worked, so completely absorbed in my task that I was unaware of the bustle of business happening on the other side of the curtain. I finished the arrangement, wrapped it and set it in the second cooler, then pulled another order and began the process all over again.

An hour later, I stopped to stretch my back and roll my shoulders, then remembered that I'd wanted to call the Maraville School Corporation. Using the delivery ruse again, I was able to discover that Norman Jones worked as a janitor at Central Elementary School, with hours from seven o'clock in the morning until five in the evening, making it difficult for me to sneak away to interview him.

Fortunately, he worked until nine o'clock on Fridays because of their roller rink and swimming pool facilities. That meant I could make a trip out there after supper on Friday and Marco would never know.

My second call was to Tara, who was no doubt on her way home from school.

"Hey, Auntie A, what's up?" she chirped, then said, "Hold on. I've got to answer this text." She was gone all of twenty seconds, then came back with, "Okay, so anyway—oh, wait. Hold on." She was gone again.

When she came back, I said, "Tara, I can't wait all day. Who are you texting that is more important than my call?"

"My best friend. She's having a boyfriend crisis."

"Didn't you just see her at school?"

There was a big sigh. "You don't understand how it is, Aunt Abby."

"Right. I was never in high school. Before you get another message, would you please do an eBay search on furniture made from skis so I know how to price Grandpa's bench?"

"Are you serious?"

"I'm afraid so."

"That is so cool!"

"It is?"

"Well, yeah! Way to go, Grandpa." There was a dead silence, then, "Sorry—I had to take that. Okay, I'll get back to you."

I had just put away my phone when Rosa carried in a cup of tea. "Grace said it's time for your break, Mrs. Salvare."

Without looking up, I said, "Thanks. You can leave it on my desk. And call me Abby."

"Okay—Abby. Is that short for Abigail?"

"Yes, but that's too formal. I don't care for it."

"Oh, but you should. Do you know that in Spanish the name Abigail means 'happiness'?" Rosa lifted her arms and turned in a circle. "And look what you do here. You bring happiness into many people's lives."

That was a different way of looking at it. I found myself smiling.

She perched on a wooden stool, put her chin on her hand, and watched me insert red carnations into an arrangement. "How did your talk with Adrian Prada go this morning?"

"How did you know about that?"

"Mr. Appleruth told me. I called to update him on Sergio's condition, which is sadly the same." She heaved a sigh and was silent for a long moment, lost in her thoughts. Then, picking up a stray pink rose petal, she asked, "So how did it go?"

"Adrian was cooperative. He talked with us for about ten minutes."

"Did he confess?"

"No."

She sighed again. "I didn't think he would crack so

easily." With a pound of her fist on the table, she said determinedly, "We will have to come up with something that makes him talk. We can't let him get away with attempted murder."

We weren't going to do anything; clients didn't run our cases or participate in our investigations. Besides, the only thing Marco and I knew for sure about Adrian was that he was guilty of making passes at Rosa.

"Actually, Rosa, until we spoke with Adrian, he still believed that Sergio had suffered a heart attack."

"Or so he says. El Diablo is not trustworthy—believe me. But he is cunning." She fingered the sterling silver lightning bolt pendant I'd seen her wear before. "We will need a clever way to outsmart him."

There was that *we* again. I had a feeling it was going to be a problem.

To change the mood of the conversation, I said with a smile, "Adrian has quite an ego. The way he was posing reminded me of a matador."

Rosa held the petal beneath her nose, inhaling the scent. "How odd that you should say that. In my language, *matador* means 'killer.' " She let that sink in. "After you told Adrian that Sergio had not had a heart attack, I suppose he tried to blame me for the fall."

"I really can't talk about an ongoing investigation, Rosa."

She slapped her hand on the table. "Why not? I am the one who hired you."

Oh, right. Awkward. Quite a temper she had there, too.

She wagged her finger at me. "You don't want to say anything because Adrian *did* blame me. Am I right?"

I inserted the last carnation. "I wouldn't be too concerned about what anyone else says. Suspects always point the finger at someone else."

Rosa muttered something about Adrian in Spanish, then said, "When will you talk to the rest of the crew?"

I tore off a big piece of wrapping paper and laid it on the table. "We're planning to go back around five this evening."

"Don't do that yet."

That did it.

"Rosa, you have to let Marco and me run this investigation. We need to interview the men while the incident is still fresh in their minds."

With a *Pffft*, she waved away my protest as though it were inconsequential. "I'm not talking about the investigation." She pointed to the arrangement. "The flowers. You're missing a carnation in the back."

I swiveled the pot for a look. Damn, she was right. The arrangement wasn't balanced. How had I missed it?

"See?" she said brightly. "I'm a natural."

"You hired the woman who hired *us*?" My husband gazed at me as though I'd lost my mind. We were on our way to the HHI headquarters and I'd just broken the news about my new employee.

"Rosa kind of hired herself. And actually she did help out a lot today. She seems to be a fast learner."

Marco shook his head. "I don't know if it's a good idea, Abby."

"I don't, either, but we really need the extra pair of hands, and Lottie thinks she'll liven things up. You have to admit Rosa is colorful."

"I'm not saying she won't work out. It's just—I don't know."

"The situation's no different than if Grace hired us to investigate something for her. Besides, Rosa's going to work only two mornings a week. I'm sure it'll be fine." Was I trying to convince Marco or myself?

"I hope so." Marco pulled into a customer parking spot in front of the HHI building and shut off the motor. A gated security fence on the right side of the building enclosed the employee parking lot, where three men in navy coveralls were standing in front of a pickup truck having a conversation.

When the largest of the men separated from the group, unchained a big black Harley, and walked it through the open gates, Marco said, "That must be Sam Walker. Let's catch him before he takes off."

I got out of the car and pulled my notepad and pen out of my shoulder bag as I hurried to keep up with Marco's rapid strides.

"Mr. Walker?" he called.

The man was about to mount the motorcycle, but paused to watch us approach, giving me a vertical sweep. "Yeah?"

Standing well above six feet tall and with a wrestler's build, Sam wore his brown hair short on the sides and straight up on top like a rooster, with the tips dyed blond.

Marco displayed his license and introduced us. "We're investigating Sergio Marin's fall. We'd like to ask you a few routine questions."

Wrestler Sam, as I'd decided to refer to him in my notes, put the kickstand down and turned toward us, folding his thick arms across his chest. "You one of them insurance cops?"

"No," Marco said. "This is a private investigation. I'm not sure you've heard the latest news, but doctors haven't found any medical condition that might have precipitated Sergio's accident, which leaves it a puzzle as to why it happened. Can you think of anything that might have caused him to fall?"

Sam pondered it briefly, then said, "Dizzy spell maybe."

"Have you ever known Sergio to have a dizzy spell before?" Marco asked.

"None I remember."

"Any of the employees have a grudge against Sergio?"

Wrestler Sam paused, as though thrown by the question. "Why do you want to know that?"

"Our client believes Sergio's fall wasn't an accident."

"What the hell else would it be?"

"Possibly attempted murder," Marco said.

Sam let out a loud laugh. "You have *got* to be kidding me."

"Not at all," Marco said.

"You seriously think someone *pushed* Sergio over?"

"You tell me."

I watched the wrestler's expression go from incredulity to outrage. He put a meaty hand on his chest. "Are you talking to me because you think *I* did it?"

"We don't think anything yet," I said. "That's why we're investigating."

"Sergio's wife hired you, didn't she?" Sam asked, his upper lip curling back in a sneer. "She would try to blame one of us."

"Mrs. Marin isn't blaming you," I said.

"Rosa wasn't even there, man," he went on, as though I hadn't said a word. "This is bullshit." He looked around as if seeking an escape hatch, his voice rising. "I ain't standing here taking this shit."

The other two men were watching now.

"Look, Sam," Marco said, "we have to interview everyone who was on the scene Monday morning, that's all. We started with you because you seemed like you were about to take off. So let's make this quick and painless. Just tell us what you observed right before Sergio fell."

"What I observed," Sam said with a sneer, "was my nail gun shooting nails through the shingles."

Marco merely gazed at him with folded arms and waited for him to realize that smart-alecky answers weren't going to cut it. I tapped my pen on the notepad and looked around as though bored.

Sam also glanced around to see what his coworkers were doing, saw them observing, then got serious. "I didn't see nothing but the ladder going backward."

"Did you hear Sergio say anything?" Marco asked.

"He yelled for help."

"Did he say, 'Someone help me'? or 'Help me, please'?"

"No, just 'Help.' "

Marco gazed at him steadily. "Are you sure it was just the one word?"

"I ain't lying to you, man," Sam said irritably. "I know what I heard."

"Then you were able to hear him over the sound of your nail gun?"

"Shit, yeah," Sam said. "I was only like a foot away."

Amazing what Marco could get people to reveal.

"Was anyone else that close to Sergio when he fell?" Marco asked.

Sam's thick neck turned bright red, as though he'd just realized how that admission made him look. "Sure, others were there. Clive, Jericho, Adrian . . ." He looked around at them again, running his hand along the top of his rooster spikes. "I guess that was it."

"Were they as close to Sergio as you were?" Marco asked.

Sam lowered his voice, as though afraid of being overheard. "Okay, I might have been wrong about that. I'm gonna say I was more like three yards away."

"That's quite a difference," I said as I wrote it down.

"Sometimes I exaggerate," Sam said.

"How about the others?" I asked. "How close were they?"

"I can't really recall, but I remember that Adrian was the closest."

"What was Adrian doing at the time of Sergio's fall?" Marco asked.

"I think he was attaching the gutter."

"You can't say for sure?" Marco asked.

"Look, I wasn't kidding before when I said I was watching my nail gun. Take your eye off it for a second and you could do real damage, know what I mean?"

"If that's the case," Marco said, "then how do you know that Adrian was the closest to Sergio at the time of his fall?"

Sam looked down and didn't reply, his neck reddening again. I made a note of his reaction, then glanced up to see the other guys approaching.

"How did you feel about Sergio being promoted to foreman?" Marco asked.

"Hell, I didn't have no problem with it," Sam said. "Adrian was pissed, though. Right, guys?"

"About what?" a moody-looking guy with a Clint Eastwood voice asked. He had icy-blue eyes that sank deep in hollows on either side of his thin nose, a triangular face, a pale red goatee, and long strawberry blond hair pulled back in a ponytail.

"Is there a problem 'ere, mate?" a lanky, brown-haired man with a narrow face, curved Roman nose, and Cockney accent asked. Both men wore the same coveralls and took the same stance—arms folded over their chests, gazes curious.

"Sergio's wife hired these PIs 'cause she thinks someone pushed him over," Sam told them.

"No kidding?" The Brit grinned as though he found it amusing. "She thinks it's one of us, does she?"

Displaying his PI license again, my husband offered his hand. "Marco Salvare, and my wife, Abby."

"Clive Bishop," the Brit said, shaking Marco's hand and giving me a friendly nod.

"Jericho," the moody guy said. His voice was so deep I had to strain to hear it. He didn't make a move to shake Marco's hand, just kept his gaze on him.

"Just so we're clear," Marco said, "the cause of Sergio's fall hasn't been determined. All we know is that it wasn't a heart attack or stroke or any other apparent medical condition."

"Probably a dizzy spell, then," the Brit said.

"Dizzy is what I said, too," Wrestler Sam said to me, tapping my notepad. "Make sure you put that down."

"There was no medical reason for him to be dizzy," I said.

" 'Ere's a reason for you," Clive said. "Sergio liked to lift his glass a little too much at the end of the day. 'E'd come to work in the mornings with some bang-up hangovers."

I made note of it, wondering why Rosa hadn't mentioned Sergio's drinking. When I looked up, Jericho's strange eyes were fixed on me.

"How do Sergio and Adrian get along?" Marco asked.

"Like two 'ounds after the same fox," Clive said, making Sam snicker. Clive seemed to be their self-appointed spokesman.

"And the fox is?" Marco asked.

Clive and Sam glanced at each other as though they shared a secret, but neither volunteered an answer. Jericho remained stone-faced. I had a strong hunch the fox in question was Rosa, and I was fairly certain Marco knew it, too, but he was working in his usual roundabout way to get them to explain. I wished he'd hurry, though. It was five forty-five and my stomach was growling.

"What do I need to know, guys?" Marco asked. "Why didn't they get along?"

When the two men again shared glances, my stomach and I decided to speed things up. "Because Adrian was hitting on Sergio's wife?"

When no one answered, I said, "Come on. It's supper time. Do you want to be here all night?"

I got a look from Marco that said, *Be patient. Don't rush them.*

Yeah, well, tell that to my stomach.

Finally Clive said, "Why don't you flip your question round the other way?"

Great. Now I had to do a quick mental rewind. "Sergio was hitting on Adrian's wife? I didn't realize Adrian was married."

" 'E's not," Clive said.

"Spell it out for us," Marco said, growing impatient at last.

"Let's just say that Adrian didn't like the way Sergio treated Rosa," Clive said.

"Are you telling us that Sergio mistreated his own wife?" I asked.

The wrestler held up his meaty hands. "We don't know that for sure."

"We've only 'eard Adrian's side of it," Clive said. " 'E's had a thing for Rosa for a long time, and it really bothered 'im that she married the bastard."

"Then you have no evidence of it," Marco said.

"Just what Adrian told us," Clive said.

"Not true," Jericho said in his low rasp. "When Rosa came to pick Sergio up one day, she had a big purple shiner. I asked her what happened, and she pointed at Sergio and said, 'It's his fault. Why don't you ask him?' "

I turned to Clive. "Was that what you meant when you said to flip my question around? That Sergio was *hitting* Rosa?"

"Now you're getting the picture, love," he said.

And it wasn't pretty. Allegations were one thing, but actual physical proof was a whole new ball game. It also put Adrian's suggestion in a new light: *Perhaps you should ask Rosa if she slipped poison in his thermos that morning.*

Maybe that wasn't such an outrageous statement after all.

CHAPTER SEVEN

I turned to the first page of the notepad and added a fifth name to our suspect list. I didn't want to believe that Rosa had a hand in her husband's fall, but why had she withheld two huge pieces of information?

"Did you do as Mrs. Marin suggested and ask Sergio about her black eye?" Marco asked Jericho.

"Not my place," he said in his weird, whispery voice.

"What was Adrian's reaction to her black eye?" Marco asked.

Jericho shrugged, his face emotionless. I saw Clive give Sam a sly grin, so I pointed at him with my pen. "You know something."

"Me?" he asked, trying to look innocent.

"Did Adrian say something to Sergio about the black eye?" I asked.

"You'll want to ask Adrian that question," Clive said.

What I wanted to do was jab him with my pen the next time he grinned at Sam.

"Did you ever witness any fistfights between Adrian and Sergio?" Marco asked all three men.

"One or two," Clive said. He glanced at the others but only Sam nodded.

"Any trips to the ER from those fights?"

"They had a few bruises," Wrestler Sam said. "Nothing else."

"Did Mr. Appleruth find out?"

"It was personal," Clive said. "No reason for 'im to know."

"Anyone else ever get into a fight with Sergio?"

"I 'ad the occasional argument with 'im over a beer," Clive said. "Nothing physical."

"How about you, Sam?"

"Sergio and me, we got into it once. He pushed me a couple times, and then I pushed back." Looking at his comrades, the wrestler said with a snicker, "He didn't try it again, did he?"

The others gazed down as though embarrassed for him. Sam apparently wasn't quick enough to preview his answers before they left his mouth.

"How hard did you push back?" I asked.

Sam's neck reddened again. "Not that hard. You know, just to let him know not to mess with me. No one ended up in the hospital or nothing."

I put an asterisk beside his answer. It was worth checking out.

"How about you?" Marco asked Jericho.

"A few disagreements." Jericho seemed outwardly calm, yet his fingers at his sides were curling and uncurling, as though the memory made him angry.

"You've all had run-ins with Sergio," Marco said. "What were they about primarily?"

"With Sergio, it was anything and everything," Clive

said. "The weather, politics, sports—but mostly 'ow we were doing our work."

"What didn't he like about your work?" I asked.

"Sergio 'ad a certain way he wanted things done," Clive said. " 'E didn't understand that his way wasn't the only way, so 'e'd throw a fit. I'd just start to whistle like I didn't care." He grinned at his friends. "Sergio 'ated that, didn't he, mates?"

"Did you ever complain to Mr. Appleruth?" I asked.

"I did once," Clive said. "Appleruth said 'e'd talk to Sergio, but nothing ever changed. If anything, Sergio criticized my work even more."

"I've already asked Sam this question," Marco said to the others, "but how did the two of you feel about Sergio being promoted?"

"I wasn't exactly thrilled," Clive said. "Sergio wasn't a pleasant bloke to work with before. Now that 'e's our boss, 'e's even worse. But 'e was selected, so what's a fellow to do?"

"Jericho?" Marco asked. "Any comment?"

"What Clive said."

I finished writing, then glanced up to find Jericho's deep-set eyes on me yet again. It was almost an appraising stare, as if he was collecting physical information. I felt goose bumps prickle my arms and I inched closer to Marco.

Sam nodded in our direction as he said to his friends, "They asked me who was working next to Sergio. I told them Adrian was."

Nothing like prompting their answers.

"That's what I remember, too," Clive said.

Jericho looked away as though bored.

"Explain something to me," Marco said. "You've got a solidly built man near the top of a ladder that's leaning against a house. How do you tip the balance in the other direction?"

Wrestler Sam said, "You'd have to throw your weight back."

"Does it make sense that an experienced man would do that?"

"If he was dizzy," Sam said.

"Wouldn't you hug the ladder if you felt dizzy?"

They pondered that for a moment. Then Clive said, "If Sergio 'ad a 'angover, all it would take is for 'is sugar level to fall and then—" He tipped his head back to mime blacking out.

"But he yelled for help," I reminded Clive.

"Maybe 'e knew 'e was about to pass out," Clive said.

Sam shook his head. "I'm telling you it was a heart attack. I saw him clutch his chest like this." He cupped his hand over the chest pocket on his left side.

"Why didn't you mention that before?" Marco asked.

"I just remembered," Sam replied.

"The doctors ruled out a heart attack," I said.

"'Ow about appendicitis?" Clive asked. "When my appendix burst, I passed out."

"The doctors would have found that," I said. "An infection anywhere in his body would've shown up in his initial blood work."

"You sure put a lot of faith in doctors," Clive said.

"Considering that both of my brothers are doctors," I said, "I kind of do." And for the same reason, I kind of didn't.

“What about the painters?” Marco asked. “Were any of them working near Sergio?”

“They were down too low to see anything,” Sam said.

So no witnesses. Very convenient.

Clive checked his watch; all shifted from one foot to the other as though ready to call it quits.

“Last question,” Marco said. “Who was responsible for slashing Sergio’s tires?”

“ ’Is tires were slashed?” Clive asked. The wrestler shrugged as if he didn’t know a thing while Jericho remained impassive.

“His tires were slashed,” Marco said, “a dead rat was left in his locker, and his coveralls were splashed with red paint.”

“Why would anyone do that?” Sam asked in mock innocence.

“To intimidate him,” Marco said. “If I were the detective running this case, I’d want to know who left those warnings, because they just might lead me to the guilty party. I’m sure that’s why the police asked Mrs. Marin for the coveralls. Someone’s DNA is bound to be all over them.”

Sam’s head whipped around toward Jericho, alarm written all over his face, but before he could say anything, Clive jumped in with “Good luck to the detectives then, mate, because whoever did it wouldn’t ’ave ’ad to touch the coveralls to throw paint on them.”

“You’re talking like you know who it is, Clive,” Marco said.

“All I’ll say is that a lot of our mates don’t like the bastard. Right, fellows? Now I’ve got a date with a pint, so I’ll be saying good night.”

"Me, too," Sam said.

"Good luck finding your *guilty party*," Clive called in a mocking voice as we walked away. Their laughter followed us to the car.

"They're not taking this very seriously," I said.

"That's why I wanted them to think the detectives were looking for DNA on Sergio's clothing. Did you notice Sam's instant reaction?"

"Yep. Maybe the three of them are behind everything, including Sergio's fall."

"Judging by their answers, they obviously feel confident that they won't be discovered."

As we drove back to town, I said, "You know what's really bugging me? Why Rosa didn't tell us that Sergio was hitting her. Or that he had a drinking problem."

"What's the first rule of investigating, Sunshine? Verify, verify—"

"I know, verify. But the black eye, Marco. That's serious."

"It *might* be serious. If Sergio was abusive, it gives Rosa a motive, which means we're going to have to have a talk with her before we do any more work on the case. Would you call her this evening and set a time?"

"Sure. But you know, Marco, if Clive is right about Sergio having a hangover, it's possible he felt like he was about to black out and called for help before he toppled."

"That wouldn't explain why Sam saw him clutch his chest."

"Maybe he was reaching for his cell phone to call nine-one-one."

"I'll find out from Reilly whether his blood work

showed any alcohol in it. So give me your assessment of the three men."

"Sam seems the type who settles things with his fists and is definitely not the sharpest knife in the block. Clive seems the smartest of the three and is quick with his answers. Jericho is just weird. First of all, he was too quiet. I couldn't get a reading on him. And then I didn't like the way he kept staring at me."

"I noticed that, too. I think you'd better let me follow up on him by myself."

"And miss out on an interview? No way, Salvare. We're a team. If he gives me one of those creepy looks again, I'll call him out on it."

"If he does it again, Sunshine, *I'll* call him out on it. It's my job to protect you."

Aw. How gallant was that?

"Did any of them strike you as being a murderer?" Marco asked.

"Maybe Jericho. I couldn't shake the feeling that there was something lurking beneath the surface. How about you?"

"I agree, and I'll add that Sam struck me as someone who would seize the chance to intimidate or possibly hurt Sergio, but I don't get the sense that Sergio's so-called accident was premeditated. I think that whoever did it saw an opportunity and took it."

Marco pulled into the public parking lot a block from Down the Hatch and found a parking space near the street. "Did you pick up on any animosity between the three men and Adrian?"

"Obviously they threw Adrian under the bus about being the nearest to Sergio and being jealous of Sergio's promotion, but other than that, they didn't say anything bad about him. But how will we know who was actually the nearest unless we can find another witness?"

Marco opened my door to let me out. "I'll call Appleruth tomorrow morning and have him check with the painters and then I may canvass the immediate neighbors in the morning."

"And I'll call Rosa as soon as I get back home." With a sigh, I added, "I really hate having her on our suspect list."

"It can't be helped, babe."

"So what's our next move?" I asked as we walked up Franklin Street.

"We need to interview the three men separately. If you're still sure you want to go, then let's pay Jericho a visit tomorrow after supper."

"It's a plan."

We paused in front of Down the Hatch, where he once again opened the door for me. "What do you say we have dinner and forget about the case for a while?"

Two hours later, as I was romping with Seedy on the floor of our cramped living room, the phone rang. I didn't recognize the number on caller ID, so I answered with a cautious "Hello?"

"Abby, how did it go?" Rosa asked in her upbeat way.

"It went well. We talked to Clive, Sam, and Jericho, and all of them were cooperative. Actually, I'm glad you called. We'd like to set up a time to talk to you again."

"We are talking now, aren't we?"

"I mean the three of us."

"If you have something to ask me, why can't you ask me now?" There was a sharp intake of breath. "Those men said something bad about me, didn't they? Abby, what could those men have told you that you need Marco at your side to talk to me?"

"They didn't say anything bad about you, Rosa."

"Then talk to me, Abby, woman to woman."

"Okay. Why didn't you tell us about Sergio's drinking?"

"What about his drinking?"

"That he often gets drunk after work and comes in the next day with a bad hangover."

"Sergio?" Her voice deepened as her temper flared. "Yes, he has a few beers after work sometimes, but so drunk he has a hangover? That is not my husband. He's too much of a control freak to let that happen."

"Is it true that he stops at a bar with the guys after work?"

"Yes, but never to get drunk."

"Then what would make them think that Sergio had a hangover?"

"My husband gets very bad headaches that make him grouchy like a bear. So ask yourself, Abby, why would these men make up such lies unless they had something to do with Sergio's fall? Did they at least confess to the *advertencias*?"

"They pretended to know nothing about them."

She exhaled in exasperation. "Then I will have to talk to them."

"Rosa, no. You have to let Marco and me do the questioning. We're trained to do it. You're not."

"And yet you are not getting any answers."

"Just have patience. Investigations move slowly at first." As if I were one to talk about patience.

She sighed heavily. "I'm sorry. I am not a patient person. Sergio would always say, 'Calm down, my little *relámpago*. Not everything moves as fast as you do.'" With a smile in her voice she added, "*Relámpago* means 'lightning.' He calls me that because I light up his life like a flash of light."

Wow. That was why Marco called me Sunshine.

"That is why he bought me my beautiful lightning bolt necklace. Now Sergio says nothing at all. He doesn't open his eyes, he doesn't even squeeze my hand. The doctor told me today that he is not very hopeful my husband will recover."

"I'm sorry, Rosa."

"I have to go," she said, her voice choked with tears. "I will see you tomorrow morning."

She hung up before I could say good-bye. I hadn't even had a chance to ask her about the black eye, but after hearing about Sergio's condition, I was glad I hadn't. I couldn't imagine what emotional state I'd be in if Marco was in a coma. Besides, would a wife talk so lovingly about a husband who had given her a shiner?

If she wanted you to believe she was innocent she would, the little voice in my head whispered.

I called Marco to tell him about the conversation, but he was too busy to talk, so to get my mind off Rosa I took Seedy for a walk. As we made our tour of the block, I noticed a FOR SALE sign in front of a big two-story and my thoughts turned back to Daisy Jones. So as soon as we were back home, I found the notes I'd tucked away and called Mr. Kerby, the landlord of the apartment complex where the Joneses had previously lived.

Using the delivery excuse, I asked Kerby if he knew of the Joneses' whereabouts, and he steered me toward a Mrs. Welldon, an elderly woman who lived in the apartment across the hall from the Joneses' rental.

"Hello, Mrs. Welldon," I said pleasantly. "I'm sorry to be calling so late. This is Abby Knight from Bloomers Flower Shop." When would I remember to add Salvare?

"From Florida, you say?" she asked in a warbly voice.

"Bloomers Flower Shop."

"You'll have to speak up, dear."

"Bloomers Flower Shop," I said loudly. Seedy got up from the sofa and hobbled into the other room. I had disturbed her postwalk nap.

"I've never heard of it."

"We're on the square in New Chapel."

"Well, I'll just have to make it a point to get out there one of these days. Thanks for your call. Bye, now."

"No, wait! I have a delivery for Sandra Jones, but I'm unable to locate her. Your landlord said you might be able to help."

"How nice that Sandra is getting flowers. You know, I believe Sandra's in New Chapel, too. Goodness, I haven't heard from her in over a year. I hope she's doing well. And that dear little boy of hers . . . what was his name? Sandra used to send him over with a plate of cookies every Friday. Bud! That was it. They were such nice neighbors, the Joneses, always willing to lend a hand. And whenever I took sick, Sandra would be right over to help. She was a nurse at one time, you know."

"What did you think of Daisy?"

"Oh, my—of course I would love a daisy, but don't make a special trip here just for me."

I raised my voice. "I meant their little girl Daisy."

"I'm not quite catching that, dear."

"I'll bring your daisies out tomorrow, Mrs. Welldon. Thank you."

I hung up the phone and turned to find Seedy peering around the corner. "You can come out now. I'm done."

She cast me a reproachful eye as she returned to her spot on the sofa.

Thursday

When I arrived at Bloomers the next morning, Rosa was already hard at work, dusting shelves in the shop, singing at the top of her lungs. She paused to call, "Good morning, Abby," and it was only then that I heard the radio playing in the background. Her voice had drowned it out.

I slipped into the parlor for a cup of coffee with Grace and Lottie while Rosa continued her aria. Both of my assistants were smiling.

"I told you she'd liven the place up," Lottie said.

"Her husband must be doing better," I said.

"Actually, his condition has deteriorated from yesterday," Grace said.

"Then why does she sound so happy?" I asked.

"Singing can be a stress-buster," Lottie said. "Herman whistles when he's stressed. It's like a steam valve."

"I hope that's all it is," I said.

"What do you mean?" Lottie asked.

"I believe Abby means that Rosa is a suspect," Grace said, then took a sip of her tea.

Lottie glanced at me for confirmation.

"You know Marco's rule," I said. "Everyone's a suspect until we rule them out."

We finished our morning meeting; then I headed to the workroom to get started on orders. I checked to see what had come in overnight, printed them out, then turned to find Rosa standing inside the curtain with a Cheshire cat grin on her face and her arms behind her back, as though she was holding something she didn't want me to see.

She had on shiny black knee-high boots and dark blue jeggings with a cream-colored sweater whose neckline was hidden behind the yellow bib apron. Perfect. Hanging over the bib part of the apron was her lightning bolt pendant.

Remembering that I was supposed to be wearing my apron, I took it off my chair and slipped it over my head as I asked her what was up.

"I have a surprise for you," she said with an impish smile. "You know those ugly eyeball pots?"

"That my mother made?"

"Those are the ones."

I couldn't suppress my scowl. Why did it bother me when someone else made fun of Mom's work?

"I'm sorry, Abby. I know you love your mother, but they *are* ugly. So I was thinking, what can I do to them so that everyone will want one? I thought and thought until I was making myself crazy. 'Ay-ay-ay, Rosa,' I said. 'Stop it.' And then it hit me. Ay, ay, ay—or eye, eye, eye. It's all about the eyes."

She brought forward my mom's hideous pot, now filled with a beautiful arrangement of silk flowers. "You see?" She began to point. "Here you have white irises. Get it? The iris is part of the eye. And here you have apple blossoms. The apple of your eye, you see? Then you have pink carnations for pinkeye, and ivy"—she pointed to her eye—"*eye*-vee for greenery. Now you can say that it is an eye-eye-eye pot."

Ay caramba! It was sheer genius. I stared at the flowers in astonishment as my mind continued to work with the theme.

"You don't like it, do you?" she said in a downcast voice.

"Rosa, it's amazing."

She brightened immediately. "I know! I amazed myself. Lottie and Grace said maybe we could have a drawing for it to get people in the shop, and then they'd want to buy the other pots, too."

"When did you make this?"

"This morning. After I put my son on the school bus I came here to work on it."

The eye pot gave me an idea. I didn't relish the idea of confronting Rosa with allegations of her ailing husband's abuse, but since Grace and Lottie were busy getting set up for the day, now would be a good time to finish questioning her. So I said, "Maybe we could do one with black-eyed Susans."

Rosa laughed as she placed her project on the table "Black-eyed Susans—like a black eye. I like that."

Not the reaction I would've expected from a victim.

"As soon as I am done dusting," she said, "I will fill the rest of the ugly pots."

“Why don’t you work on them later?” I pulled out a stool, perched on it, then patted the one beside me. “I’d like to talk to you about something else right now.”

“This sounds serious.” She sat down and propped her chin in her palm, studying me with her luminous brown eyes. “Are you going to fire me?”

Chapter Eight

"No, Rosa, I'm not going to fire you. You're doing a great job."

She looked heavenward, made the sign of the cross, and whispered, *"Gracias a Dios."* Then she said, "So what can be so serious?"

"This is really awkward, and I hate having to ask you, but it's important that we know everything."

She patted my knee. "Go ahead, Abby. Don't be afraid. I won't bite."

I inhaled, then blew it out. "Did Sergio ever mistreat you?"

She tilted her head the way Seedy did when she was puzzled. "Mistreat me how?"

"Did he ever hit you?"

"Sergio?" Her startled expression changed to anger. She shook her head, her long curls bouncing around her shoulders. "Never did my Sergio hit me, Abby. Never! Who said such a mean thing?"

"All three of the men we talked to yesterday. They said that was why Adrian and Sergio didn't get along—that Adrian didn't like the way Sergio treated you."

She smacked her palm against the slate top. "They are lying!"

"Just let me finish."

She muttered something under her breath about the men, then huffed in disgust and made a forward motion with her hand. "Fine. Go ahead."

"When we asked if they had any proof, Jericho told us that you came to pick up Sergio once and had a black eye. When he asked you how you got it, you told him it was Sergio's fault and you said to ask him how it happened."

"Yes, it was Sergio's fault. He put his big work boots right in my way. I told him a hundred times to leave them outside, but would he listen? No. He is as stubborn as a mule. So one morning I came into my kitchen from the garage and tripped over them."

"Wait," I said, grabbing a pen and pad of paper from my desk. "Let me write this down. How did you get a black eye?"

"When I fell, I hit my face against the corner of the chair's seat. It was Sergio's fault that I hurt myself, but he didn't leave his boots there to *make* me fall. He left his boots there because he was lazy. If he had ever raised a hand to me, Abby, I would have picked up my heavy skillet and hit him over the head."

The fierceness of her expression left no doubt in my mind that she spoke the truth.

"These men," she said scornfully, "they know only one side of Sergio, but I knew his other side, his soft side. He would do anything for me, Abby." Her mouth began to tremble. "He was grumpy, yes, and I know that he could be a critical, demanding boss, but he was a good husband."

Rosa got up and plucked a tissue from the box on my

desk to wipe her eyes. "What else did they accuse Sergio of? Pushing the ladder himself?"

"No, but one of them thought he might have gotten dizzy and passed out from not eating that morning."

"How do they know what Sergio ate that morning?" She tossed the tissue in the trash can under the table and sat back down. "The doctors can tell you what he ate. They would know what was in his stomach. It was the same thing he eats every morning. Huevos rancheros. He refuses to eat anything else. Believe me, Abby, there was nothing wrong with him Monday morning. He slept well—this I know because his snoring kept me awake—and woke up as hungry as a horse."

"Was he diabetic?"

"No. He took no medicine, Abby—nothing, not even for high blood pressure. There was no reason for him to pass out. Someone pushed him backward, and I'm telling you: It was Adrian Prada, and those other men know it. They just don't want to get in trouble with Adrian because he will be foreman next."

"How do you know that?"

"Everyone knows he is next in line. He will not only be boss but he will make a much bigger salary, too. Do you see why he wants Sergio dead? Money and power."

More like money, power, and lusting after Rosa.

"Did Sergio ever get into a fistfight with any of the men?"

She shrugged. "He never told me about anything like that."

"Then you never saw any cuts or bruises?"

"I saw cuts all the time—it was the rough nature of the job—but bruises from fights? Not that I am aware."

"Then you don't know about a fight between Sam and Sergio?"

"If it happened, Sergio didn't tell me."

I finished writing it down. "That should take care of it. Thanks for understanding."

She put her arm around my shoulders. "That's okay, Abby. You're doing your job. Now I have to do mine." She pinched her nose and pretended to wave away dust motes. "Some of those armoire shelves have not been cleaned in a long time. But I will take care of them from now on. Don't worry about a thing." She paused at the curtain to say, "I hope my singing isn't bothering you. I promise I will stop when the shop opens."

"That's fine. And I'm sorry, but I forgot to ask how your husband is today."

"Not good," she said with a sad sigh. "Worse than yesterday."

And yet she sang happy songs. So maybe I did have one more little bomb—why she seemed so cheerful when her husband's health was failing.

"Rosa—"

"If I think about Sergio," she continued, "I will cry, and believe me, I cry loud, and that will scare away the customers. So instead I sing something that makes everyone smile. Then I smile back and feel a little better. I'm sorry. What were you going to say?"

I grabbed the eye pot. "Would you find a good spot for this?"

Over my lunch hour, I made the thirty-minute trip to Maraville to see Mrs. Welldon, using my GPS to navigate the streets of the big, sprawling urban city. I pulled into a visitor's spot in the parking lot in front of the five-story apartment building, one of a dozen identical buildings in the complex, and entered a small vestibule where the mailboxes were located. Tenants' names were posted on each box with a buzzer below. I found the Welldon name, pressed the buzzer, and waited.

"Yes?" I heard the warbling voice say.

"This is Abby Knight from Bloomers Flower Shop. I have flowers for you."

"Well, aren't you sweet? Come right up."

She buzzed me in and I headed for the elevator. The building was old and in need of new carpeting and paint but otherwise seemed solidly built. I exited on the fifth floor and located Mrs. Welldon's unit at the far end of the hallway.

"Come in, dear," she said, swinging her door wide. She was a diminutive white-haired woman with an elfin face that was as wrinkled as a prune. She had on a purple jogging suit with pink stripes down the legs and fuzzy white slippers that seemed too big for her petite frame.

"Here you go," I said, holding out the bouquet of daisies. "Compliments of Bloomers Flower Shop."

"Oh, my! Look how many there are. Let me put them in some water." She shuffled up the hallway in her oversized slippers. "I was just about to have lunch. Won't you join me?"

"I wish I could, but I need to get back to the shop." In fact, I was allowing myself only ten minutes to question her about the Joneses. I sniffed the air, my stomach growling at the delicious aroma wafting from her kitchen. "Smells like bratwurst."

"You're close," she called. "It's polish sausage and sauerkraut."

Yum. I hadn't had that dish since I was a kid, when my best friend Nikki Hiduke's Polish-descended mother would invite me over for dinner.

My stomach rumbled a warning that it needed food soon. If I didn't eat now, I'd have to pick up something on the way back to New Chapel, and during the noon hour there was always a line at the drive-through. So what was the difference if I spent ten minutes eating Mrs. Welldon's scrumptious lunch or waited in line for junk food?

I slipped off my jacket and followed her into the kitchen. "Maybe I'll stay after all."

Her kitchen had the tallest cabinets I'd ever seen, and when she opened one to take out bowls, I noticed that the shelves above the second one were empty, no doubt because she couldn't reach them. The ceramic-tiled countertops were burgundy and the linoleum was gray with burgundy flecks. Her refrigerator was small and old-fashioned and her stove had seen a lot of use.

She dished up two bowls, poured two glasses of iced tea, and sat down across from me at a small round table covered with an oilcloth covering in a bright floral print.

"Tell me what you think of it," she said as I forked a bite.

I chewed blissfully as the salty, sour, and sweet juices coated my tongue, and after swallowing I sighed. "Mrs. Welldon, this is absolutely the best sausage and sauerkraut I've ever had."

"I'm so glad you like it. I don't often have company,

so this is a real treat for me. Now tell me, dear, were you able to locate Sandra?"

"Not yet, but I did find out that her husband is a janitor at a school here in Maraville."

"Yes, he had taken that job before they moved away."

"Do you know why they moved?"

"Sandra said the apartment was too small for them. Frankly, I was surprised. The apartments are quite roomy."

"So tell me about the children."

She smiled sweetly. "Bud was a dear little boy, so thoughtful. Sandra is doing a fine job of raising him."

"What about Daisy?"

"Beg pardon?"

"Their daughter, Daisy?"

Mrs. Welldon looked upward, as though thinking. Instead of answering, however, she forked another bite, chewed slowly, swallowed, then took a drink of tea to wash it down. She glanced up to find me watching her. "Did you want more food, dear?"

"No, this is plenty. I had asked about Daisy."

She looked confused. "You did? I'm so sorry. My mind isn't what it used to be. I'm ashamed to say I've forgotten about her. But rest assured Sandra is a fine mother, and Norm is such a kindhearted man. I couldn't have asked for better neighbors."

"How long did they live here?" I asked.

"Oh, heavens, seems like they were here only a short time, but as you'll find out one day, time moves a lot faster when you're as old as I am. If I had to guess, I'd say two years."

"But you definitely do remember now that there was a little girl?"

"Daisy."

"Right."

"That's what I'm saying. Her name was Daisy. Didn't we already establish that, dear? Better finish your meal before it turns cold."

I ate another bite and savored it for a moment. "This truly is the best I've ever had, Mrs. Welldon. But getting back to the Joneses, did Sandra ever tell you anything about how she met Norm? Where they grew up?"

"You're a curious young lady, aren't you?"

"Well, you know, there's nothing like a romantic 'how we met' story."

That seemed to satisfy her. "Sandra did mention Bowling Green a few times. She said it was such a cozy, friendly place to live. I remember asking her why she left if she liked it so much, and she said that their circumstances had changed. What those circumstances were, I don't know."

"Did you ever notice anything unusual about them?"

"Now let me think. Unusual . . . unusual . . . Well, I have to say I found it rather unusual that Sandra and Norm were against public school educations, especially since Norm worked at a school. But homeschooling is becoming something of a trend these days, isn't it?"

"I really don't know much about homeschooling. Did Sandra ever say why they were against public education?"

"She told me that she could do a better job, that schools weren't focusing enough on the three R's." Mrs. Welldon shrugged. "To each his own, I guess."

"Did the children seem happy?"

"Oh, my, yes. That little Bud would just skip up the

hallway singing his little songs, his blue eyes sparkling so. It did my heart good to see him."

"And Daisy?"

"Oh, well, of course her, too." She took another bite. "I must say, this did turn out well, didn't it?"

"It did, Mrs. Welldon. Thank you so much for inviting me." I took my empty bowl to the kitchen and set it in the sink, then gave her a gentle hug. "Enjoy your flowers."

As I drove home, I reviewed what I'd learned. Clearly, Mrs. Welldon's memory wasn't as sharp as it could have been, but if she remembered Bud, why had she had such a difficult time recalling the cute little girl with the curious green gaze?

I wished I could share my thoughts with Marco, but I didn't want to tip my hand. If my investigation came to nothing, it was best he didn't know. If I did find something concrete on which to base my suspicions, I'd bring him on board at that time.

Meanwhile, I had to plan my Friday evening trip to Maraville's Central Elementary School so that no one would know I had left New Chapel.

As soon as we'd had a quick dinner that evening, Marco and I headed northeast to an unincorporated part of the county, where homes were nestled into a lush valley dotted with trees and ponds, many with barns on their properties. We'd left as early as possible to make use of the remaining daylight. Unfortunately, the brief spell of warm March weather had vanished, leaving temperatures in the thirties with a brisk wind that rattled the bare tree branches and made my teeth chatter.

"Did you have any luck finding a witness this morning?" I asked Marco.

"I caught quite a few neighbors still at home, including people at the two houses directly across the street from the Victorian, but none of them saw Sergio fall. I also spoke to Appleruth and asked him to find out which painters were on the job that day so we can interview them. He said he'd talk to them individually and weed out those who couldn't have seen the accident."

"Doesn't sound promising."

Using Marco's GPS, we traveled up a winding country road past the Art Barn, where my mom had taken classes. Deeper into the country, Marco stopped in front of a lone mailbox on a post beside a gravel road and checked the address printed on the side. "This is it."

"All I see is a rutted path, Marco."

"It has to lead somewhere." He took a right onto the narrow road and followed it through a thicket of pine trees until we came out into a clearing. Fifty yards ahead stood a small, ancient mobile home.

"It sure is isolated out here," I said, looking around at the surrounding trees.

"You can wait in the car if you feel uncomfortable, Abby."

"Right. Like there's never been a slasher movie where the innocent young woman decides to stay in the car." I pulled up the hood on my coat and tightened the scarf around my neck. "Let's do this, Salvare."

Marco killed the engine and turned up the collar on his jacket. We got out of the car but hadn't taken more than two steps when Jericho appeared from around the back of his trailer, a shotgun in his hands. Marco grasped my arm and brought me to a stop.

"What should we do?" I whispered.

"Be ready to jump back inside the car."

"Jericho," he called. "We'd like to ask you a few additional questions about Monday morning."

"Why?" came the low rasp.

"Forgot to ask them before," Marco called.

Jericho moved slowly toward us, taking our measure. He was wearing a camouflage jacket and pants and military-style black boots. He stopped directly in front of Marco, standing with feet spread and arms crossed, his pale, hollow-eyed gaze shifting from Marco to me. "What do you want to know?"

Marco held up both palms. "Do me a favor and put the weapon down. Army Ranger training still makes me uneasy when someone is carrying, especially when I've got my wife with me."

Jericho studied Marco for a long moment, then emptied the chambers and dropped the bullets on the ground at his feet. "Good enough?"

When Marco continued to eye the shotgun, Jericho laid it on the ground behind him. "Now?"

"Thanks, man," Marco said. "I'll make this as quick as I can."

Jericho folded his arms and braced his legs, clearly intending to conduct his business right there. "Go ahead."

A strong gust of wind blew the hood off my head. I couldn't suppress a shudder as I pulled it up and hugged my coat tighter around my body.

"Oh, hell," Jericho said. "She's freezing. Just come inside."

We followed him to the trailer, but when he opened the door to let us go in, Marco took one look at the dark interior and said, "No, man. You first."

Jericho gave him a quizzical glance, then climbed the two metal steps, went into his mini abode, turned on a light, then motioned for us to enter. Marco signaled for me to let him proceed first and then climbed the stairs, staying just inside the portal until he took a quick survey of the room.

He turned to hold out his hand to assist me up; then I stepped in to see a very small but tidy living room/dining area/kitchen. The living room had just enough space for a beat-up brown tweed sofa, an end table with a white ceramic lamp, a green recliner, and a tiny TV. The dining table was a plank of polished wood that extended from the wall, with wooden benches on either side. The decor was sparse but immaculate.

The kitchen consisted of a short avocado laminate counter on the opposite wall from the table, a white-enameled sink, a small white refrigerator and stove, and a few walnut cabinets above the counter. On the counter was a metal baking pan holding what appeared to be a small, skinned animal about the size of a squirrel. I shuddered, revolted by the sight.

Noticing the direction of my gaze, Jericho said, "Tomorrow's supper."

Okay, then.

Beyond the kitchen I could see a hallway that led to the back. Through the open door, I saw a bed with a white comforter neatly pulled up.

"Cozy digs," Marco said.

Jericho gave a slight nod to acknowledge the compliment. "Beer?"

"No, thanks," Marco said. "We won't be here that long."

Jericho indicated the sofa with a tilt of his head. "You can sit down if you want."

As we headed for the sofa, I spotted a door off the living room that I assumed led to a second bedroom at the front of the trailer. We had just sat down when Jericho's phone rang. He pulled a small flip phone out of his pocket and looked at the screen.

"I need to take this."

"Go ahead," Marco said.

He walked past the kitchen and headed up the hallway. "Yeah?" he answered. "Just a minute." When he got to the bedroom at the back, he shut the door.

"Tiny place," I said, glancing around. "I don't know how he stands it. I'd be claustrophobic."

"That's because you *are* claustrophobic."

I noticed the door to the second bedroom standing partway open and got up.

"Where are you going?" Marco asked as I pulled out my cell phone.

"I want to see what's in this front room."

"Abby," Marco whispered as I switched on my phone's flashlight. "Don't."

"Just a quick peek."

I opened the door wide enough to see inside, then shined the light around the small room. In front of a window I saw a table loaded with tubes of oil paint and a jar full of artist's brushes. In front of a swivel stool, I saw a canvas on an easel that had a partially finished portrait of a nude woman on it, her back toward me.

"It's his art studio," I whispered.

"Fine, now get back out here."

"One minute."

Around the perimeter of the room were stacks of canvases in various sizes. More hung on the walls, all of them of women in various nude poses. What was really odd was that all of the women had identical long, curling dark hair. Had he painted the same woman over and over?

I focused the beam on the portrait nearest me and felt a chill run through my body.

Rosa Marin stared back, a sweetly seductive smile on her face.

I moved to the next canvas. It was of Rosa, too. With a cold feeling in the pit of my stomach, I swung the beam around the room. The walls were filled with nude portraits of Rosa Marin.

Chapter Nine

I returned to the sofa in a state of shock, wishing I could take a scrub brush to the image in my brain of Rosa's naked body. The good news was that I'd had the presence of mind to snap a quick shot before leaving the room. But all I could think of now was that if she had posed for Jericho—many times, apparently—were they lovers? Wouldn't they have to be? Which led to the bigger questions: Had they conspired to murder her husband? Was Rosa playing us?

"Are you okay?" Marco asked as I sat down beside him.

"You won't believe what I saw."

Before I could pull up the photo, the door opened and Jericho came out. "Business call," was all he said. He sat in the recliner and waited for Marco to speak. He was totally at ease, elbows resting on the chair arms, face impassive. A man good at keeping secrets.

I slipped my phone into my purse and took out my notepad and pen as Marco said, "I appreciate your taking time to talk to us and I'll keep it brief. Let's start with who is next in line to be foreman."

"You asked that before. It's Adrian." Jericho's gaze shifted to me and his eyebrows drew together ever so slightly. I realized then that I was frowning at him and tried to return to a neutral expression. Using the top end of my pen, I pushed against the wrinkle that always appeared between my brows when something was bothering me.

"Does Mr. Appleruth decide on a foreman on an individual basis," Marco asked, "or is Adrian just the next one in line?"

"Adrian has the most seniority, so unless he screws up, he gets the job."

"Is Adrian aware of that?"

"Everyone is aware of that."

I wrote it down and added, *If true, Adrian lied to us.*

"Is the foreman's position something everyone aspires to?" Marco asked.

"I don't know." His voice, as well as his expression, were flat.

"Would you like the position?" Marco asked.

He shrugged as though he couldn't have cared less.

"Do you know what Sergio was doing right before he fell?" Marco asked.

"Painting the trim under the eaves."

"Did you see him painting?"

"It didn't register at the time. I know it now because people have said it."

"Did you see who was close to him?"

"The guys say Adrian. I wasn't paying attention to what anyone else was doing."

"What were you doing at the time?"

"Nailing shingles."

"Who else was nailing shingles?"

"Sam."

"What was Clive doing?"

"He kept us supplied."

"So he was up and down a ladder?"

"Yeah."

"Was the ladder near Sergio's ladder?"

Jericho lifted one shoulder. If he'd been any more laid-back, he'd have been snoring.

"Did you hear Sergio say anything when he fell?"

" 'Help.' "

"Then what happened?"

"I stopped nailing and looked around. That's when I saw Sergio falling backward."

"So you had your back to him initially?" I asked.

He picked at a hangnail. "Yeah."

"And you could hear him call for help over the nail gun's noise?" I asked.

"It isn't a continuous noise."

"What were the others doing when you glanced around?" Marco asked.

"They were on their feet watching Sergio."

Marco waited for me to finish writing, then asked, "Did you ever witness Sergio drunk?"

"I never hung around the bar that long."

"Better things to do?" I asked, tapping my pen on the notepad.

Jericho gave me a skeptical glance, and I realized I was frowning at him again. "You could say that."

"Like what? Paint?" I asked.

His gaze narrowed. "How do you know I paint?"

"Mr. Appleruth said you've displayed canvases at the

Art Barn. If we wanted to see some of your work, could we find them there now?"

"Maybe a few of the older pieces."

Marco gave me a *What are you doing?* expression. Turning back to Jericho, he said, "Did you ever witness Sergio coming to work with a hangover?"

"Possibly. Could be he was just more bad-tempered than usual."

"What made Clive think it was a hangover?" Marco asked.

"I don't know."

Jericho didn't know much apparently. Marco rubbed his palms on his jeans, something he always did when he felt frustrated. Looking at me, he said, "Anything you want to add?"

I smiled my thanks at him, then turned to Jericho. "Have you heard any of the rumors about Rosa Marin having an affair with another man?"

I could feel Marco's gaze burning a hole in my cheek. If I glanced his way, he'd only give me another *What are you doing?* look, so I stayed focused on Jericho.

"I don't listen to rumors."

Marco put his arm around the back of the sofa and discreetly touched my shoulder. I still didn't look at him. "What do you paint? Landscapes? Portraits?"

Jericho's focus shifted toward the partially open studio door then back at me, his gaze narrowing further. "Whatever strikes my fancy."

More like *who*ever.

"What's it to you?" he asked.

"I'm a big fan of art. I'd love to see some of your work. Do you have any pieces here?"

"I don't show them anymore." He rose. "Anything else?"

Marco stood up, too. "That should do it. Thanks for your time."

"Where were you going with that?" Marco asked the moment we were out the door. "And what rumors were you talking about?" He sounded slightly annoyed.

"Marco," I said breathlessly as I hustled alongside him in the fierce wind, "there were nude paintings of Rosa all over Jericho's studio. I was hinting that I knew about them to see what he'd reveal."

"Do you hear what you're saying? You actually wanted Jericho—a suspect—to know you were snooping around his house?"

Marco was furious. Not many things upset him, but any situation that put me in danger sure did, especially when I created it.

"What's one of the biggest rules I've taught you, Abby? Never tip your hand." He opened the car door for me and I climbed in, feeling about two inches tall.

He slid behind the wheel and sat for a moment, key in the ignition, while I traced a drip down the passenger-side window. I couldn't tell whether he was trying to calm himself down or was doing some serious thinking. Whichever, I knew to leave him alone until he was ready to talk. Finally he said, "Are you sure it was Rosa?"

"I'm sure. I even took a picture. I'll show you."

He started the engine. "Let's get away from here first. Jericho may be watching."

As we drove back up the gravel road, he said, "What rumor were you talking about?"

"There isn't any rumor, just my feeling that there has to be something going on between Jericho and Rosa."

"Based on what?"

"The number of paintings I saw. I could perhaps understand a wife wanting to surprise her husband with a fantasy portrait of herself, but being painted by her husband's coworker? Multiple times? No way."

Marco said nothing as he turned onto the country road, but his fingers were tapping the steering wheel, so I knew he was mulling it over.

"So," I continued, "after I saw them, my next thought was that if Rosa and Jericho are or were lovers, they might have teamed up to get rid of Sergio."

"First rule, babe."

"Verify."

"Right. We'll have to talk to Rosa again, but this time I want to be there."

As if I couldn't handle questioning her by myself? Really? "Then we'll have to go see her together, because if I call her to set something up, she'll insist that I talk to her woman to woman."

"Then let's go after dinner tomorrow night."

One problem: I had planned to go see Norm Jones then. "Isn't the bar kind of busy for you to take off on a Friday night?"

"I forgot it was Friday. Saturday during the day, then."

"Works for me." I was glad now I hadn't shared my investigation of the Joneses with him. If it amounted to nothing, Marco would never know. But if my gut feeling was right, I wanted to wow him with my skill so he'd never doubt me again.

"Give me your assessment of Jericho," Marco said.

"After seeing those paintings, the red flags are up. Jericho is a man with secrets. He'd make an excellent poker player. And did you notice the difference in what Adrian Prada told us about who the next foreman would be and what Jericho said? Adrian pretended like he didn't know, and Jericho said everyone knew it was Adrian."

"What went through your mind when Jericho said Clive was up and down the ladder?"

"Same thing that went through yours. I wanted to know where that ladder was in relation to Sergio's. And now I want to know why Clive didn't mention anything to us about being on a ladder in the first place."

"None of the three mentioned it before. Maybe Adrian Prada can tell us more about Clive's movements. He doesn't seem to be in tight with the other three."

When we stopped at a light, I took the opportunity to show Marco the photo of the painting. Before I handed him my phone, I enlarged the image so he could see Rosa's face—and nothing else.

He studied it a moment. "How many paintings were there?"

"On the walls, maybe seven. There could be more, because he had paintings leaning against each other on the floor."

"I'll call the Art Barn tomorrow to find out what he's displayed in the past."

My cell phone rang, so I closed the photo file, then checked the screen and saw my cousin's name. "Hey, Jillian, what's up?"

"What are you doing right now?" she asked.

"Marco and I are on our way to the bar."

"And then what?"

"I'm going to collect Seedy and take her home."

"No, you're not. You're going to pick me up and we're going to see—are you ready?—The. Best. House. Ever."

Yay?

The Best House Ever was a tiny robin's egg blue cottage with white trim that sat at the back of a long, narrow lot on a street of older homes. To get to TBHE, we had to walk up a flagstone path overgrown with weeds and through a rose arbor filled with dead vines and fight our way past thorny barberry shrubs that stretched their sharp branches across the small porch and snagged our clothing. Then, because no lights had been left on for us, we had to use our cell phone flashlights so Jillian could see to unlock the door.

"Are you sure this is the right house?" I asked, trying to peek in a dark window.

She shined the beam on the brass numbers beside the door. "Seventeen Eighty-Nine. This is it."

"The address or the year it was built? Does anyone live here? It looks neglected."

"It hasn't been occupied for a while, but I was assured that the inside of this cute little cottage will make you flip." Jillian hit a switch inside the door and a light came on behind a frosted dome in the ceiling, illuminating a front hallway barely big enough for four people. There was an arched doorway on either side of us, so we entered a room on the right, where Jillian flipped another switch—that did nothing.

Using light from both phones, I was able to see a

small, low-ceilinged room with white stucco walls and dark wood floors that creaked when we stepped on them. There were two narrow double-hung windows facing the street and a small brick fireplace.

"Isn't this a darling room?" Jillian asked.

"I do like the fireplace, but the ceilings are low and with only two windows, and a north-facing house, it'll be dark in here during the day."

"Don't judge it until you've seen the rest."

I opened the bifold glass doors on the front of the fireplace and something rustled inside. I shined my light on it and saw two beady eyes peering out from under a pile of half-burned logs. "Ew!" I quickly shut the doors and backed away. "I think there's a mouse in there."

"Don't be silly. How could a mouse get down the chimney?"

I rubbed my arms. "I hate mice, Jillian. You know that."

"You hate spiders, Abby, not mice."

"I know what I hate, Jill." I followed her into a bedroom lit by another domed light on the ceiling. The room had the same two windows facing the street, the same white walls, and a minuscule closet. The room was so tiny that a bed and dresser would fit, but nothing else.

"It's too small," I said.

"This is the nursery, Abs. It's supposed to be small."

"We don't need a nursery. We need a guest room."

"Yeah, for all those guests that stay with you." She left the room and went up the hallway toward the back. "Come see the master suite."

I followed her into a room identical to the first. "This isn't a master suite. It's just another cramped bedroom."

"This is a cottage, Abs. It's supposed to be small. But don't judge it until you've seen the rest."

I followed her into a kitchen that was just large enough to fit the sink and small counter attached to it, a few cabinets above the sink, and an old oven across from it. "Where's the refrigerator?"

She opened a screen door onto an enclosed back porch. "Here it is. Oh, look. It's your eating area, too."

And the laundry room, apparently, with the dryer stacked on top of the washer. "Jillian, this is horrible. I don't want to come out here every time I need something from the fridge, and I certainly don't want to eat out here. It's old and dirty."

"You'd have to rehabituate it, that's all."

My Harvard-educated cousin liked to make up words, a habit that annoyed me no end. "*Rehabituate* isn't a word. You mean *rehabilitate* or *renovate*."

"I mean you buy this for a song and put some money into it, open it up, and make it your dream house."

"More like my nightmare house. Does it even have a basement?"

She shined her light around the porch, then opened the back door and looked out into the yard. "There it is."

I leaned out and saw double doors built into the ground à la the tornado shelter in *The Wizard of Oz*. All it needed was a squadron of flying monkeys and a pair of red shoes. I backed into the house, turned around, and headed for the front door.

"Wait, Abs."

"Don't tell me not to judge it yet," I called back, "because the jury is in and the verdict is a big thumbs-down."

"Abby, wait!"

I stopped at the front door. "No, Jillian. I'm done."

"Abs."

"I've told you what I'm looking for, but you're not listening to me."

"You're not listening to me, either! Help me, you idiot."

Chapter Ten

"You are not having a baby, Jillian."

"I am *so* having a baby. Don't tell me what I'm suffering isn't labor, because this is laborious! Can't you speed it up? You drive like Grandma."

"Grandma passed away five years ago, Jill."

"Exactly."

"Fine, I'll go faster. Last time you said I was driving too fast."

"Apparently you learned that lesson too well."

I gritted my teeth and made the fifteen-minute drive to the hospital in silence while my pregnant cousin groaned, moaned, panted, and gasped. I couldn't not take her. What if she really was in labor?

"Pull up to the ER," she directed.

"Let's use the front door this time."

Between pants she ground out, "Pull. Up. To. The. ER!"

When I went around the circular driveway to get to the big glass doors, an ambulance was parked ahead of me and two paramedics were unloading a patient. Holding her bulging stomach with one hand, Jillian reached over and leaned on the horn, causing the paramedics to turn and give us dirty looks.

"I'm having a baby!" she called, rolling down her window. "Bring another stretcher."

They rolled their patient inside and a minute later a woman came out, peered at the occupant leaning out of my window, and stood with arms akimbo. "Jillian, what you up to, girl, making all that racket?"

"Bring a wheelchair, LaBrea. I'm in labor."

I stared at my grimacing cousin. "You know her, too?"

"Don't look so surprised. I got to know some of the staff when we took Lamaze classes. Here she comes. You'd better get around to my side so you can help her."

As soon as Jillian was on her way inside, I drove around to the front of the hospital, found one empty parking space in a far back row, and made the trek in the gusty wind, muttering unflattering things about my cousin. And then I felt bad. How could I be angry at her for having a baby?

I took the elevator to the fifth floor and headed to the nurses' station. "I'm looking for Jillian Knight—I mean Osborne," I said to an aide sitting at a computer.

"A nurse is in with her right now. You can have a seat in the waiting room."

I texted Marco to let him know what was going on, then bought a cup of cocoa to warm myself up.

He texted back: *Should I call Claymore?*

I replied: *Let me get more information first.*

I went to the nurses' station and said to the aide, "Can you find out how my cousin's doing?"

"You're Jillian's cousin?" Giving me an appraising glance, she said, "I guess I should have known by that red hair. You know, I had thoughts of dyeing my hair your color. I always thought it would be such fun to be a redhead. You know what they say. Reds are wild." She looked at me again. "You don't look wild."

"My cousin, please?"

"Right behind you."

I turned and saw Jillian waddling toward me. "Oh, you have cocoa! Give me some!" She stretched out her arms and wiggled her fingers like an impatient child.

"You're not having the baby?" I asked as she slurped my hot beverage.

She shook her head.

"You said you were in labor."

"I *was* in labor. False labor." She noticed my glare and handed my cup back. "It's still labor. So, are you ruling the cottage out?"

When we got onto the elevator, I had a sudden thought, so I punched the button for the second floor, where the intensive care unit was located. "We're going to take a little side trip, Jillian. I want to see how my client's husband is doing."

"Give me your cocoa, then. I'll wait downstairs in the lobby. Oh, wait! Cocoa! Wouldn't that be a great baby name?"

"If the baby was a kitten." I handed her my cup, stepped off the elevator, and followed signs to the ICU wing. The nurses' station was the central hub of a giant wheel, with patient rooms around the outside of the circle.

"I hate to bother you," I said to a nurse at the station, "but can you tell me how Sergio Marin is doing?"

"Are you family?"

"A friend."

"I'm afraid I can't give out that information unless you're immediate family," she said.

"I understand, but is he holding his own?"

She looked past me and said, "Hey. What are you doing? You can't go in there."

I turned to see who she was talking to, but saw only two nurses' aides moving a medicine cart from one room to the next, an old man on a cane doing a slow walk around the circle, and a young woman standing outside a room crying into a tissue.

"What's happening?" a nurse at the back side of the station asked.

"Some man I've never seen before just went into room nine."

The other nurse took off.

"I really can't tell you anything about your friend," the first nurse said to me. "Those were his wife's wishes."

"Okay. Sorry to have bothered you."

I turned away just as a hulk of a man in a black overcoat came out of a room, followed by the second nurse. "Next time bring ID with you," she said crossly.

When she got back to the nurses' station, she said to the other nurse, "He claimed to be a brother, but didn't have identification on him to prove it."

"Who doesn't carry a driver's license or credit card?" the first nurse asked.

Who, indeed?

My curiosity aroused, I turned to look at the man. He was striding rapidly around the back side of the circle, the brim of his black baseball cap pulled down low as though to shield his eyes. He turned up his coat collar, glanced back at the nurses' station, and saw me watching, then quickly exited through a door to the stairwell.

I felt a familiar tightening in my gut, a signal that my internal radar had just gone on full alert. "Who's the patient in room nine?" I asked.

"Your friend," the nurse said without looking up.

Sergio. With an unauthorized visitor.

My heart beat faster. I called across to the other nurse, "What was the man doing when you went in?"

"I couldn't tell. His back was to me."

"Was he near Sergio?"

"He was leaning over him."

"Call security," I told her as I took off toward the stairs. "That man may have tried to hurt Sergio. And check to make sure he's breathing!"

I tugged open the heavy door to the stairwell and stood on the landing trying to decide which way to go. I could hear someone's shoes pounding the cement steps, but I couldn't tell whether it was coming from above or below. I decided to try the logical direction and go down, but when I exited onto the main floor, the lobby was filled with people and I couldn't find him.

I pulled out my cell phone and called Marco. "It's me. I'm still at the hospital. Listen to what just happened."

I gave him a quick rundown, and he said loudly, "I can barely hear you over the noise here, Sunshine, but first thing I need to know is, are you all right?"

"I'm fine."

"Next time you think there's danger, would you do me a favor and have a nurse call security instead of going in pursuit?"

"I did that, too." I glanced around the crowded lobby.

"But I haven't seen even one security guard hurrying toward the stairwell or the elevators."

"It's possible the nurses checked on Sergio before they called for security and he turned out to be fine. Just to be on the safe side, call Reilly and let him know what happened. Maybe he can get a security detail out there."

"Okay. See you later."

"There you are," Jillian said, waddling up to me. "Let's go home. My back hurts."

Because of the gusty wind, I held Jillian's arm as we exited the hospital. We were just about to cross the street to get to the parking lot when a pickup truck came roaring out of the lot and headed in our direction.

I pulled Jillian back to the curb, then waved my arms at the driver. "Hey!" I shouted. "Slow down!"

"There's a pregnant lady at risk here!" Jillian called, patting her abdomen.

As the truck passed by, I saw a large man wearing a baseball cap and coat with the collar turned up sitting in the passenger seat. A smaller man wearing a hoodie was driving. Neither one looked my way.

I dug for my phone as I ran to the middle of the pavement, hoping to get a photo of the back of the truck, but by the time I had the app open, the vehicle was too far away to get much of a shot. "Could you read the license plate, Jill?"

"It looked like three-four-one, but I couldn't make out the letters that followed."

"I'll have to enlarge my photo when I get home. Maybe I'll be able to see the rest." I typed the numerals into my notes, then went back to where Jillian stood and offered my hand.

"Oh, thanks," she said, and handed me the empty cocoa cup.

"Sorry to bother you at home, Reilly," I said into my phone as I sat on the sofa with Seedy in my lap. "I thought you should know that when I was at the hospital this evening with my cousin—"

"Did she have her baby?"

"No. False alarm. Anyway, I stopped by the ICU to ask how the painter was doing and saw a nurse chase a man out of the room."

"Okay. And this is important why?"

Seedy was wiggling, so I set her on the floor. "First of all, he claimed to be Sergio's brother but didn't have any ID on him to prove it. Who doesn't carry some form of ID? And second, the way the guy was dressed made me suspicious. He had on a bulky black overcoat with the collar turned up and a baseball cap pulled down over his eyes as though he didn't want anyone to see his face.

"Anyway, after the nurse chased him out of the room, he glanced my way, then took the stairs instead of the elevators. And then, when Jillian and I were crossing the street, a man wearing a hoodie and a guy who could have been the same man—with a dark baseball cap pulled down low and a coat collar turned up—nearly ran us down. They were in a black or navy pickup truck, and all I could make out were the first three numbers—three-four-one. I tried to take a photo but it's too blurry to be of any help."

Reilly was silent, so I said, "Did you get all that?"

"Just writing it down."

"The police need to put a guard at Sergio's door,

Reilly. If he's the victim of a murder attempt, that man might have been there to finish him off."

"I'll agree that the man's behavior sounds suspicious, but there's nothing I can do about a security detail unless the detectives decide his accident was a murder attempt. What I can do is search this partial plate number and see what kind of matches I get."

"Great, because we have four suspects, and that truck might belong to one of them."

"There's one hitch. You said you saw the first three numbers. A pickup truck's plate should start with the letters T-K, not a number, so that plate might have been stolen, in which case you probably won't find one of your suspects on the list. But I'll see what comes up and let you know."

"Thanks, Reilly. And while I've got you on the phone, when you talked to the Joneses on Monday about Sergio's fall, are you positive that nothing struck you as being off?"

"Are you still on that kick? No, Abby, nothing off or strange, and I interviewed them at some length. They were nice people with cute kids."

"Did you know that they moved out that same day?"

"No."

"Did you see any signs that they were in the process of packing?"

"No, and I wish I knew where you were going with this."

"Wouldn't you think that if someone were moving, you'd have noticed packing boxes or other signs of their leaving?"

"I didn't get any farther than the front hallway, Abby.

I didn't see anything but them. And so what if they moved and you didn't know about it?"

"I just thought it was odd that they were gone when we went back early the next morning, especially because they'd paid their rent through the end of the month. Could you run Norman Jones through your criminal database and see if you get any hits?"

"Not without cause. I'll call you when I know something about the license plate."

I hung up with a frustrated huff. "*You* take me seriously, don't you, Seedy?"

She placed a red rubber ball at my feet and gazed up at me with her tail wagging.

Friday

Bloomers was so busy all morning that Grace, Lottie, and I didn't even have time for a tea break. I did manage to carve out fifteen minutes to put together an arrangement to take to the Joneses, one that I hoped Sandra couldn't resist. And what could be more irresistible than roses, sweet peas, and peonies in shades of blush, pink, and cerise? I added variegated euonymus for my greenery and put it all in a crackle-finish cream ceramic vase. It was elegant and yet relaxed.

"Gosh, it's pretty," Lottie said as she passed through. "Someone's gonna love opening the door to that."

Exactly what I was counting on.

If I hadn't had to walk Seedy, I probably would have worked through lunch as well, eating a sandwich on the run. But a dog had to do what a dog had to do, so I took her across the street to the courthouse square and let her sniff out the perfect tree.

While Seedy was exploring, I called Marco and told him where I was, and in a few minutes he walked across the street to join us. Seedy spotted him coming and wagged her tail hard, then went back to sniffing.

"This is my first break today," I told Marco. "Business is so good, I'm almost afraid to talk about it for fear of jinxing myself."

We sat down on a bench while Seedy explored. "I just got off the phone with Reilly," Marco said. "I asked if the detectives had decided whether to call Sergio's accident attempted murder, but there's been no decision yet. I did have some luck when I called the Art Barn. I spoke with a woman who teaches there, and she remembered Jericho as a painter of abstract art. She said she can't remember anyone ever painting or displaying nude portraits."

Seedy saw a man strolling across the lawn and hobbled back to us, ducking behind my legs and watching the man warily. "It's okay," I said, picking her up. "He's not going to hurt you."

"Do you have time to join me for lunch?" Marco asked as we crossed the street to go back.

"I wish I did. We're on for dinner, though."

He gave me a kiss and then headed back to the bar. I watched him for a moment, feeling my heart expand with love. "How did we get so lucky, Seedy?"

She licked my chin, clearly in complete agreement with me.

My plan was to follow Norm Jones home from the school where he worked so I could interview the Joneses together. So as soon as Marco and I finished dinner, I stopped at Bloomers to pick up the arrangement, took Seedy back to the apartment, then headed west on the highway toward Maraville. I wasn't familiar with the sprawling urban city except for the big shopping mall just off the highway, so when my GPS led me north and then west and then north again, I started to lose track of where I was.

When I finally spotted Central Elementary School, nestled deep in a subdivision, I breathed a sigh of relief. A long brown-brick building, it had a playground in the back surrounded by a chain-link fence, a shallow parking lot in front, and a bigger one on the side. Unfortunately, Norm's beat-up blue van was in neither. I drove around the school twice just to be sure he hadn't parked at the curb, but with no luck. Had he driven something else?

Taking the arrangement with me as my excuse to ask questions, I went through the front entrance and saw the glass-fronted office up the main hall to my right. But it was locked and there was no one around to ask for help. I heard far-off voices and followed them toward the back of the building, then up a hallway to the right, coming out onto a lobby with three sets of double doors. I opened one door and saw a roller rink inside filled with kids and adults skating, laughing, and calling to one another, making it hard to hear anything else.

An older man in brown coveralls was leaning against a broom inside a glass-walled snack room watching the skaters with a smile. Guessing him to be a maintenance man, I headed his way.

"Do you work here?" I asked him.

"You brought flowers for me? Gee, you shouldn't have." He winked.

"Sorry, maybe next time. These are for the Joneses. Is Norm around?"

"Someone's sending Norm flowers *here*?"

"Actually, they're for Sandra. I would have delivered them to their house, but I don't have their new address."

The man rubbed his neck and glanced around the rink. "You know, I don't think Norm is here tonight. Seems like he told me he had to go see his kid's karate class perform this evening."

"You don't happen to know where he lives, do you?"

"Sure don't. You'd have to check with the office, and they won't be in until Monday."

A little girl skated in and around the room, calling, "Mr. Paisley, Mr. Paisley, watch me skate backward!"

"I'm watching, Amber," the janitor said. "Go ahead."

"Norm's wife is an old friend of mine," I said, before Mr. Paisley could walk away. "We lost contact after high school, and I've been trying to get in touch with her ever since I heard she moved to Maraville. Do you know Sandra?"

"Just to say hi. Only time I've seen her is when Norm's old beater quits on him and I have to give him a ride home. I keep telling him to junk that van and get a truck like mine, but he says he can't afford it. So I let him use my pickup when he needs to transport things. He used it just last week, in fact."

"How long has he worked here?"

"About a year, give or take."

"Has he ever said what he did before he came here?"

"Janitorial work—somewhere in Ohio from what I

remember." He gave me a puzzled look. "Why all the questions?"

"I just want to be sure my old friend Sandy has herself a good man. Know what I mean?"

"Sure do. Yep, sure do. Tell you what. Give me your name and number and when I see Norm I'll have him give you a call."

That idea made me uncomfortable. "Actually, I'd rather he not know." I held up the arrangement. "I want this to be a surprise. Thanks for your help."

"Just call the office on Monday, then," he said.

I left disappointed that my trip hadn't been productive. The only new piece of information was that Bud was taking karate. I returned the arrangement to Bloomers and walked Seedy, then got on the Internet and used the databases that Marco always used when he was trying to track someone down. I plugged in as much information as I could about the Joneses—their names, his occupation, their Bowling Green connection, their two past addresses—but nothing came up.

I searched the county's tax records, tried searching for them both separately and as a couple, and even looked for them on Facebook and Twitter, but after reviewing over one hundred Sandra Joneses, and even more Norman Joneses, in all their variations, I gave up. Their names were too common.

When Marco got home, I was lying in bed with an open book on my stomach and the bedside lamp on, still puzzling over the invisible Joneses. I needed to find out what his solution was for that kind of situation without telling him why.

"What are you doing up, babe?" he asked, slipping under the covers with me. "It's late."

"I fell asleep watching a movie and now I'm wide awake and wondering how the movie ended." I rolled onto my side facing him. "So what *does* a private detective do when someone he's investigating seems to have no history?"

"Keep digging."

"What if he's dug all the way to China and still can't find anything?"

Marco's eyes searched mine. "Are you sure this is about a movie?"

"Well, it's not about me." Which wasn't exactly a lie. I traced a line down his chin, down his throat, and paused at the V of his undershirt. "So how would the case be resolved?"

Marco picked up my hand and began to kiss my fingers, one by one, a good indication of where his thoughts were headed. "Here's how I'd end it. The detective would try everything he knew, tap every contact he had on the police force, but still not find anything. Then one day, as he's leaving his office, a black van pulls up to the curb and two men in dark suits yank him inside and tell him to stop his investigation or else. Why? Because the people he was following were in the witness protection program. Hence no history."

Was that why I couldn't find anything on the Joneses? Because they had fake identities?

"So in your version," I asked, "what does your detective do next?"

"Decides not to mess with the feds." He raised my chin to gaze into my eyes. "Forget about the little Jones girl, Sunshine."

Apparently I wasn't as clever as I'd thought.

It seemed I had two options, then. Option one was to keep digging and watch out for dark vans parked in front of Bloomers. Option two was to call it a day.

But calling it a day just wasn't an option for a Knight.

Chapter Eleven

Saturday

The sound of a door closing woke me. I lay there half asleep trying to figure out whether Marco had just come in or gone out. Then I heard a kitchen cabinet bang shut and the question became moot, so I rolled onto my back, folded my arms behind my head, and stared up at the ceiling as bits of my dream came back to me.

It had been about Daisy again. We'd been drawing pictures at a child-sized picnic table in the middle of a grassy yard, just like in the first dream. Daisy had handed me her picture and said, "Will you help me find my puppy, please?"

I'd looked at the drawing and was relieved to see that the brown-and-white dog had all four of its legs.

"Of course I'll help you," I'd said. Then she'd pointed over my shoulder, and I'd turned to see a black van parked at the curb.

I shuddered at the memory.

"Look who's finally awake, Seedy," Marco said, depositing the dog on the bed beside me. "It's a nice, sunny day outside and we've just been for a walk around the block; haven't we, little girl?"

"Did you have fun?" I asked Seedy, giving her a hug.

Marco pressed a kiss on my forehead, then started for the door. "Coffee's made, bread is in the toaster, and almond butter is on the counter. Anything else her highness would like this morning?"

"Nope. Sounds perfect. I'll be right there."

"Good," he called from the kitchen. "I'd like to get over to Rosa's house as soon as possible because I'm going to have a busy day at the bar."

I tossed back the covers and slid my feet onto the floor. "Looks like we'll have to find something to do on our own today, Seedy." In a whisper, I added, "What do you say we work on our hobby?"

She wagged her tail and gave her familiar little yip. How nice that she was in complete agreement. And I already had a new plan of attack. I'd take a bouquet to Mr. Mallory, the owner of the old Victorian, show him my ID to prove who I was this time, and wheedle more information about the Joneses out of him. Seriously, who could resist a short, busty redhead carrying an armload of flowers, with a three-legged dog at her side? The man would have to be heartless.

An hour later Marco and I were on our way to Rosa Marin's house, a neatly kept older bungalow on the south side of town. We parked in Rosa's driveway and hadn't even reached her porch before the door opened and she stepped outside. She had on a long-sleeved navy T-shirt with faded skintight jeans and black ballet slippers.

"Buenos días!" she called cheerfully. "How nice of

you to bring me a report. This can only be good news. Come in, come in!"

Marco and I exchanged glances as we stepped inside.

She showed us into her cheerfully decorated living room and asked us to sit on a floral-print sofa while she went to find her son.

"This is Peter," Rosa said, guiding the boy into the room with her hands on his shoulders. Small of stature, he had dark hair and eyes like his parents, with his mother's attractive features. "Petey, this is Mr. and Mrs. Salvare."

After we'd greeted him, Rosa whispered in his ear, "What do you say?"

Shyly ducking his head, Petey said, "Nice to meet you."

"That's my boy," Rosa said proudly, hugging him.

"May I watch TV now?" he asked.

"Yes, Petey, you may." She gave him another hug, then kissed the top of his head before sending him away.

"He's so polite," I said once he was gone.

"Good manners will open doors, I tell him," Rosa said.

"Who takes care of him while you're at work?" asked Marco, always the pragmatist.

"My mother. She lives across the street. Would you like some coffee? Tea? Water?"

"No, thanks," we said in unison.

"But you must let me bring you something!"

After settling on glasses of iced tea, Marco and I conferred while Rosa prepared the beverages in the kitchen.

"She's expecting good news," I said quietly. "I feel bad now about why we've come."

"Why don't you explain what you saw at Jericho's

first," Marco said. "I'll pick up the questioning after we get her response."

"It's going to be awkward, Marco. She's bound to be embarrassed, to say the least. She might be too surprised to speak."

I clearly did not know Rosa Marin.

"Nude paintings?" Rosa barely got her glass of iced tea on the side table beside her chair before jumping to her feet and crying angrily, "Of me? And there are more than one?"

"Seven," I said, "that I saw."

"Un diablo!"

As Marco and I sat on the sofa with blue plastic glasses in our hands, Rosa paced from one side of the living room to the other, her hand to her forehead, her voice rising even further as she talked. "Why would Jericho have done this terrible thing? *Dios mío,* he has to be a devil!" She stopped and turned to us. "We have to do something about them."

"Unless Jericho displays them in public or puts them up for sale, there's nothing we can do," Marco said.

"But they are paintings of my body!"

"It doesn't matter," Marco said.

Rosa wasn't buying it. She crossed her arms underneath her bosom, her eyes angry slits. "If my Sergio were here he would burn his house to the ground!" She began pacing again. "There may be nothing you can do, but this is *my* revenge. I will take a knife to them and turn them into ribbons."

Marco rose and stepped in her way, catching her in mid-rant. "Rosa, you can't take this matter into your own hands. Do you want to end up in jail? Sit down so we can discuss it calmly. Please."

She was full of fury as she glared at Marco, her nostrils flaring. "I cannot *believe* that devil painted me!"

"We feel the same way," I said. "Please, sit down so we can figure this out."

"What is there to figure out?" she asked, letting Marco guide her back to her chair. "That man must pay! Justice must be done."

Marco waited until she was settled, then said, "Did you ever pose for him?"

Her eyes widened. "You think I would pose for a man I barely know?"

"It doesn't matter what I think," Marco said. "It's my job to ask questions."

She pointed a long red fingernail at me. "*You* believe I would do this, Abby—pose naked in front of this *demente*? Me, a happily married woman?"

"That's kind of what you think when you see a nude painting of someone," I said.

"Dios mío!" She made the sign of the cross. "What is happening to my life?"

"Mama," Petey said from the doorway, "is everything okay?"

"Everything is fine," she said, forcing a smile. "Go watch TV. Go. Now!" She kept up the smile until he was out of the room, then sprang up and began to pace again, wringing her hands. Stopping in front of us, she whispered passionately, "I have never, never, *never* posed for Jericho—or any other man—not even with clothes *on*! I tell you, he is *loco*. Why else would he paint me? He will not get away with this! I will report him to Mr. Appleruth and *then* I will burn down his house."

"No one is going to burn down anyone's house," Marco said firmly. "We need to figure out why he did it. Let's focus on that for now."

"I know why," she said, her upper lip curling back. "It's because he hates my husband. He was going to show them to Sergio to make him think I cheated on him."

"Do you know that for sure?" Marco asked.

Rosa pointed at her heart. "I know it in *here*."

Marco gave me a look that said, *Will you try to get her to sit down?*

I got up and ushered her to her chair. "You sit right there so we can get back to working on your case, okay?"

"You must believe that I am an honest woman who would never let another man see me that way."

"We do," I said.

Marco waited until she was seated, which was on the edge of her chair, her hands clasped. Then he said, "You need to know that Jericho didn't show us the paintings. Abby spotted them in his studio while he was out of the room."

Rosa looked at me in surprise, and maybe even a little admiration. "You were snooping?"

"The bedroom door was open," I said. "A little."

"So he does not know you know about them?" Rosa asked.

"No," Marco said, then cast me a reproachful glance as he added, "And we don't want him to know. So you have to promise not to say a word about them to anyone."

"But I tell my mother everything."

"Not even your mother," Marco said. "This is very important." He was talking to her as though she were a child. "Do you promise?"

"How will I report Jericho to Mr. Appleruth?"

"You can't, Rosa," Marco said. "That will have to come later."

Scowling, she folded her arms and didn't say anything for a long time. Then with a last huff, she said, "All right. I promise."

"Good," Marco said. "To be fair, we haven't verified that Jericho is the artist, but we intend to find out."

"Who else would it be?" she asked. "They are in his trailer."

"It appears that way," I said, "but the first rule of investigating is to verify everything."

"So bear with me," Marco said, "because I need to ask you a few questions that might be embarrassing."

She pushed up her sleeves. "I think it's a waste of time, but go ahead."

"Have you ever been alone with Jericho? And that could mean even while you were still working for Mr. Appleruth."

"Not that I can remember—unless maybe he came into the office when I was there by myself. But he never talked to me. He always acted shy around me."

"Did you ever flirt with him?" I asked.

She wrinkled her nose. "No, I never liked Jericho. He has the crazy eyes."

"Did you ever pose for an artist?" Marco asked. "Ever have your portrait done?"

She shook her head. "Never."

"Did Sergio ever take a photo of you naked?" I asked.

"I am too modest for that," she said, reaching for her glass.

Seriously, had she looked in a mirror lately?

"Why do you need to know that?" she asked.

"Sometimes people share photos," I said, trying to be tactful.

"Not my Sergio. There is no way he would have shared anything so private. He didn't even like other men looking at me."

"Did you ever see Jericho or any of the other men take a photograph of you?" Marco asked.

"Not that I am aware of. Why?"

"It's always possible that Jericho painted you from a photograph," Marco said.

"If he took a photograph of me, I did not know about it."

Marco glanced at me to see whether I wanted to ask anything, and I gave a small shake of my head. "Okay, Rosa," he said, "that's all we need to know."

"I have not changed my mind about Adrian Prada," she said, walking us to the door. "But if Jericho is as *loco* as he appears, then maybe he and Adrian acted together to injure my husband."

"We'll work on that," Marco said.

"How is Sergio today?" I asked.

Rosa's expressive mouth curved downward. "No better. Maybe a little worse. And my poor Petey. Every evening he asks when his papa will be coming home, and I have no answer for him."

I gave her a hug. "Thanks for the tea, Rosa. And please don't feel obligated to come to work if you need to be at the hospital."

"Thank you. Both of you."

"So no burning down anyone's house," Marco warned her.

She fingered the lightning bolt pendant. "I won't."

I saw a gleam in her eye that told me she had something else in mind.

On our way home, I said, "I believe her story, Marco."

"And yet the paintings exist."

"Maybe Jericho carries a secret passion for Rosa and painted her from his imagination. Maybe he even caused Sergio's accident, thinking he might have a chance with her."

"The problem is, Sunshine, that we can't question him without giving away that we know about the paintings, and then we run the risk of having him press charges against us for invasion of privacy. But maybe we can get one of the other men to talk. In fact"—he glanced at his watch—"here's an idea. I've got time before I need to be at the bar. Let's pay Clive a surprise visit right now."

"I've got an even better idea. We're out of groceries, and the store is on the way. Let's stop there first."

Clive Bishop rented a room by the month at the Thrifty-Inn Motel. Built in the 1950s, the one-story, white-brick, fifteen-room inn sat at the juncture of two highways on the southwest edge of New Chapel. There had been a few drug busts at the hotel in recent years, but with increased police surveillance, it was basically a low-key operation.

An old man seated on a stool behind the counter in the motel office gave us Clive's room number and told us that he was in.

"Great guy, that young Brit," the man said, scratching his chin through a scraggly gray beard. "Very outgoing. Usually has a funny story for me, although I can't always catch everything he says with that *furrin* accent and all. A nicer feller you'd never want to meet. Come the weekend, though, you won't see him leave his room at all. Just holes up there with a couple cases of beer and a bucket of chicken. And don't try catchin' him on a Saturday night, either. That's when he entertains the ladies, if you get my drift."

"I didn't get his drift," I said to Marco as we headed up the sidewalk that ran in front of the long chain of rooms. "Is Clive throwing parties?"

Marco put his arm around my shoulders and said with a smile, "Think about it."

We stopped at the third door from the end and Marco knocked. In a moment, Clive opened the door. In white stockings, with his big toe poking through the left sock, he wore a gray hooded sweatshirt and baggy sweatpants. His eyes looked bloodshot and his hair was ruffled as though he hadn't yet put a comb to it.

"I don't see you carrying a six-pack," he said with a wry grin, "so you blokes must be here on official business. Have you come to tell me that Sergio didn't make it?"

"No. He's holding his own," Marco said. "We just wanted to talk to you without the other men present. I've found that people are often more open without someone listening in. Have you got ten minutes for a few questions?"

"Still on the hunt for your guilty party, mate?"

"On the hunt for information, is all," Marco said as I tried to peer discreetly around Clive to see into his room.

"I'd invite you in," he said, "but I'm not exactly set up to entertain more than one person at a time, so how about that picnic table across the way? I'll grab my jacket and meet you there."

He shut the door, blocking any further view.

"Well, Miss Obvious," Marco said as we crossed a sparse grassy area behind the motel, "what did you see?"

"Not much. A dirty white wall, an unmade bed, and a brown recliner beside the bed. Looked like a pretty depressing place to live."

"You missed the sack of empty beer bottles just inside the door."

"But I caught the bloodshot eyes."

After checking for spiders and ants, I sat down on a narrow bench beside Marco at a splintering wooden picnic table that had weathered to a dirty gray. As Clive limped across the grass, one hand on his lower back, clearly in pain, Marco said, "He must have been on quite a bender last night."

I readied the notepad and pen as Clive took a seat on the opposite side.

"I appreciate your taking the time to talk to us," Marco said. "I have just a few questions, so this shouldn't take long."

Clive spread his arms. "Ask away, mate."

"How much do you trust the men you work with?" Marco asked.

"One 'undred percent. They're good blokes."

"Would you include Sergio in that statement?"

"That's a loaded question, isn't it?" Clive said with a smile. "Of course, I trust Sergio."

"Do you remember everyone's position on the roof at the time of his fall?"

Clive rubbed his forehead, grimacing as though thinking made his head hurt. "I remember that Adrian was working at the roof's edge, and Jericho was about three yards up from there."

"And Sam?"

"I don't 'ave a good recollection of Sam. Sorry."

"But you're sure he was on the roof."

"We're roofers, aren't we?"

"Could he have been on the ground getting a load of shingles?"

Clive scratched his sideburn. "Maybe."

"But wasn't that your job on Monday?"

"Can't really remember. We change jobs from site to site."

"Can you remember what you were doing when Sergio fell?"

Now he rubbed his forehead again. "Sorry, mate. I've got a killer of an 'eadache. I want to say I was nailing shingles." He mimed pulling the trigger of a gun.

"Jericho said you were hauling shingles to the roof."

Clive shrugged. "Maybe I was, then."

As I wrote out Clive's answer, Marco changed subjects. "I understand that Jericho does oil paintings."

"And a good painter he is, too."

"Then you've seen some of his work?"

"A few things."

"What does he paint?"

Clive scratched the sideburn again. "A bit of this, a bit of that. You know, a mix."

"Such as landscapes?" I cut in.

"Landscapes, sure."

"People?" Marco asked.

"Not that I remember. What are you getting at?"

"You work closely with these guys," Marco said. "You must get to know each other pretty well."

Clive shrugged. He seemed almost jolly. "Can't be 'elped, can it? We talk while we work."

"So when one of you has a girlfriend, the others know?" Marco asked.

"Like I said, we're mates."

"Do you have a girlfriend?" Marco asked.

"A number of them." He winked at Marco.

"Pay-by-the-hour variety?"

Clive grinned.

The drift just came in. I scowled to let him know I was disgusted.

"How about Sam?" Marco asked.

"He broke up with his girlfriend about a month ago. Poor bloke doesn't understand women at all." Clive tapped his forehead. "For a big guy, Sam's got a tiny brain. It's why I call 'im T-Rex."

"How about Jericho?" Marco asked. "Any girlfriends?"

"Well, he's my mate, so I 'ate to say anything bad about 'im, but—" He made a circular motion next to his temple.

"He's crazy?" I asked.

"Maybe offbeat is a better way to put it. You know those artsy types. Always in their 'eads, aren't they?"

"Give us an example," Marco said.

"Some of the things that Jericho shares don't always make sense. 'E'll say 'e's got a girlfriend and tell us 'ow beautiful she is, but won't tell us 'er name. Or 'e'll come in all steamed up about his latest painting, bragging that it'll fetch a thousand dollars, it's just that brilliant. But then 'e won't show it to us."

"Does Jericho have a girlfriend currently?" Marco asked.

"That's what I mean. 'E says 'e does, but 'e won't tell us anything about 'er."

"Have you ever seen him out with a woman?"

"Not once in the year I've been 'ere. I think 'e's just a big talker."

"Do you ever spend time at his trailer?"

"Sure. Sometimes Sam and I'll spend a whole weekend out in the country, mostly in the summer, though."

"And while you're there, does he show you his paintings?" I asked.

"Sometimes, and other times 'e'll be dark and mysterious. When 'e's like that, I'll try to joke 'im out of it. 'Girl troubles?' I'll ask, giving 'im a jab in the ribs. 'Is there any other kind of trouble?' 'e'll say, and then 'e'll be better."

"Can you describe the paintings you've seen?" I asked.

"Back when I first hired on, 'e showed us some landscapes 'e'd done, country scenes mostly. The last painting 'e showed us was one of those really modern art pieces." He rubbed his forehead again. "I can't think what they're called at the moment."

"Abstracts?" I asked.

"That's it."

"How long ago was that?" Marco asked.

"Four or five months, I'd say." Clive folded his arms across his chest. "Why all the interest in Jericho's paintings?"

"Just part of our investigation," Marco said. "I like to get to know people."

"That's a little scary, mate. What do you know about me? Or maybe I don't want to know."

"You're here on a work permit visa," Marco said. "You're divorced, no children. A history of larceny."

"Petty larceny," Clive said with a smile. "You know 'ow teenagers are."

"We don't consider auto theft and home invasion petty larceny here in the States, Clive." Marco had obviously been doing some homework.

"I did my time and came out a reformed man," Clive said, still smiling.

"Any of the four roofers own a pickup truck?" Marco continued.

"All of us do," Clive said.

"Describe them, if you would."

"Mine's silver, Sam's is navy, Jericho's and Adrian's are black. Sam also 'as a Harley, but 'e'll only take it out in good weather."

As I wrote, Marco asked, "Do you remember where you were Thursday evening about eight o'clock?"

"Probably 'ome. Why?"

"A stranger was seen entering Sergio's hospital room," Marco explained. "Big guy, black baseball cap and overcoat, later seen riding shotgun in a black or navy pickup truck with a smaller man driving. He claimed to be a brother but had no ID on him. Puzzling thing is, Sergio doesn't have a brother."

"And you think the fellow was out to hurt Sergio," Clive said. "Look, it's no secret I didn't like the bloke much, but I wouldn't 'ave tried to harm 'im. I really can't see any of my mates doing that, either."

"If I told you that the detectives have gathered evidence showing that Sergio's fall was not an accident," Marco said, "what would you say?"

"I'd be stunned, that's all. Just stunned."

Marco leaned forward. "If you had to pick one of your coworkers as the culprit, Clive, who would it be?"

"I can't pick one of my mates. It's not right."

"Why? Are you afraid word would get back to him?"

"No. That's not what I meant."

"What did you mean, then?"

"I mean I won't pick one of them."

"You won't say who you think might have done it?" Marco asked. "Then you do have someone in mind."

His jolliness gone, Clive slapped his palm on the table and got up. "I'm not playing your little game. I'll not point a finger at any of my mates."

"It's Sam, isn't it?" I asked before he started away. "He's who you'd pick."

Clive swung around, his eyes blazing as he stabbed a finger at me. "I did not say that!" Then he limped away as fast as he could.

"I'll bet he wanted to say that," I said.

Marco's cell phone rang. He pulled it from his pocket and checked the screen. "It's Reilly. He must have news on the case."

"Hey, Sean, what's up?" he asked as we walked back

to the car. He listened a few minutes, then said, "Where is she? Okay, we'll be right there."

"Where is who?" I said as he unlocked the car.

"Rosa. I hope the groceries will hold. We have to go bond her out of jail."

Chapter Twelve

"You tried to break into Jericho's trailer?" I asked Rosa in a whisper after they'd brought her out of the women's holding cell.

"I wanted to see those paintings," she said with an innocent shrug. "He would not open the door."

"So you smashed the glass? What were you thinking?"

"I wanted Jericho to tell me why he did such a horrible thing. Do you see that a man who would paint naked pictures of another man's wife would also slash his tires and leave dead rats in his locker?"

"He said you threatened to cut the paintings to ribbons," I told her.

As we received curious stares from the people around us, Marco moved us toward the exit.

"A man like that would push Sergio's ladder to make him fall," Rosa concluded.

"What did you intend to do if he confessed?" Marco asked.

She looked up, thinking, then shrugged. "Call the police, I guess. And then cut the paintings."

Marco shook his head as he opened the door for us. "She's even more impulsive than you are," he said quietly as I passed through behind Rosa.

"Than I *was*," I corrected. "I've learned a lot of self-control over the past two years. In fact, I've learned a lot about investigative work in general." And I was going to prove that to him soon.

When we were in Marco's Prius, I asked Rosa where her son was.

"My mother is taking care of him."

"What would Petey think if you had to sit in jail for a week?" Marco asked.

She huffed and stared out the window, her arms crossed.

"You're lucky Jericho didn't press charges," Marco said, watching her in the rearview mirror.

"He would not dare," Rosa said hotly. "If he did, I would make him take me to court and then I would demand that he produce the paintings so that everyone would know what kind of man he is. That is the kind of man who would push Sergio's ladder."

"Do you understand that you might have put us in jeopardy?" Marco asked.

"How?" she asked.

"Because Jericho now knows that one or both of us poked around in his house," Marco said. "If he's the man who tried to kill your husband, what would stop him from trying to hurt us?"

Immediately, her forehead creased. "I did not think about that. I was trying to help. I am so sorry."

"You have to let us run the investigation," Marco said, "or we'll have to pull out."

"Please don't do that," she implored. "I will not cause a problem again. I promise."

She was silent until we parked in front of her house. Then she leaned between the seats, put a hand on each of our shoulders, and said, "Thank you for coming to get me and for talking the cops out of making me post a bond. I'm sorry I caused you trouble. I just want to find the man who pushed my husband."

"That's what we want, too," I said.

"Good," she said with a smile. "So what's our next step?"

"What *is* our next step?" I asked Marco as we headed to the apartment.

"It's your next step, Sunshine, because obviously Rosa wasn't listening to me. You'll need to have another talk with her. Make it absolutely clear that either *she* keeps out of it or *we* get out of it. I'm dead serious about that, Abby. I'm not going to let her put you in danger again."

Marco didn't get angry often, but he was now. I patted his arm. "I'll talk to her. Rosa means well. She's just impatient." I poked his shoulder playfully. "Like me."

"One impatient woman is all I can handle, babe."

"It's all you'd better *want* to handle, Salvare."

One corner of his mouth curved up as he glanced over at me, so I knew he was softening. "Why don't we review what we learned from Clive?"

I opened the notepad. "I don't have much. It felt like we were spinning our wheels with Clive. But I did have a hard time believing he couldn't remember what he was doing when Sergio fell. That moment should be etched in his brain."

"I think he's suffering from a hangover, but point taken. What else?"

"You didn't tell me that Clive has a history of auto theft and home invasion."

"Sorry. I didn't mean to spring that on you. But it does make Clive look like more of a suspect, given that he fits the description of the driver you saw at the hospital."

"Which goes along with my next point. Three of them own dark-colored pickup trucks, and two of them—Sam and Jericho—are big enough to match the man I saw at the hospital. Did Reilly ever get back to you about the license plate number, by the way?"

"No. I'll call him from the bar this evening."

"Then we have Clive's report of Jericho being secretive about both his alleged girlfriend and his paintings. I'll bet there is no girlfriend, Marco, except in his mind."

"If he fantasizes about Rosa, that could explain why he paints her nude."

"Only a man would think that way," I teased.

"Really? What would a woman do if she fantasized about a man?"

"A normal woman? She'd buy a few romance novels and continue the fantasy."

"And if she wasn't normal?"

"Stalk the guy."

Marco pretended to shiver. "I think I prefer the nude paintings."

"Of course you do, honey," I said, patting his leg. "You're a man."

"Moving on," he said.

"Clive is loyal to his friends," I said. "If he knows who pushed Sergio, I don't think he'll ever say so."

"It might be more than a matter of loyalty, Abby. Maybe Clive doesn't want to end up like the rat in the locker."

"Really?"

"Think about how upset he got when you called him out on Sam."

"True."

"What I keep noticing with the three men is that they all agree that Adrian was the closest to Sergio, and yet none of them will say much more than that. They'll hint at things and then deny them. It makes me wonder whether it's because they're afraid Adrian will be their next boss, or because they know he didn't push Sergio."

"How do we find out?"

"By asking more questions. I'm going to start with Sam. He seems the easiest to crack."

I clicked on my cell phone's calendar to make the entry. "Okay, what day and time?"

"I'd like to be at his house when he gets home from work on Monday, but without you this time, Abby."

I glanced at him in surprise. "Why?"

"Because, of all the suspects, Sam seems the most volatile, and I don't want you in harm's way."

"Marco, I'm your partner. I should be there."

"There is no *should* in this, babe. You don't have to be with me for every interview."

"But the interviews are the best part. How many times have we interviewed suspects together over the past two years? And how many turned out to be dangerous during the interview? One? Come on, Marco, you weren't this nervous before we got married. The only difference now is that I've got this pretty ring on my finger." I wiggled my fingers for him to see.

A muscle in his jaw ticked. He knew I was right, but he couldn't admit it.

"Let me put it this way, Salvare. Just try to keep me away."

As we carried groceries up the outside stairs into the kitchen, Marco said, "I hate to leave you alone on your Saturday off."

"Don't worry about it. I know it can't be helped. Besides, I've got things to do."

"Such as?"

I pretended to ponder it. "Oh, maybe take Seedy for a walk . . . Lounge on the sofa with that new mystery I picked up last month and haven't had a chance to read. How often do I have an opportunity to do that?"

"Sounds like a relaxing afternoon. You're probably sick of eating at the bar, so don't feel you have to meet me for dinner."

"Marco, there's nowhere I'd rather be than with you."

He drew me into his arms for a kiss. "I was hoping you'd say that. And I'm sorry for before. You're my life, Abby. I'd never forgive myself if something happened to you."

"Don't you think I feel the same way? We're in this together, Marco, for better or for worse. For richer or for poorer. Till—"

He put his fingers over my lips. "Stop right there."

On his way out the door, he stopped to rub Seedy's head. "Keep Abby out of trouble, okay?"

She wagged her tail. She was amazingly good at keeping secrets.

An hour later, with Seedy on her leash, and armed with an enticing arrangement of spring flowers, I walked up to the front door of an impressively large brick home and rang the doorbell.

"Okay, Seedy, look adorable," I said, stroking her head. "We need to charm Mr. Mallory into giving us information about the Joneses."

But it wasn't the man who owned the old Victorian who answered. It was a fiftysomething woman in a black velour jogging suit. "Oh, my gracious heavens, is that for me?"

I hadn't even considered that Mrs. Mallory might be home. Now we'd have to charm them both. But before I could ask whether her husband was at home, she opened the storm door, talking a mile a minute.

"I can't believe Bob actually remembered my birthday! He never does, you know, even with all the hints I drop. And he never let on at all when he left this morning to go fishing. Well, it's a good thing he remembered—let me tell you. Who leaves his wife alone to go fishing on her birthday? Please come in!"

"I have my dog with me."

"I don't mind one bit. Please!"

I stepped inside but Seedy hung back, so I handed the woman the arrangement and scooped Seedy up, setting her on the carpet in the foyer. "She's shy. She's a rescue."

"Well, that poor little thing. Isn't she a dear, missing one leg. Oh, these are from Bloomers," she said, checking the envelope attached to the wrapping paper. "I love that little shop. Wait while I get you a tip, dear."

"Mrs. Mallory?" I called as she hurried up the hallway. "There's no need for that. I own Bloomers."

"Well, then how about a cup of coffee and a piece of birthday cake? I just brewed a fresh pot and I'd love to hear more about your rescue pup." With a big smile, she motioned for me to follow. "Come on back to the kitchen."

Half an hour later, I was the one smiling. Not only had I eaten the most delicious dark chocolate birthday cake ever and washed it down with two cups of caramel-flavored coffee, but I also had another piece of information about the Joneses: the names and phone numbers of the two references Norm had put on his rental application. Both lived in Bowling Green, Ohio.

"See how well we work as a team?" I asked Seedy as we drove home. "Mrs. Mallory couldn't resist us."

My cell phone beeped to signal an incoming text, but I ignored it. It was followed by a second beep, and then a third. Just as I was pulling into a parking spot near the apartment, the phone rang.

"Oh, good," Jillian said. "You're there. You ignored my texts so I was afraid something had happened."

"Nothing happened. I was driving. I'm one of those rare people who refuses to put my life on the line to see what people like you want. I would have called you back in a few minutes."

"Whatev. Just drop what you're doing and come get me so I can show you the perfect house. The. Perfect. House, Abs."

"At least it's not The. Best. House. Ever."

"No jokes, Abby. I'm serious about this one."

"I won't hold my breath."

"You'll see. It's the model home in a new development and it's going to sell fast. How soon can you get here?"

"I have to take Seedy home, so twenty minutes."

"Okay, Grandma."

"Fifteen."

"Fine. Just hurry."

"Oh, my God."

"Didn't I tell you?" Jillian asked, gleefully poking me in the shoulder. "Didn't I?"

"I can't believe it."

"And you doubted my ability to find you The. Perfect. House." She sighed dramatically. "O ye of little faith."

I stood in the middle of the spacious living room and gazed around in astonishment. "Everything is brand-new."

"I know! Isn't it exciting? You'd be the first owners."

Wow. I couldn't believe it. A nine-foot ceiling. Tan walls with white trim. Two-tone beige carpet. Five big windows. A little over our budget, but otherwise perfect. It seemed too good to be true. "Before I step one foot out of the room, are you sure it has two bedrooms?"

She waved the listing papers in front of me. "Two bedrooms, Abs."

"And a basement?"

"And a basement. It's got everything on your list and more."

"Pinch me. I think I'm dreaming." I turned around just as Jillian pinched the soft flesh under my arm. "Ow! It's just a saying, Jill."

"Are you going to stand there rubbing your arm or do you want to see the other surprises this house has?"

"I'm afraid to leave here. I'm afraid that when I walk out, the rest of it will be a huge disappointment."

Stepping behind me, Jillian put her hands on my shoulders and pushed me through the living room into the dining area and from there into the kitchen.

"Granite counters, Abs," Jillian said, running her hands along the smooth black surface. "Stainless steel appliances. Light cherry cabinets—and look at these sleek handles."

I felt tingles of excitement in my stomach. "Show me more."

We walked down a hallway and stopped to see a guest room, also painted a warm tan with white trim. It was large enough to fit a double bed, dresser, nightstand, and chair—or a crib, changer table, rocking chair, and dresser, if that time ever came.

I gave her a thumbs-up. "So far so good."

Our next stop was the guest bathroom across the hall. It had a decent-sized tub, a white toilet, and an oak commode larger than the one in Marco's apartment.

"Look at this," Jillian said, running her hands over the shiny counter. "More granite. Oh, wait—Granite! That'd be an awesome name."

"Please tell me you wouldn't do that to your baby."

She sighed loudly. "You're such a spoilsport."

We entered the master bedroom, and that was the moment I knew I was in love. Not only was it big enough for our queen-sized bed, Marco's dresser, and two nightstands, but it also had a perfect spot for my great-grandmother's cedar chest, still in storage in my mom's basement. I'd always dreamed of having a place for it.

"Right here beneath these windows," I told Jill.

"You're right. The chest would be perfect there. And did you notice the view?"

"A park behind the house! Seedy will love that."

"This is one of six homes that border the park," Jillian pointed out. "It's a premier lot, but because of the economy right now, you might be able to get the house at preconstruction prices."

I took another look around, my excitement growing. "Show me the basement, quick."

"Park," she said as we headed down the hallway. "My son, Park Osborne."

"Don't."

The basement turned out to be an unfinished area with the furnace and hot water heater on the far end, and the laundry tub and washer and dryer hookups on the near end behind the stairs. But it had potential. I could see Marco carving out space for a workshop, and maybe even a man-cave.

"Well?" Jillian asked as we headed upstairs. "I don't hear any 'Thank you, Jillian's."

"Thank you, Jillian. This *is* my dream house. You were right."

She peered out the living room window. "Oh, great. Here comes someone else to look. Call Marco and get him over here. If you want the house, you have to make an offer today."

"Today?" I asked as I dialed his number. "He won't want to decide that quickly."

"Hot properties move fast, Abs. Follow me."

We stepped onto the back deck just as Marco answered. "You won't believe it, Marco. Jillian found us our dream house. It has everything, including a deck, a fenced-in backyard, and a park behind the house. And the best part is that it's brand-new."

"But?"

"No *buts*. This house has it all. It's a little above our price range, but Jillian said we might be able to get a preconstruction price."

"So there is a *but*."

"Fine. There's a *but*. Jillian thinks it'll move quickly, so we need to make an offer soon. But you do need to see it first."

"So there are two *buts*."

"I'm serious, Marco. Can you get away?"

"I've never heard you this excited about a house before, Sunshine. Okay, I should be able to leave for half an hour."

"Leave now. Hurry."

By the time Marco got there, the other couple was standing in the kitchen discussing whether to make an offer.

"I'm going to take photos," I told him at the front door. "Jillian will take you through."

"You realize this is the model home," he said, "in a new subdivision."

"So?"

"So this is one of the first houses to be completed. That means they'd be building all around us."

"And?"

"Noise, Abby. Construction dust. Workers. Trucks—big ones—rumbling in and out of the neighborhood."

"Temporarily." I readied the camera app on my phone.

"There's a couple in the kitchen who might make an offer. We have to move fast."

"Come on," Jillian called, and Marco followed.

While they were looking at the house, I ran around snapping photos and planning furniture arrangements. By the time we met back in the living room, Marco had come to a decision. "It *is* a great house, Abby. If you really like it, then we should put in an offer."

I wrapped my arms around his waist and hugged him. "Let's do it, Salvare. Get the paperwork ready, Jillian."

"Yeah, about that . . . ," she said, looking just the tiniest bit chagrined. "I'd love to write your offer, but you signed an agreement with Lorelei, so she'll have to do it."

"Three *buts*," Marco said.

"Then what will happen?" I asked my cousin.

"Then she'll submit it to the developer and give him a day to respond."

"She'd better be home," I said as I pulled out my phone. I found our Realtor's number and crossed my fingers as I counted the rings. "Hello, Lorelei? I found a house."

"Think about it, Buttercup," Marco said as we headed to our cars. "We might be home owners by tomorrow."

"I'm so excited, I don't know if I'll be able to sleep."

That was the beginning of one of the longest twenty-four hours of my life.

After meeting Marco for dinner at the bar, Seedy and I returned to the apartment that now seemed tinier than ever. In truth, it had never felt like home to me, not because it had been Marco's bachelor pad but because there wasn't much I could do to make it feel like mine. It spanned the second floor of an old house, with steps going up the back, a tiny kitchen and even tinier eating area, a bathroom with a handheld shower that Marco had installed over the tub, a small living/dining room, and a cramped bedroom, all sparsely decorated.

I'd added as many feminine touches as I could squeeze in, and Marco had made room for me in his closet, but the clothes were so smashed into it that they always came out wrinkled. And forget about space for my cosmetics in the bathroom medicine cabinet. I had to keep a plastic bin full of my supplies on top of the toilet.

"I won't miss this place, Seedy."

She was circling in her doggy bed, ready to take a nap, but when she heard her name she paused and wagged her tail.

"Want to go outside?" I asked her.

She didn't even look at me. She found just the right spot and lay down.

"Okay, fine. I'll have to find something else to do."

After the excitement of the afternoon, I was still keyed up and very glad I had a project to work on. I pulled out the list Mrs. Mallory had given me and made a call to the first name on it, a Mark Dillon in Bowling Green, Ohio. He had worked with Norm Jones at Bowling Green Elementary. The phone went straight to voice mail, so I left a message and moved on.

The second name was Steve Conroy, but a recording said I'd dialed a number no longer in service. I did an Internet search for variations of "Steven Conroy, Bowling Green, Ohio," but the only thing that popped up was an obituary. I sure hoped that wasn't our man.

As I continued to search, my phone rang, and I saw an out-of-town number from Bowling Green on the screen. Trying to sound professional, I responded, "Salvare Detective Agency."

"Hi, this is Mark Dillon. I got a call from someone in your office just a little while ago."

"Hello, Mr. Dillon. This is Abby Salvare. I was the one who called you. I'm checking references for a business client, and your name was on the list."

"You're not trying to sell me something, are you? Because I'm on the Do Not Call list."

"No, this is a legitimate business call, Mr. Dillon. If you'd like to look our detective agency up on the Internet, I'll give you the Web site."

"I've never talked to a private detective before. What do you need to know?"

"First of all, do you still work for Bowling Green Elementary School?"

"I did until a few months ago. I'm retired now."

"Thank you. Do you recall a janitor there by the name of Norman Jones?"

"Sure do. I worked with Norm for many years. Great guy."

That was consistent with what everyone else had said. "Did you ever meet his family?"

"You bet. We used to have dinner with them once a month. My wife and I even babysat for their kids a number of times."

Huh. Then maybe my internal radar *was* off.

"So you do remember Bud and Daisy?"

"Who?"

"Bud and Daisy, Norm's children."

"Norm's kids are Dan and Elizabeth. Are you sure we're talking about the same Norman Jones?"

"Norm the janitor who worked at the same school where you worked? His wife's name is Sandra?"

"Sandra? Not the Norm Jones that I worked with. His wife's name was Martha."

My radar starting beeping. "How about if I describe Norm to you. He's a big man, on the overweight side, with brown hair balding on top, and he drives a beat-up Chevy van, or at least he does now, maybe not when you knew him."

"Young lady, I don't know who you're talking about. Norm Jones passed away over a year ago."

Chapter Thirteen

"Norman Jones is dead?" Goose bumps sprang up on my arms.

"He'd better be. I went to his funeral."

Then who was the man pretending to be Norman Jones? And where did Sandra fit into the picture? "Do you have Norman's wife's address or phone number so I can talk to her?"

"Martha followed Norm about five months later, I'm sad to say. It broke her heart when he died."

"I'm so sorry."

"Looks like your information is a little out-of-date."

"It appears that way. So let me ask you this. Do you happen to know a Steve Conroy?"

"Yes, ma'am. I worked with Steve for many years. He passed away about a year before Norm. The cancer got him."

"Then he was also a janitor?"

"Yes, ma'am."

My mind was racing trying to figure out what was going on. Why would the man I knew as Norman Jones, a janitor in Maraville previously from Bowling Green, take the name of a deceased janitor? And then use another deceased janitor as his reference?

"This might be a long shot, Mr. Dillon, but is there anyone you worked with maybe a year ago who fits the description of the man I thought was Norman Jones? Large, balding, brown hair, beat-up Chevy van?"

"Well," he said slowly, "you could be talking about Ed Birchman. He was a tall, heavy guy with brown hair, bald on top. I don't remember the van, though."

"Did Ed have a wife named Sandra?"

"That might've been her name. He was a real private guy. Didn't like to socialize with the rest of us."

"Did he ever talk about his children?"

There was silence for a moment; then he said, "I seem to recall something about a boy."

"How long did you work with Ed?"

"Maybe a year at the most. He moved around a lot from what I understood."

"Did he ever say where he came from?"

"Somewhere in Indiana. Mary something."

"Could it have been Maraville?"

"I suppose that sounds right. It's been a while, young lady."

"Did Ed ever mention why he moved to Bowling Green?"

"I think he said he had family here, a brother or something."

"You've been very helpful, Mr. Dillon. If you remember anything else about Ed, would you call me? I'll give you my number."

"Hold on while I get a pen."

For a long time after I hung up, I sat there staring at

my notes, pen tapping on the pad, trying to make this new information fit in with Marco's theory. Would someone in the witness protection program be given the name of a person who'd passed away?

And it bothered me that Norm Jones, or Ed Birchman, had used a retired janitor and a deceased janitor as references. That didn't sound like a decision that a federal agency would make if they were trying to keep someone's identity hidden.

I wanted to run it by Marco, but he'd know immediately why I was asking. I couldn't ask my dad, either—he would worry that I was getting myself into something dangerous. And Reilly would blab to Marco . . . unless I was able to play it as innocently as possible.

I scrolled through my phone contacts until I found his number.

"Hey, Reilly, do you have a minute? I have a question for you."

"Make it quick," Reilly said. "I'm on duty."

"Sure. How much do you know about the witness protection program?"

"A little bit. What do you want to know?"

"When the feds come up with names for their protected witnesses, do they ever use people who are deceased?"

"What kind of question is that? Marco's not getting involved in a federal case, is he? 'Cause he'd better stay clear. Is he there? Let me talk to him."

"Pause for a breath, Reilly. It's just a general question. I fell asleep during a movie and don't know how it ended."

"Jeez, Louise. You scared me for a minute. Maybe the

names are computer generated—I don't know. And you know what? It's better you don't know."

"Okay, but they probably wouldn't use a dead person's name, would they?"

"I wouldn't think so. Why aren't you asking Marco this?"

"He's working, so I thought maybe you'd know. Sorry I bothered you. I'll just Google it."

"Right, and have guys in black trench coats at your door."

"Reilly, are you getting paranoid in your old age?"

"Who's old? I'm forty-two, and you're damned right I'm paranoid. So I'm telling you to be careful."

"Fine. I won't do an Internet search on the WPP. And hey, this is just between you and me, okay?"

"Why? What are you keeping from Marco?"

"That I bothered you while you were on duty." Channeling Jillian, I added, "Duh."

I hung up, then immediately started a search on Ed Birchman. The search engine came up with someone by that name in Chicago, but not in Maraville. I tried other combinations, but it wasn't until I accidentally typed "Ted" instead of "Ed" that I hit pay dirt—a Ted Birchman living in Maraville, Indiana. I called the number on the screen and an elderly man answered.

"Hi. This is the Salvare Detective Agency, Abby Salvare speaking. I'm checking references for a business client. May I speak with Ted Birchman?"

"Junior or Senior?" he asked in a friendly voice.

"The Ted Birchman associated with Bowling Green, Ohio."

"That would be my son, Ted Junior," the man said. "He lives in Bowling Green."

"Is he by any chance a janitor?"

Mr. Birchman's voice became icy. "No, he is not. He's a respectable businessman."

"Then do you happen to know an Ed Birchman who *is* a janitor?"

In a voice vibrating with hostility, he said, "I have no son named Ed."

Click.

Well, that was telling. I hadn't asked if Ed was his son.

I did a search for Ted Birchman in Bowling Green and learned he was the head of an insurance agency. I was about to call him when I heard the back door open. As Seedy hobbled off to greet Marco, I stuffed my notes inside a floral magazine, knowing Marco would never pick it up, and slipped it beneath a pile of unread magazines on the coffee table. Then I snatched the book I'd said I wanted to read, flopped onto the sofa, and pretended to be absorbed.

"Hey, Sunshine," he said, moving my feet so he could sit down. "Enjoying your leisure time?"

I rolled to a sitting position so I could cuddle up next to him. "I sure am."

"Sean Reilly called as I was leaving the bar."

Uh-oh. My pulse jumped up about twenty beats. Had Reilly ratted me out? "What did he want?"

"From the partial plate number you gave him, he got several hits, but none of our four suspects were on that list."

My breath came out in a rush of relief. Reilly hadn't

told him about my call. "That's great . . . ly disappointing."

"But he also got a hit on a stolen plate with those numbers. Someone may have used it on the truck so as not to be traced."

"Well, we know Clive was a car thief, and I said before that he could have been driving that truck. So maybe he and Sam are accomplices." I moved so I could see my husband. "It'll be exciting to see whether you can make Sam squirm."

"Exciting?" Marco shook his head in exasperation. "Abby, you're going to give me an ulcer."

Sunday

"Have some more roast beef, honey," Mom said, passing the platter around the dining room table.

"You've hardly touched your food, Abracadabra," Dad said. "What's up?"

Marco and I were at my parents' house for dinner, sitting at the big cherry dining room table with my brother Jordan, sister-in-law Kathy, and niece Tara, while Seedy and her puppy Seedling romped in the living room. My other brother Jonathan and his wife, Portia, were on a cruise somewhere in the Mediterranean.

I glanced at Marco and he nodded his okay. "Well," I said, "we didn't want to say anything until we got the official word from our Realtor, but Jillian found us our dream house."

The comments began to fly too fast to respond:

"She did?"

"In New Chapel, I hope."

"That's wonderful, honey!"

"What does it look like? How many square feet?"

"Congratulations, Abracadabra."

"Did you say Aunt Jillian found it?" The last came from my niece, Tara. "Seriously?"

"Seriously," I said. "Jillian has been taking me to see houses and the last one was perfect for us. It's the model home in a brand-new subdivision. We're waiting to find out whether the developer has accepted our offer."

"That news calls for apple pie à la mode," Mom said, bringing in a steaming pie from the kitchen. "Tara, would you get the ice cream and a scoop?"

As we ate dessert, Mom said, "By the way, Abigail, Rosa is a wonder. All of my eye pots sold. People love them."

"So does that mean you're making more?" I asked.

"No, I'm bored with that project. But I have something new that I'll bring down tomorrow."

"Bring it out now, Grandma," Tara urged. "We want to see it." She poked me in the leg. My mom's art always made her howl with laughter.

"It's not ready," Mom said. "I want it to be perfect."

My cell phone rang, so I jumped up to take it in the living room, where Seedy and Seedling had curled up together on the sofa. I saw our Realtor's name on the screen and my heart began to race in anticipation. "Lorelei, what's the good word?"

In a somber voice, she said, "I'm afraid I have bad news."

Marco came in and held my hand, his expression hopeful until I said, "What's the bad news?"

"Someone else offered more money and the developer accepted it."

"Oh." I mouthed to Marco, *We didn't get it.*

"I'm sorry, Abby," Lorelei said softly.

"Me, too."

"We'll just keep looking, that's all," she said.

I hung up, tears blurring my vision. "Someone offered more."

Marco put his arms around me and held me, rubbing my back. "We'll find another house, Sunshine."

"But look how long it took to find that one, Marco. *Months.*"

"I know. But we can't give up. There's another one out there somewhere."

I wiped away a tear and straightened my shoulders. "You're right. Giving up is not an option."

I turned and the whole family was standing just inside the doorway, watching us with sad expressions.

"We're sorry, honey," Mom said, and came to give me a hug.

"It wasn't meant to be, that's all," I said.

But, oh, how I'd hoped it was.

Monday

"I have a house for you to see," Lorelei sang over the phone as Seedy and I walked the two blocks from the parking lot to Bloomers. "Will you have any time today?"

"Lunchtime," I said. "What's it like?"

"Ideal for two young people just starting out, and it's at the low end of your price range. Shall I pick you up or do you want to meet me there?"

"We'll meet you."

I stopped to type the address into my phone, then opened the yellow door and let Seedy hobble in ahead of me. She sniffed the air, then headed straight for the purple curtain. Mondays were Lottie's breakfast days, and Seedy could smell it cooking.

In the kitchen, Lottie was just pushing down the toaster. "I heard the bell jingle," she said. "Eggs will be up shortly." She looked down at Seedy, who had put her paw on Lottie's leg and was gazing up expectantly. Seedy had perfected the *poor me* expression.

"Your eggs are coming up, too," Lottie said, making Seedy wiggle with happiness.

Grace came in carrying a tray with coffees, cream and sugar, and three scones.

"What's the flavor today?" I asked, plucking one from the plate.

"Date," she said as I took a bite of the scone. "Did you get your house?"

The bite seemed to stick in my throat. I poured cream into one of the coffee cups and took a sip, then shook my head.

Lottie glanced at me over her shoulder. "I didn't hear what you said."

"She didn't get it," Grace said gravely, taking a seat on one of the stools at the narrow counter. "I'm so sorry, love."

"It wasn't meant to be, I guess," I said.

"Gracie," Lottie said, piling eggs onto our plates, "this would be a great time for a quote."

Grace was in mid-sip of her coffee, so she held up a finger to signal that it was coming. Then she slid off her stool, assumed her lecture pose, and said, "As the oft-quoted poet James Montgomery wrote, 'Hope against hope, and ask till ye receive.' " Resuming her seat, she said, "Words to live by, dear."

"That goes along with what I was telling you the other day, sweetie," Lottie said. "Send out those positive thoughts and something positive will happen."

I pressed my fingers into my temples and closed my eyes. "Okay, I'm sending out positive thoughts right now that I want to find my dream house."

"What's that noise?" Lottie asked.

"It sounds like someone's banging on the front door," Grace said.

"Maybe it's opportunity knocking," I said, hopping off the stool. "I'll go see who it is."

Think positive, think positive, think positive, I told myself as I pulled back the purple curtain and walked into the shop. And there at the door, framed in yellow, was my very pregnant cousin looking extremely distraught.

I unlocked the door and let her in. "What are you doing here so early?"

"I have to use the bathroom," she said, practically running through the shop.

"That's why you're here?"

"No, silly," she called over her shoulder. "I have news that just couldn't wait."

Chapter Fourteen

I paced in front of the worktable wondering what had gotten my cousin out of bed before ten in the morning. Lottie and Grace waited calmly in the kitchen doorway.

Jillian emerged wiping her hands on a paper towel. If she'd come to share a serious problem, she certainly wasn't showing it. "Sorry," she said with a shrug. "My bladder was duressed to the max."

I sighed. "There is no such word, Jillian. You mean stressed."

"Do you know what it feels like to have a seven-pound dumbbell lying on your bladder while you're trying to sleep?" she countered.

"Of course not."

"Well, your time will come," she said, tossing the towel in the wastebasket. "Then you'll see how duressed a bladder can be."

"Honey," Lottie said, "I had four dumbbells lying on my bladder. You want to talk about discomfort? Try having quadruplets."

"Excuse me, Lottie, dear," Grace said, to move the

conversation along. "Jillian, what news did you bring us, love?"

Jillian waddled over to one of the stools at the work-table and sat on it. "Sorry. My feet are duressed, too. Anyway, I heard about you not getting the model house, Abby, so I contacted the developer about the cost of new construction and he dropped off the information a little while ago."

"You got up early for me?"

She held out her arms for a hug. "You're welcome."

"Thank you, Jill. I'm touched." Seriously.

"I was up anyway. Dumbbell on the bladder, remember?" Jillian dug through her enormous tote bag and pulled out a manila envelope. "All the specs on the model you saw are in here, along with information about the subdivision."

"I appreciate your efforts," I said, taking the envelope, "but the problem is that we can't wait for a house to be built. We need to move soon."

"That's what you said six months ago. You're not going to find what you want in an existing home, Abs. You have way too much meticulosity."

"Seriously, Jill?"

"It's a word," she said with a pout.

Right. Another Jillian word. I opened the brochure and showed the photos to Grace. Lottie had slipped out of the room.

"It's a lovely home," Grace said.

I sighed. "Isn't it?"

"They put these houses up in five months," Jillian said. "I'll bet Marco's landlord would give you a month-to-month lease."

"Five months would be August. Even if he let us extend the lease, I don't think we'd want to stay in that cramped apartment for that long."

Lottie slipped in beside me and showed me the information on her cell phone's dictionary: *Meticulosity: Being meticulous.* Jillian had finally gotten it right.

"Anyway," I said, "our Realtor is taking us to see a little cottage today that she promises we'll love."

"Sure," Jillian said, rolling her eyes. "Because you've had great luck with her so far. At least show the information to Marco and see how he feels about it."

"Build a house?" my gorgeous groom said as we pulled up behind Lorelei's car. "It would be next winter before we could move in."

"Jillian said five months, but I agree with you, Marco. We need something soon, and we don't know the first thing about having a house built. We're better off buying a house that's available now and affordable—like Lorelei said this one would be."

We turned to look at the cottage to which our Realtor had sent us, and my hopes fell. It was made of brick that had been painted white, and much of that paint had worn off. It had no landscaping—not a shrub or a tree or even any decorative grass—not much of a lawn, either, and no porch. Basically, it had zero character. But that could be added.

Lorelei was waiting inside the front door and waved excitedly as we walked toward her. "You're going to love this charmer," she said, practically bouncing as she held the door open for us.

We stepped straight into the living room entranceway, which consisted of four square feet of linoleum made to look like red bricks. The rest of the small rectangular room was carpeted in forest green shag that had seen better days—make that decades. If that wasn't disgusting enough, the walls had been papered in a floral print of gigantic mauve and white orchids on a shiny forest green background, with the ceiling painted pastel green.

It had two narrow windows facing the front and a brick fireplace on the outside wall that had been painted over with a thick coat of white paint that, like the outside, had chipped off in many areas. But at least it matched the linoleum by the front door, which was more than could be said for the mantel, a thick slab of roughhewn dark wood.

"Well?" Lorelei chirped, hugging her clipboard against her jacket.

"It's really green," I said.

"But it's floral," she said, as though I hadn't noticed fifty giant flowers staring at me. "Right up your alley."

Which is where the wallpaper and carpet would end up if we bought the house.

"We could strip the walls," Marco said, looking around, "and paint the ceiling . . . and tear out the carpeting and linoleum . . . and have the brick sandblasted."

"Let's see the kitchen," Lorelei said, exiting through a doorway.

When we entered the kitchen, she was leaning against the counter, smiling. "Look how roomy it is. You can fit a good-sized table in here."

"More linoleum," I muttered to Marco.

"More wallpaper," Marco muttered back.

The walls were covered in what appeared to be the reverse of the living room paper—mauve background with lots of green leafy vines and white orchids, with a grass green laminate counter. The refrigerator was small and white, while the freestanding range with oven was black. There was a makeshift shelf over the range with an outlet built into the wall. I assumed it was for a microwave.

The linoleum here was brick patterned, too, but in a yellowed white with texture added, as if that would fool anyone into believing it was actual brick.

"What kind of wood is this?" I asked, running my hand across the face of a cabinet door. It was rough and not at all shiny.

"I'm not sure," Lorelei said, although her expression said differently.

"It's stained plywood," Marco said.

"It could be painted," our cheery Realtor said.

Marco looked out the window over the sink. "Not much of a backyard."

But I was looking *at* the sink, a stainless steel variety that had lost its shine from hard scrubbing and appeared to be badly scratched. Ditto for the green counter.

"We can strip these walls," Marco said, "and the linoleum."

"We'd have to replace the sink and the counters and buy a microwave," I said.

"Let's see the bedrooms," Lorelei called as she went through another doorway.

"I don't like it," I whispered to Marco as we followed her up a hallway carpeted in mauve shag.

"At least it has good bones," he said. "We'd have to

invest some money to modernize it, but I'll bet we could get it for a steal."

"And it's already at the low end of your price range," Lorelei said. "Now, on your right is the bathroom."

"Is this the only bathroom?" Marco asked.

Lorelei checked her clipboard. "Yes."

I peered in, almost afraid to see what horrors lay in store. "More green," I whispered to Marco.

The countertop was made of forest green cultured marble with white streaks running through it, the walls were a lighter green, and the floor was covered in white linoleum tiles. It had a bathtub/shower combination with a sliding frosted-glass door and a toilet with—surprise—a green seat.

"I'm starting to feel like a leprechaun," I said.

"Oh, a leprechaun," Lorelei said with a laugh. "Because of your red hair and being so short."

Not what I'd meant at all. "Actually, it's because of all this—" I opened the sliding glass shower door and it fell off its track.

"It can be fixed," Lorelei said as Marco attempted to put it back. "Or replaced."

"We'd have to paint the walls and get rid of this floor, too," I said.

"On to the master bedroom," she said, darting away.

We moved through the next doorway into a small bedroom painted pumpkin orange with brown shag carpeting. "At least it's not green," I said, "but it's kind of small."

"My furniture should fit," Marco said. He opened the pumpkin-colored bifold closet doors and immediately shut them. "Stay back," he said to me. "It smells like something died in there."

Lorelei opened one side and peeked in. "You're right. I'm not sure what that is—the Realtor told me the owner had the mouse problem under control."

"Good-bye," I said, and walked out.

"But there's one more bedroom," she called as I escaped back the way I'd come.

"That's okay," I replied. "This isn't the house for us."

"We'll just keep trying," she shouted.

We drove back to the town square in silence. I assumed that Marco was as depressed as I was, but as he parked the car, he began to chuckle.

"What's so funny?"

"Your leprechaun comment. I was picturing a colony of them living there."

"I don't think even a leprechaun could have taken all that green."

"If we bought it, we'd have to set off a bomb inside."

"To get rid of the mice or the house?"

We laughed until our sides hurt. As I wiped tears off my face, Marco said, "We'll find the right place, Sunshine. We just have to think positive."

My thoughts exactly. I was positive we'd already found the right house, but it had gotten away from us.

Bloomers was so busy that afternoon that I took only one break when my mom brought in her newest objet d'art. I had hoped to have a little extra time to work on the Jones project, but by three thirty I knew that wasn't going to happen. I was beginning to think I'd need to hire a full-time person to manage the shop so that Lottie and I could work on arrangements together.

I was definitely not complaining, however. No way. I'd hoped and prayed for my little shop to succeed, and it was finally happening.

"Get ready to be amazed, Abigail." Mom set a shopping bag on the floor and removed two boot-sized shoe boxes. I thought I saw the curtain flutter behind her and guessed that my assistants were eavesdropping from the other side.

With a big *"Ta-da!"* Mom opened one of the boxes and laid the contents on a clear space on the slate-topped table so I could look at it.

It looked back at me. Not a pleasant experience. "You made a fish," I said, trying to sound cheerful. "Out of all those wiggly eyes."

She took another fish out of the second shoe box and laid it beside the first one. "I had a whole box of eyes leftover, so I decided to keep the theme going."

By my estimate, each fish measured sixteen inches long and seven inches at its widest point. Their bodies were completely covered in wiggly white eyes with black pupils, which I supposed represented fish scales, with the fins and tails painted a shiny metallic green. What I couldn't figure out were the one-inch metallic green cups they appeared to be trying to swallow, or the metallic green plates behind them.

"Can you guess what I call them?" Mom asked.

I knew what I'd call them, but she'd never hear it from me. "Tell me."

"Walleyes."

I studied them for a moment. "Because they're fish and they have eyes?"

As Grace sailed through the curtain bearing a cup of

coffee for each of us, Mom turned one fish over so I could see the picture hanger on the back.

"How clever, Maureen," Grace said, placing a cup in front of her. "You've made walleye wall art."

"Thank you, Grace, but they're more than that." Mom held both fish with their mouths up and tails down. "They're sconces."

Better than a pair of choking fish, but still, *sconces*?

She turned to me, her eyes lit with excitement. "I know the perfect place for them, too. On the wall on either side of the armoire in place of those pewter ones you have there now."

She put her arm around my shoulders and said to Grace, "It's so gratifying being able to help my daughter make her little shop a success."

Or a little shop of horrors.

After a quick supper Marco and I drove to the house in town that Sam Walker owned. We went over our questions on the way there, and I wrote them in the notepad so Marco could refer to them if he needed to.

Sam's place was a ranch house with white aluminum siding, an attached two-car garage, and a patchy lawn. One of the garage doors was open, revealing Sam's black motorcycle inside. We walked up to the garage and found the former wrestler polishing the chrome trim. A bench and a set of barbells sat behind the motorcycle, and a hook next to the interior garage door held two navy baseball caps. His black pickup truck occupied the second bay.

"Oh, hey," Sam said, rising. "I thought I heard car doors slam." He had on grease-stained blue denims with a dark blue sweatshirt.

"Got a few minutes to talk to us?" Marco asked.

"You kinda got me trapped here," Sam replied, holding up a white cloth and a can of chrome polish for us to see.

"We won't be here long," I said, taking out the notepad and pen.

"I don't have no chairs for you. Sorry."

"Nice truck," Marco said, circling around the vehicle. He paused briefly at the back to check out the license plate, then moved on around it. "Looks brand-new. Drive it much?"

"Winter mostly. I ride my Harley whenever I can."

"Ever let any of your friends borrow it?"

Sam went back to his polishing, crouching down on one side of the bike. "My friends got their own trucks."

"Did you have it out last Thursday evening?"

"I haven't had it out all week. Why?"

"Truck just like this one nearly ran my wife and her pregnant cousin down as they were leaving the hospital."

Sam swiveled to look at me. "No kidding?"

"No kidding," Marco said.

"The dude must've been wasted," Sam said.

"The thing is," I said, "the guy in the car was the same one I saw a nurse chase out of Sergio's hospital room. Big man about your size, wearing a dark overcoat and baseball cap like those back there." I pointed to the caps hanging by the door.

"When I heard that he had claimed to be Sergio's brother," I said, "I had the nurse call security."

"So?" he said.

"Sergio doesn't have a brother," I said. "So maybe the guy was there to make sure Sergio never woke up."

"Why are you telling *me* this?" Sam asked.

"Where were you Thursday evening?" Marco asked.

It took a moment for Sam to get the picture. Then he tossed down his rag and got up, his hands balling into fists as though he was about to throw a punch. "You think I was that dude?"

Marco moved between Sam and me, and I could tell by the tensing of his shoulders and the widening of his stance that he was prepared to defend me. "Are you?"

The wrestler's neck turned an angry red and his nostrils flared. I expected him to paw the ground next. I took a step back. Hell hath no fury like a wrestler cornered.

Chapter Fifteen

"If that's why you're here," Sam snarled, "you can get the hell out of my face. I don't like Sergio, but I sure as hell ain't gonna go after him—or run down two women. What kind of guy do you think I am?"

"I don't enjoy having to ask these kinds of questions, Sam," Marco said calmly, "but it's part of what I do, and I do it to the best of my ability. Isn't that what you do?"

Sam shifted from one foot to the other. "Yeah."

"I apologize for offending you, but I had to ask," Marco said. "Let's talk about work, okay?"

Sam rolled his head, as though loosening tight neck muscles. "Yeah, I guess," he said in a subdued voice.

"Who was hauling the shingles to the roof on the day of Sergio's accident?"

"Probably Clive, but I don't wanna say for sure. We take different jobs every day and it's hard to remember."

"I'd like you to think back to when you heard Sergio call for help," Marco said.

"You turned around and saw what?"

"Didn't you ask me this already?"

"Bear with us," Marco said. "We just want to make sure we have an accurate report."

Sam gave Marco a disgruntled look. "I heard someone cry, 'Help,' so I turned around and saw Sergio grab his heart and then his ladder went backward." He shook himself, as though he didn't want to recall it.

"You're sure he put his hand to his heart and not his stomach?" I asked.

"It was like this." He demonstrated by putting his hand over his sternum. Then he thought about it and moved his hand down. "Or maybe here."

"That would be your stomach," I said.

Sam shrugged. "It happened fast, you know? I didn't really think about that when I saw him falling."

"What else did you notice? Where were the other roofers?"

He picked up the cloth and started to polish again. "Adrian was working on the gutter and Jericho was near me. I guess that means Clive was our supplier, so he could've been anywhere."

"Shouldn't he have had a good view of anyone who might have pushed Sergio?" Marco asked.

"Not if he was on the truck."

The questioning was going nowhere. I felt it and I was sure Marco could feel it, because he changed subjects.

"Ever have a rat problem here?" Marco asked.

"Nah, just mice, why?"

He nodded toward a black shelving unit against the side wall. "You've got some rat poison there."

I looked over and saw a box of poison sitting on the top shelf. I wouldn't have noticed if Marco hadn't pointed it out.

"I got it by mistake," Sam replied.

"Where do you think the dead rat came from that Sergio found in his locker?" Marco asked.

"I don't know nothing about that, dude."

"That's not what I asked."

"Could've been anyone put the rat in the locker," Sam said carelessly. "Sergio doesn't have no friends there."

"What do you think it meant?"

"Maybe that he's a rat."

"How about the slashed tire?" Marco asked. "What does that mean?"

"How about you ask the dude that did it?" Sam answered irritably.

"How do we find that dude?"

"Hell, you're the detective. How should I know?" He dipped the cloth into the wax and started to polish again. "So what did the cops ever find out, you know, when they tested the paint on Sergio's coveralls?"

Did someone have a guilty conscience?

"The results haven't come back yet," Marco said. "Do you know something about the coveralls?"

"Just wondering, is all."

"I wonder about that, too," Marco said. "First Sergio got the warnings; then the so-called accident happened. They're a little too coincidental, don't you think?"

"They don't have to be connected," Sam muttered as he worked.

Marco squatted down on the other side of the bike so he could look Sam squarely in the face. "Why don't you tell us what you know about the coveralls?"

"I don't know anything. Like I said, I was just wondering."

I saw a muscle in Marco's jaw twitch and knew he was getting frustrated. He changed directions again. "Have you ever seen any of Jericho's paintings?"

"Yeah, a few."

"Does he paint portraits?" I asked.

"You mean like pictures of people? I never saw none."

"Clive said Jericho has become secretive about his paintings," Marco said.

"Secretive," Sam repeated, as though trying on the word for size. "I'd call it more . . . temperamental. Yeah. That's a good word for Jer. He only shows his paintings when he's got a good temperament."

"Does Jericho talk about his girlfriends?" Marco asked.

"Kind of. Jer's been mentioning this hot chick for a couple of months now but won't tell us anything about her—well, except that she's hot."

Obviously Marco had found a topic that Sam could warm up to: women. "Has Jericho ever mentioned that he took his girlfriend anywhere—to dinner, to a game, the kinds of things you'd do on a date?"

"Nothing. Not even that he got her into the sack." Sam made a circling motion next to his head to indicate he thought that was crazy.

"Maybe he won't tell you anything because the woman is married," I said.

Sam gave me a blank look, as though to say, *What's that got to do with it?*

"Do you think Clive is right to suspect Sergio of hitting his wife, Rosa?" Marco asked.

"I hate to say 'cause I've only heard stuff."

"Didn't you see her black eye?" I asked.

"No. That was Clive and Jer. But Jer's the one you need to ask. He talks to Rosa."

"Often?" I asked.

"I don't know about that. She don't come by much anymore. But he'll go out to the car to talk to her when she does come."

"Do you think Jericho could have feelings for Rosa?" I asked.

Sam snorted. "What for? He's got a hot chick."

"How about Adrian?" Marco asked. "Any sparks between him and Rosa?"

Sam shrugged. "They've known each other since they were kids, so I guess he likes her."

"We're talking about more than liking her," I said.

Sam gave me a baffled glance. "Like he's in love with her?"

"That's what we're asking you," Marco said.

"I don't hang out with Adrian," Sam said, running his hand back and forth across the top of his Mohawk. "You'd have to ask him."

"Doesn't Adrian go out for drinks with the rest of you?" I asked.

"Yeah, but all he does is brag about his hookups and how much the women like him. I never heard him say anything about being in love with Rosa."

"I'm confused," Marco said. "Weren't you in agreement with Clive when he said Adrian and Sergio were like two hounds after the same fox?"

Sam blinked at him as though trying to comprehend.

"The fox being Rosa Marin," I explained.

"I thought he was talking about the foreman's job."

Sam was definitely not the sharpest thorn on the bush.

"Okay, let's talk about the foreman's job," Marco said. I could tell his patience was just about gone. Or maybe that was my patience I felt ebbing. "Was there ever a question of who was going to get the position?"

"To me there was," Sam said, ruffling his hair again.

"Explain," Marco said.

"I was hoping Mr. Appleruth would choose Adrian. He would have made a better foreman."

"Do you think it's fair that Sergio got it because he has a family to support?" Marco asked.

Sam shrugged. "What does it matter now?" He put the lid on the can and tossed the cloth into a plastic bin. He was ready for us to leave.

"One more question," Marco said. "Do you think it's possible that Adrian pushed Sergio's ladder?"

Sam sighed, as though frustrated. "Look, no one pushed Sergio's ladder. He got dizzy or sick or something and fell, that's all."

"Not what I'd call a productive interview," I said as Marco took me home. "It's like we're going in circles with these three guys. One will make a statement, the other two will agree, and then when we question them individually, they'll modify their story. At first I thought Sam was playing dumb, but now I don't think he's playing."

"Keep in mind that it doesn't take a genius to kick someone's ladder away."

"I'll give you that. And out of the four men who work with Sergio, Sam most closely fits the description of the man in the hospital room. Plus, it was obvious that he's concerned about being linked to the coveralls."

"I'm almost certain Sam was behind those warnings," Marco said. "There's just no way to prove it without a DNA test, damn it."

"I'm leaning toward Sam being our number one suspect."

"I don't know, Abby. No matter what else the three men say about each other, they all agree that no one was close enough to push Sergio's ladder. Maybe it was a collaborative effort."

"True, they did all have the means, motive, and opportunity, but I don't get any bad vibes from anyone except Jericho, and that's only because of the paintings. And then there's Sam, who is sticking by his story that he saw Sergio put his hand to his heart or stomach. How do we explain that when the doctors report no medical reasons for Sergio's fall?"

"I need to call Reilly to see if those tox reports came back. That might give us an answer. And I'd like to interview Adrian Prada again. The first time we talked to him, we didn't get to go into any great detail about what happened Monday morning. I'll phone Appleruth first thing tomorrow to see where Adrian's working so we can shoot over there and catch him during a lunch break."

"I'll make sure I'm free at noon."

Marco hit his fist on the steering wheel. "Damn, it's frustrating. There's a piece of the puzzle just beyond my grasp."

"We'll find that piece, Marco. You haven't earned a reputation as the best detective in town for nothing."

"Thanks, babe." He pulled up in front of the house, then reached over and put his hand on my knee, raising my hopes that something romantic was coming. "So here's what I'm thinking we'll do when I get home tonight."

Oh, baby. "Yes?"

"Let's go over all the notes again. I want to see whether anything jumps out at me." He patted my knee.

Well, that was disappointing. It appeared that if I wanted a little romance, the "anything jumping out at him" would have to be me. In the meantime, I had a few hours to kill, and I knew just how I was going to do it.

"Ted Birchman?"

"Yes, ma'am."

"Mr. Birchman, this is Abby Knight"—oops—"Salvare from the Salvare Detective Agency, and I was wondering if I could ask you about your—"

"About my brother. I know, Ms. Salvare. My dad phoned me this morning. He was pretty rattled by your call."

"Oh, I'm sorry."

"Dad had to cut off communication with my brother years ago, and it still troubles him."

"I truly didn't mean to upset your dad, Mr. Birchman. I was just checking references for my client."

"Ed used me as a reference? That's hard to believe, Ms. Salvare—if that's really your name."

"That's my name, Mr. Birchman. The Salvare Detective Agency is one hundred percent legit. If you'd like to see our Web site, I'll give you the link right now."

"Why don't you do that."

I waited as he checked.

"Okay," he said. "Sorry if I doubted you, but when it comes to my brother, I've learned to be cautious. Now tell me why you want to talk to me, because I know Ed didn't use me as a reference."

I decided to tell him as little as possible. "You're right. He didn't use you. But in checking the references your brother put on his rental application, I found two discrepancies. It's our policy to investigate in those instances before the lease is signed."

"What kind of discrepancies?"

"Before I answer that, is your brother and his family in the witness protection program?"

Ted laughed loudly. "Oh, my God. Is that the story he gave you?"

"No one gave me that story, Mr. Birchman. I found out that your brother is going by the name of a man who is now deceased, so I wondered if he had to assume another identity for security reasons."

"If Ed assumed someone else's identity, it was not for the witness protection program, I assure you. But it probably *was* for his own security—to keep himself out of jail. He's a scam artist. He's been in trouble all over the Midwest, so it's not surprising he's using a phony name. So what's his latest ruse?"

"I don't know that there is a ruse. All I know is that he's currently holding a janitorial job in Maraville, Indiana, and before that he put on his application that he was employed as a janitor in your city."

"Ed hasn't lived in Bowling Green for quite some time, Mrs. Salvare. He was probably fired from his last job and didn't want to list it on his application. That's what he does. He gets a job, stays somewhere for a while; then, when the police get too close, he pulls up stakes and moves."

"That's exactly what your brother did in my town. The police were at his house because of a roofing accident, and the next day he and his family were gone."

"Which means he's up to his old tricks. If I were you, Mrs. Salvare, I would tell your client to rent to him by the month, because he won't be there long."

"I'll pass along your advice. By the way, have you met his children?"

"Children? Ed has more than one? All I ever heard about was a son. Bud, I think his name was."

"He has a daughter, too. How long ago did you speak with your brother?"

"Oh, well, let me think. Maybe six years ago?"

"That's about how old his daughter is."

"He never even bothered to call me and let me know."

Hearing the regret in his voice, I said, "I'm sorry, Mr. Birchman. I didn't mean to bring up a painful subject. I have two brothers and can't imagine not having any contact with them."

"Thanks. I appreciate that. Believe it or not, my brother and I were close at one time. Then our lives went in completely different directions. I only found out about Ed's son because one day, about ten years ago, my brother showed up at my door needing a place for Sandra, him, and the baby to stay until he found an apartment. According to Ed, he had been evicted from his home in Maraville right after Bud was born. But who knows what the real story is? I'll say it again, Mrs. Salvare, tell your client to be cautious."

I thanked him for his help and hung up just as Seedy pawed at my leg, her leash in her mouth. "Is it time for a walk?"

She was so excited, she hobbled in a circle.

"Okay, let's go. I need to do some thinking anyway." I jotted down notes about the conversation and put them with the others in my floral magazine, then grabbed my jacket.

As we strolled up the sidewalk, I reviewed my conversation with Ted Birchman. If his brother was a scam artist, then judging by the beat-up van and the rentals he'd lived in, Norm/Ed clearly wasn't a successful one. He and Sandra must have decided to teach the children at home so they could move at a moment's notice without disrupting their schooling. At least they cared enough about the kids to want them to have an education. Still, what a terrible way to grow up.

I waited while Seedy did her business; then we started back up the street. What was I going to do about my case now? Norm had left New Chapel, and without any proof of a scam, the local police wouldn't investigate him. So what would be the point of my continuing to poke around?

Yet I still wondered about the look Daisy had given me. Was she tired of being on the run? Had that glance been a silent plea for help? If so, was there anything I could do for her?

"I think I've reached the end of my project, Seedy," I said as I let her into the apartment. "Now what can I do next?"

Chapter Sixteen

Tuesday

"Maybe I should have an all-pink wedding," my customer said as we sat at a table in the coffee parlor going through photographs of wedding bouquets. "I think my bridesmaids would look nice in pink."

Which is what she'd said about the color blue twenty minutes earlier. I showed her several ideas for pink arrangements, but she merely sighed unhappily and took another sip of coffee. "I don't know. Maybe yellow is the way to go."

In the thirty minutes I'd been working with the young woman, I had learned four things: Her name was Darla Green; she was twenty-two; she worked as a receptionist at her father's auto parts store; she had no backbone.

"What are your favorite colors?" I asked.

"Melon and aqua."

"Then why not go with that?"

"Because my mother said she would disown me if I did."

"Why would she disown you if you decided to use your favorite colors?"

"Because Mother hates them. She wants me to go with bright spring colors."

"Okay, so who's getting married here, Darla, you or your mother?"

She seemed baffled by my reaction. "Well, me, of course."

"Then if you want melon and aqua as your colors, you should be able to have them."

"But my parents are paying for everything. What am I supposed to do?"

"Tell your mother that you don't want spring colors."

"As if that were possible." Darla sighed miserably. "What a nightmare this is turning out to be. Mother said no to beef, so we have to have chicken and polish sausage for our reception. Polish sausage! Who does that? She said no to the band we wanted, too. And forget champagne. White or red wine is it."

"Maybe you could compromise," I said. "I understand that your mom and dad may be working on a budget, so have a lower-cost sparkling wine instead of champagne, and maybe forgo the beef *and* polish sausage and just stick with chicken. You could use a DJ instead of a live band, and—"

"They can afford the champagne and the beef and the band, Abby. My dad makes over two million dollars a year."

"Then I don't understand."

"It's Mother," Darla said, sinking her chin onto her palm. "If she doesn't get her way, look out. It's just easier to give in to her."

A bully in designer clothing. "You know what I'd do, Darla? I'd work with my fiancé to save enough money to pay for a nice little ceremony of my own."

"A small wedding?" She wrinkled her nose.

"Believe me, you don't need a humongous affair to start off married life, especially if it means giving in to a tyrant. You could have a cozy little ceremony in the gazebo, for instance, at Central Park."

Her eyes widened. "You're right."

"You bet I'm right. That way, you can have your melon and aqua flowers and whatever else you want that fits in your budget."

"But what do I tell Mother?"

"I'd tell her to take a—"

"Break," Lottie said, pulling out a chair at the table, while Grace moved in to refill Darla's coffee cup. "Take a break, sweetie. I'll work with Darla to wrap this up." Smiling at the young woman, Lottie slid the photo album over and said, "Let's get you all fixed up, hon."

I sat at the table in the workroom, my chin in my hand, while Grace explained that Darla's mother, Edna St. Pierre, was one of our best customers. Her last name was different from Darla's because she had remarried. The bill for wedding flowers would have been enormous and we would have been paid in cash.

"Guess I shouldn't be giving personal advice to customers," I said.

"Your heart was in the right place, love," Grace said.

"I hate bullies, Grace."

Grace put her hands on my shoulders. "And what about mothers? Isn't there anything you've done for your mum that you didn't want to do?"

Every piece of art my mom had ever created flashed through my mind.

"I'm just frustrated, Grace. We're going in circles on Rosa's investigation. I want to find my dream house, and that's not happening. And I keep having disturbing dreams about little Daisy Jones. I had another one just last night."

"Abby, listen to me," Grace said, sitting on a stool beside me. "You'll find that lovely little house. The one that's meant for you hasn't appeared yet, that's all. And something is bound to turn up in Rosa's case. As far as Daisy is concerned, you felt there was something about her that needed investigating, so you did. Now you know her father is a scoundrel, but you said yourself that the children seemed well cared for, so you have to let it go."

"I'd like to do that, but the dreams haunt me."

Grace's brow wrinkled as she pondered my dilemma. "Try this. Imagine blowing up a balloon, and every puff you put into it is some of that worry, until it's filled to bursting. Then imagine releasing that balloon into the stratosphere. Up and up it floats until you can't even see it. And as the old saying goes, out of sight, out of mind."

I closed my eyes and pictured the balloon rising farther and farther into the air. Then a bird flew past and punctured it, and there went that image.

But I didn't want to disappoint Grace, so I thanked her for her help and plucked an order from the spindle. Twenty minutes later, I was back in my groove. Flower therapy worked every time. If only I could make arrangements in my sleep.

* * *

Shortly after noon Marco and I drove to the job site where the HHI roofers were working, a huge two-story residence in one of New Chapel's priciest neighborhoods. The day was sunny and fairly warm for March, so the workers were taking advantage of it, some sitting on the low stone retaining wall surrounding a courtyard, others seated on a blanket, leaning their backs against the side of the house, their lunches on their laps.

I saw Jericho, Clive, and Sam side by side on the retaining wall, but Adrian was leaning against his pickup truck parked on the street talking on the phone. He saw us approaching and ended his call.

"Well, if it isn't my *amigos* come to see me again," Adrian called gregariously. He glanced over at his fellow workers, then said quietly, "It is a good thing you caught me out here. You are not popular with one of my *compañeros*."

I turned to look and saw Jericho glaring at us.

Adrian said to me, "Is it true that you broke into his studio, *chica*?"

"No, it's not true," Marco said.

I would have offered a bit more explanation, such as that we had been invited into Jericho's trailer, but Marco kept the interview moving along. "We'd like to follow up on a few things we touched on before. I know your time is limited, so we'll be quick. Do you mind?"

He waved his arm. "Ask away."

"Good," Marco said. "First, think back to the morning of the accident, when you heard Sergio call for help. Would you describe where you and your coworkers were positioned?"

"I believe I have already told you that I was working

a yard or two away from where Sergio was. Jericho and Sam were on the same side of the roof, but Clive I do not remember seeing."

"Could he have been bringing up a load of shingles?" Marco asked.

Adrian nodded. "This is possible."

"Were you working on the gutters?" I asked, looking at the notes I had made previously.

"Yes."

"Who was closest to Sergio?" Marco asked.

"No one was close to him."

"If I told you there was evidence that one of the roofers pushed Sergio," Marco said, "how would you respond?"

"I would say that's not possible. Falling from that height is certain death. Not one man here would push Sergio no matter how he felt about him personally."

"What if Sergio was being abusive to Rosa?" Marco asked.

"I don't know what you have been told, but Sergio would never lay a hand on Rosa. The old *bastardo* truly loves her. And besides, I would not let that happen. There was a time when he did not treat her with the respect she deserved, so I had to straighten him out, but that is all finished."

"*You* decided that Sergio was not treating Rosa with respect?" I asked.

"As a friend of her brother, it was my duty to protect her."

"Was it your duty to harass her, too?" I asked.

"I beg your pardon?"

Marco said, "What my wife is referring to is a comment we heard about you flirting with Rosa when she worked at HHI."

"Ah! Now I understand." Adrian turned his dimpled smile on me. "When it comes to a beautiful woman, I am a hopeless flirt. I mean nothing disrespectful by it. It is just in my nature."

I felt my cheeks grow hot. The rogue was flirting with me as he spoke! I wanted to be offended, yet I couldn't deny his charisma.

"But believe me," Adrian continued, "when I tried it with Rosa, she set me straight. She is a strong woman, that Rosa. Even though I know she would prefer me to that old man she is married to, she is loyal to Sergio. After all, he is the father of her son."

"What about Rosa's black eye?" I asked. "All of your coworkers believe Sergio hit her."

"And what did Rosa tell you? That Sergio left his boots in the way and she fell over them? That is what happened. I asked Rosa myself, and Rosa cannot lie to me. Her face gives away everything she thinks in her head."

Another point she and I had in common.

"The others"—Adrian glanced toward his coworkers—"they do not understand Rosa as I do."

"Have you ever seen any of them flirt with Rosa?" I asked.

Adrian's eyes narrowed. "Why is this important?"

"It's a routine question," Marco said. Unfortunately, he said it just as I said, "We believe one of them has a crush on her."

Oops.

Adrian got up close to Marco and said quietly, "Are you speaking of Jericho?"

When Marco said nothing, Adrian stepped back. "There is no need to answer. I have suspected him of having a passion for Rosa for many weeks now."

"Why would you suspect that?" Marco asked.

"I saw him taking a picture of her one day when she came to pick up Sergio. He did not know I saw him." Adrian rubbed his fist into the palm of his hand. "I can put a stop to that."

"Hold on, *amigo*," Marco said. "There's no law against taking a photo, but there is against assault. Nothing that we've told you has been verified. Leave it at that and let us handle it."

It was a stare-down between the two men for a long, tense moment. Then Adrian turned his fierce gaze on Jericho, sitting a good fifteen yards away. "I will leave it for now, but I will be watchful. Are we finished?"

"Just two more questions. Have you been to see Sergio in the hospital?" Marco asked.

"Why would I do that if Sergio would not want me there? We are not friends. Does Rosa *want* me to visit him?"

"The reason I ask," Marco said, "is that someone claiming to be Sergio's brother slipped into his room Thursday evening before being chased out by a nurse. Fortunately, no harm was done, but the man had nothing on him to prove his identity."

"Sergio does not have a brother," Adrian said. "What did this man look like?"

"A big man in a black overcoat with a dark baseball cap pulled down over his eyes," Marco said. "He was spotted leaving the vicinity in the passenger seat of a dark pickup truck being driven by a smaller man wearing a hooded sweatshirt."

"This does not make sense to me. You have described two men who sound like Sam and Clive, but I cannot believe that either of them would sneak into a hospital to hurt Sergio, just as I refuse to believe any of them would have pushed Sergio's ladder."

"There's one problem with that," I said. "The only people near Sergio when he fell were the four of you roofers."

"There must be another answer," Adrian said with a shrug, his diamond insignia ring glinting in the light, "because if you are looking for a killer here, *mi amiga*, you are looking in the wrong place."

"There *is* nowhere else to look, Marco," I said as we drove back to town. "We've interviewed all four men twice, and in Clive's case three times. We've gone through their interviews twice, and nothing new has emerged."

"Then we've missed something. Let's go back over the events of Monday morning. Tell me everything you remember."

"First thing I remember is you, Lorelei, and me standing in front of the Victorian discussing the condition it was in. Seedy was watching Sergio, and I remember two painters on scaffolding on the right side of the house. I also remember noticing the roofers and thinking how tricky it must be for them to work on such a sharply pitched roof. Let's see. What else?"

"Okay, back up. With all the men who were working on the house that day, why would Seedy have been watching Sergio in particular?"

"I don't know, but I remember thinking it was odd because she doesn't normally pay attention to men."

"Was he doing anything that might have attracted her attention?"

"No. He was just painting the gingerbread trim."

"Did she try to get to him after he landed on the ground?"

"No."

"So what would have made her watch him?"

"Maybe she sensed something was wrong. You know how dogs can tell when someone is about to have a seizure or go into diabetic shock?"

"Seedy's never been trained for that, Abby. And if she did sense something, why didn't she want to go to him after he fell?"

"Because she's shy around men."

"Point taken. Okay, go on."

"The next thing I remember is that we were discussing whether to see the inside of the house when I heard a cry from the roof that made me turn around. I don't recall where anyone else was at that moment because I was focused on Sergio. I only remember that after he hit the ground there was pandemonium from all directions as everyone tried to reach him. Lorelei and I got there first and pushed the ladder off Sergio, and I checked for a pulse. Then Sam started shaking Sergio, and you told him to stop."

"Okay, right there we have a red flag. Is Sam really that stupid that he would shake a man who had just fallen from a great height?"

"After the conversations we've had with Sam, yes, I do believe he might have acted without thinking."

"I'm not one hundred percent convinced about that, Abby. If someone was out to kill Sergio and then discovered that he was still breathing, a good hard shake might snap his neck like a twig."

"So you're saying that someone is Sam?"

"I'm not saying he's the only one involved, but yes."

"Then Sam is a lot smarter than he seems, and I don't get that feeling when we talk to him."

"Let's move on. Does anything else stick out in your memory?"

"Let's see. The paramedics came, then Sandra Jones and the two kids came out, and Seedy and I walked over to talk to them. Then Norm Jones came home and they went back into the house. I returned to you and Reilly, and we talked for a few minutes. Then we went home. Oh, wait. Back up. Seedy found a red marker right where Sergio had been lying. Remember that? I wonder what happened to it after we handed it over to Reilly."

"Why don't you give Reilly a call and see if he was able to find out whether the toxicology report has come in, and then you can ask him to look into the marker for us."

"I'd better use your phone, then. He doesn't always answer when he sees my name pop up on his screen."

"Maybe he's just busy. I don't think he avoids you."

"Wanna bet?" I pulled out my phone and dialed Reilly's number, then put the call on speakerphone. "See?" I said when it went to his voice mail. "Now watch this." I used Marco's phone, only to have that call go to voice mail, too.

"You were saying?" Marco asked.

"Okay, maybe he's busy right now, but it's happened to me several times, Marco. I'm not making it up."

Marco's mouth curved up just a bit, a look he always got when he was about to tease me. "You're kind of cute when you're paranoid."

"*Kind of* cute?"

"I don't want you to get a swelled head." He put his hand on my knee. "Know what we should do when I get home tonight?"

"If you tell me we need to go over the notes again, I won't be responsible for what happens to you."

"I was thinking more along the lines of a romantic evening, just you and me, a few candles, some soft music, and a bottle of bubbly."

"Now *that* sounds like a plan, Mr. S."

Marco's phone rang, so I checked the screen and handed it to him. "It's Reilly."

"Hey, Sean, we just tried to reach you." Marco listened a minute, then said, "Okay, thanks. I appreciate it. Oh, one other thing. Remember the red marker Seedy found on the ground? What did the detectives do with it?" He listened another minute, thanked his buddy, and ended the call.

"The tox report is in," Marco said, "but there aren't any red flags on it—no drugs or toxins in Sergio's system and only what they consider an allowable amount of alcohol. So we're right back where we started—with nothing."

"What about the marker?"

"Sean said he'll look into it. My guess is that it fell out of Sergio's tool belt, but rule number one is . . . ?"

"Don't ask leading questions." At Marco's bemused glance, I said, "Just kidding. It's V-cubed."

"V-*cubed*?"

"That's my shorthand for verify, verify, verify. So what did you think of Adrian's answers?"

"It's the same damn conversation we've had with all of them," Marco said. "A bunch of nos. No one was close to Sergio before he fell. No one would do that to him despite how much they disliked him. And with zero witnesses, there's not a single way to prove otherwise.

"Then we have the doctors giving us their no as far as an obvious medical condition that might have caused Sergio's fall. Now we've hit another wall with the tox results. I hate to say this, Abby, but I think the only way we'll ever find out what happened to Sergio is for him to tell us, and I don't have a good feeling about that happening—not when Rosa keeps reporting that his condition is deteriorating."

"Where is this leading?"

Marco sighed. "I've never failed to close a case to a client's satisfaction before, Sunshine, but we've taken this as far as we can. The investigation is over."

"I know it's difficult for you to say that, Marco, and I don't fault you for your decision, but how do we tell Rosa? She's counting on us."

"She's holding on to a delusion, Abby. We'll just have to be honest with her. We've explored every option and haven't discovered one piece of evidence to support her claim."

"I hope Rosa doesn't get it into her head to keep investigating on her own. Look what happened when she tried to confront Jericho."

"If she does, she does, Abby. There's not a thing we can do about it. When does she work at Bloomers next?"

"Tomorrow."

"We'll have to talk to her then."

And by *we*, I was fairly certain he meant me.

What would a plan be without a flaw? In our case, our romantic evening had two: Seedy and a cell phone that wasn't put on mute.

As soon as we had poured the wine, lit the candles, turned on soft music, and closed the bedroom door that evening, Seedy began to whine and scratch the wood with her nails. Marco turned up the volume to cover the noise, but that only made Seedy bark, and there was no way romance could happen for me when my dog was barking a few yards away.

Marco put her in the bathroom and shut the door, prompting her to howl and scratch harder. It didn't seem to bother him—typical one-track-minded male—but I kept imagining the deep grooves in the door that we'd have to repair before we moved, and that did nothing to keep me in a sexy mood.

If Seedy wasn't distracting enough, my cell phone began to ring, prompting a string of unintelligible mutterings from Marco. The phone was sitting on the dresser, and as it rang, it vibrated across the top and dropped onto the wooden floor with a clatter. Trying to block out the image of a shattered screen, I also tried to ignore the beep that signaled that the caller had left a phone message, but then text messages began to come in, making a loud ding every time.

"Someone really needs to reach us," I said. "I should probably answer it."

"Go ahead," Marco grumbled, "but I'll bet it's just your cousin."

Chapter Seventeen

Marco pulled his shirt on over his head, grumbling about Jillian being a pest and about leaving our phones in the living room from now on, as I sat on the bed listening to the message.

"It was Lorelei, not Jillian," I said as he went up the hallway to let Seedy out of the bathroom. "I'm supposed to contact her ASAP. She has another house for us to see."

"It could have waited until morning," he said, still in grumble mode. "We're not going to see it tonight."

Seedy sat down in the bedroom doorway and gazed at me as though she couldn't believe I'd had the audacity to lock her out. Now two members of my family were peeved.

"He did it, not me," I told her, pointing at my testy husband.

"Come on, girl," Marco said. "Let's go for a walk and work off some energy."

I wasn't sure whether he meant his or Seedy's.

"You know, Abby," he said, snapping her leash onto her collar, "maybe Seedy needs a playmate."

"Another animal crammed into this tiny apartment?"

Marco sat down beside me on the edge of the bed. "I mean when we move."

"Then I'd have two dogs at Bloomers. Two dogs to board when we go on vacation. Two vet bills to pay. Two—"

"I get it. Come here."

I laid my head on his chest as he wrapped his arms around me and stroked my back. "I'm sorry I snapped at you. It isn't your fault that call came in. It just seems I'm frustrated at every turn."

"I understand, Marco, and from now on we *will* leave our phones in another room. But we do need to move soon. In a house, we could put Seedy at one end and ourselves at the other, and then we wouldn't hear her."

"Don't bet on that happening," Marco said, getting up.

Speaking of whom, Seedy was now standing at the side of the bed, whining to be lifted up.

"We'll have to train her to stay in a room without us," he said.

Ah, there was that royal *we* again.

As soon as Marco and Seedy left, I returned the Realtor's call.

"Abby, I'm glad you got back to me," Lorelei said. "I found a wonderful house for you, but you need to see it soon because there are already two buyers who are very interested, and I'd hate for you to miss this opportunity. The owners had to relocate, so you could move right in. Would you be available tomorrow morning?"

"Are you sure this house is what we're looking for, Lorelei?"

"It has two bedrooms, a basement, a garage, a fenced-in backyard, and it's just three blocks from the town square."

The house did sound perfect. I arranged to meet her at eight o'clock, and then said a prayer that this would be the one.

Wednesday

I quickly realized that the reason the house had interested buyers was not only because of its location near the town square, but also, and probably the bigger factor, because of its rock-bottom price. Otherwise, I doubted anyone but a dedicated rehabber would have touched it. The bungalow-style house was ninety-three years old, and in some of the rooms, so was the wallpaper. There were big, drafty fireplaces in the living room, dining room, and both bedrooms, a massive oak staircase, ancient appliances, steam heat, and no central air.

"Don't you love the high ceilings?" Lorelei asked as we stood in the master bedroom looking up at an antique iron chandelier. "You could take that down and put in a fan/light combination."

"We could have a cozy fire up here in the evenings," Marco said, crouching down in front of the blackened brick hearth.

A fire was what I was picturing, too. The heavy drapes around windows on either side were so close that I couldn't imagine how they'd avoided being set ablaze by an errant spark. I peeled back a loose piece of the yellowing pale pink floral wallpaper next to the door and found older wallpaper beneath it. Who knew how many layers there were?

I knew I had to come clean with Marco. I simply wasn't a fan of old homes.

"Despite the drawbacks, it has good bones, Abby," Marco said, knocking on the thick plaster wall as we headed back down the hallway. "Look at these doors. Solid oak throughout. Six-inch crown molding, brick fireplaces, a bay window in the dining room . . . there's a lot to like here."

"And a lot to fix here, too, Marco. The baseboard trim and crown molding are in horrible shape, the wood floor needs refinishing, there are cracks in the plaster, and there's no counter space in the kitchen. And with a one-car garage, one of us has to park outside."

"But at this price we could build a new garage and renovate the house."

There was that *we* again.

"Remember, you can move right in," Lorelei said. "And you couldn't ask for a better location. Plus it has a big basement."

"Let's go see it," Marco said, smiling.

Lorelei wasn't lying. It did have a big basement, a big, dark, damp, musty-smelling dungeon of a basement with a forty-year-old furnace, spiderwebs in the corners, and a water line six inches up from the cracked cement floor.

"It floods?" I asked Lorelei.

"My information says the owners had the problem fixed, and it would come with a ten-year guarantee." She glanced at me, saw my concerned expression, and said, "Let's take another look upstairs."

"It has potential," Marco said as we walked back to the town square.

"The potential for a flooded basement. And did you see the size of those spiderwebs?" I shuddered at the memory. "I'm sorry, Marco, but I have to give that house a no. I want a basement that I'm not afraid to use."

"You didn't like it at all?"

"No. I'm sorry."

"Hey, babe, don't be sorry. You like what you like."

"But *you* liked it."

He put his arm around my shoulders and drew me close. "Buttercup, I wouldn't be happy in any house if you weren't happy there. We'll just keep looking."

"Let's stick to houses that aren't more than thirty years old, okay?"

"If that's what my wife wants, that's what she'll get."

Why did that make me feel guilty?

When I walked into Bloomers, Grace was setting up the coffee machines in the parlor, Lottie was filling the glass-fronted display case with fresh flowers and ready-made floral arrangements, and someone was singing off-key in the workroom.

"Is that Rosa?" I asked as I sat at a table in the parlor to have my morning coffee with Grace and Lottie.

"She sounds a bit like a parrot screeching, doesn't she, poor thing?" Grace said.

"What did you think of the house?" Lottie asked.

"Great location," I said.

"And?" Lottie asked.

I put my chin in my palm. "Great location."

"Fight on then, love," Grace said. "As that famed commander James Lawrence said in the Battle of 1812, 'Don't give up the ship.' "

"I'd take a ship at this point, Grace." I paused as the

caterwauling grew louder. "What's Rosa doing back there?"

"She's putting together an order," Lottie said. "She wanted me to show her a few of my techniques, so I gave her a lesson on a simple arrangement of mums and left her to it. She took to the lesson very quickly. Reminds me of you when you first started."

"I hope I didn't sing like that." I finished my coffee and stood up. "I'll go see how she's doing. I need to talk to her anyway."

"How's her investigation going?" Lottie asked.

"It's not," I said. "The tox report came back clean, so medically there was no reason for Sergio's fall, and we've interviewed his coworkers multiple times and haven't found a single piece of information that supports Rosa's belief that someone pushed him."

"Then you need to let *me* talk to the men."

I turned to see Rosa coming into the parlor carrying a beautiful arrangement of spider mums, button mums, and carnations in bright spring colors.

"Great job, Rosa!" Lottie exclaimed, clapping.

"Brilliant," Grace said.

I wouldn't have gone *that* far.

"I did do a great job, didn't I?" Rosa said, setting the flowers on the table. "Thank you." She pulled out a chair and sat down. "Now tell me what is happening with my case."

I gave her a quick review of the interviews we'd done and the results of the toxicology report, while she sat with her arms folded and her mouth pursed. Before I could tell her that we were calling it quits, she said, "It is time for me to step in."

"Rosa, you're not a trained investigator," I said.

"This is what you keep telling me, but I wait and wait for you and Marco to find out who tried to kill Sergio, and nothing happens. Take me along on your next interview and watch how I will get the men to talk."

"Sweetie," Lottie said to her, "I don't think you'll have much luck getting Marco to agree to that."

Both of us were now sweeties?

"He will agree if I ask him," Rosa said. "I don't want to sound like I have a swollen brain, but people cannot say no to me."

"I believe she means a swelled head," Grace said.

"Same thing," Rosa said.

Personally, I liked "swollen brain." In any case, Rosa certainly held a high opinion of herself.

"This is why I must go with you on your next interview, Abby," she said.

I kept my mouth shut. I'd tell her about our decision in private.

"Now that the matter is settled," Rosa said, "let us talk about those ugly fish hanging by your beautiful cabinet. You must do something before they scare away the customers."

"I can't get rid of them," I said. "My mom made them. It would hurt her feelings."

"Maybe you can add flowers or something to make them look better, Rosa," Lottie said, "like you did with her eye-eye-eye pots."

"That *was* quite ingenious," Grace said, nodding approvingly. "And Maureen did tell me she loved them."

What was this? Rosa to the Rescue Day? And why hadn't Mom told *me* she loved them?

"No," Rosa said firmly. "Adding flowers to them will only make them uglier. To fix them, I will have to spray silver all over the wiggly eyeballs."

"My mom will never go along with that," I said.

"Actually, Rosa does have a good idea," Grace said. "Silver would make the eyes look like fish scales."

"That is exactly what I mean," Rosa said to Grace. "You get it."

Lottie raised her hand for a high five. "I got it, too."

Were we keeping score? "But seriously," I said, "considering that they are *fish* sconces, why waste the paint? We're better off leaving them on the wall for another day, then taking them to the basement and letting Mom think they sold."

"But that is dishonest," Rosa said. "How can you lie to your mother?"

"I don't lie to my mother," I said, bristling. "Usually. Back to my point, who's going to buy fish sconces anyway?"

"Fishermen," Lottie said. "We can market them to their wives. They're always looking for fish-themed gift ideas."

"I like it," Rosa said.

"You're all forgetting one thing," I said. "My mom has to agree to it, and I'm not going to be the one to suggest it. She'll never forgive me for wanting to ruin her creation."

Rosa slapped her palm on the table. "Then I will tell her. She will say yes—don't worry."

Good luck with that. If anyone was more stubborn than Marco, it was my mom.

I heard a melody playing in the distance and turned my head toward the doorway. "Is that 'La Cucaracha'?"

"Oh!" Rosa jumped up. "That is my cell phone."

As she dashed off to answer it, we cleared the table and headed off to our different zones. Bloomers Flower Shop was about to open for business.

I put Rosa's arrangement in the glass display case, then went through the curtain and heard sobs coming from the kitchen. There I found Rosa leaning up against the wall, her hands over her face, crying her heart out.

"What happened?" I asked.

"Sergio," she said. "He is worse. I have to go to the hospital now."

I drove Rosa to the hospital and stayed while a doctor explained that Sergio's organs were shutting down. While they let her see Sergio, I sat in the intensive care waiting room until a nurse came by to give me a message from Rosa.

"She said to tell you thanks for all your help and that her mother is on her way, so there's no need for you to sit here."

"Is Sergio . . . ?" I didn't want to finish my thought, but the nurse understood.

"Rosa may be here all day," she said. "We just don't know."

I felt bad for leaving. At the same time, I knew that Lottie and Grace needed me there. "Would you tell Rosa to let me know if she needs anything?" I asked the nurse. "Make sure she knows that all she has to do is call me and I'll come back."

"I'll give her the message," she said.

I returned to Bloomers and dug into my orders, but my thoughts were never far from Rosa and Sergio. We closed the shop at five and then I headed down to Marco's bar for dinner.

"Any word from Rosa?" Marco asked as he joined me at our booth in the back.

"Nothing. I wish there was something I could do. I'm glad now that I didn't tell her we were pulling out of the case."

"If this makes you feel any better, Reilly called. He said the marker was in the evidence locker, but nothing had been done with it because there isn't an investigation. So I phoned Appleruth, and he said that although the men typically carry carpenter's pencils, it's quite possible that Sergio had a marker with him."

"So it's another dead end."

"Another in a long line." Marco stretched out his legs and leaned back. "I think the detectives were right not to open an investigation."

My cell phone rang just as Gert the waitress showed up to take our orders. "I'll have whatever he has," I told her, then answered the call.

"*¿Eres Abby?*" a woman with a heavy Spanish accent asked.

"Am I Abby? Yes, I am."

Apparently believing that I understood the language, she said, "*Yo soy la madre de Rosa. Mi hija me dijo que te llamara. Su marido ha muerto.*"

I knew she was talking about Rosa, and I could tell from the sadness in her voice that the call was not good news. "I'm sorry, but I don't understand what you said."

"*Perdóname*. My daughter Rosa . . . she asks me to call you."

"Is everything okay?"

"No. *Su marido*, Sergio, is dead."

Marco and I drove to the hospital where we met Rosa's mother and many members of her extended family, all gathered in the waiting room with their Rosary beads in their hands. The women had red, swollen eyes and the men stood around with their hands in their pockets looking grim. Rosa's son was staying with his cousins.

Rosa came out shortly after we got there and immediately threw her arms around me and wept on my shoulder. "What will I do without my Sergio? He is my life, Abby."

Just as Marco was mine, and I didn't even want to think of life without him. In a choked voice I said, "I'm so sorry, Rosa. I can't begin to imagine what you're going through."

She took my hand and Marco's hand and said through her tears, "I know without a doubt that someone did this to Sergio. It is more important than ever that we find him."

"Rosa," Marco began, but she interrupted.

"No, do not *Rosa* me! You have not seen what I discovered today when I asked to see my husband's body. Sergio has a bruise right here—" She pressed her fist against her abdomen in the soft V below her rib cage. "Someone punched him. That is why he fell."

"Are you sure it's not a new bruise?" Marco asked. "Sometimes when a patient is transported—"

"This is not a new bruise," she said in a rising voice. "I have a son. I know bruises. This one is mostly yellow with a little purple in it. It is about this big, like a quarter." She made a circle with her thumb and finger.

"Then it couldn't have been the result of a punch," Marco said. "It's too small." He made a fist with his right hand and showed her.

Rosa tapped his wedding band. "But it could have been made by a ring. Go back to see Adrian and look at the big ring he wears on his right hand—then tell me this bruise did not come from that ring. You will see that I have been right all along about Adrian."

"Adrian wasn't in the right proximity to punch him," Marco said.

"How else would you explain it?" she asked.

"Did you ask the doctor for an explanation?" I asked.

"He said there was no serious internal trauma, so perhaps Sergio had been in a fight. 'Then tell me why Sergio fell,' I said. 'Rosa, we have performed many tests, but we cannot always explain why someone gets dizzy,' he said. 'Maybe Sergio looked around too suddenly. Maybe he had an inner-ear disturbance. Maybe he was simply up too high.'" She made an angry motion with her hand. "No one here will believe that someone wanted my husband dead."

"Rosalita," her mother said, taking her arm, "come sit down."

"Marco," I said quietly as Rosa's mother led her to a nearby chair, "Sam did say he saw Sergio put his hand there before he fell."

"It would have been physically impossible for Adrian to punch him in the gut while he was on the ladder."

"I understand that, but what about a punch from the night before? I know the doctor said there wasn't any internal trauma from it, but he's still only making educated guesses. Maybe Sergio did get into a fight at the bar after work that caused him some kind of distress the next morning."

"The accident happened on Monday morning, Abby. The fight would have had to take place on a Sunday."

"So? Sergio might have gone to watch a hockey game or something. Clive told us Sergio'd suffered a few bruises from some of the fights he was in."

"Where are you going with this?"

"I remember Adrian's insignia ring, Marco, and its diameter was about the size of a quarter. I think we need to talk to him again."

Marco led me farther away. "I know you want to help Rosa, but our investigation is over. With no internal trauma to show for it, we'd never be able to prove that Adrian is responsible for Sergio's death. It'd be a waste of everyone's time."

"Not to Rosa. Even if a direct punch didn't cause Sergio's fall, at least knowing how he got the bruise might answer that question for her."

I walked over to Rosa and asked, "Did Sergio go out to a bar with any of his coworkers on Sunday evening?"

Rosa rubbed her temples. "I don't remember. Maybe. He did do that sometimes." She turned to gaze through the doorway and said in a voice choked with tears, "They are packing his clothing for me. They'd stored it in the closet so he could wear it home." Big tears rolled down her cheeks and she wiped them away. "They said I should go home and rest—as if that will be possible. Tomorrow I will have to make arrangements for his funeral." She began to cry again. Her mother put her arms around her and her relatives gathered close.

"Let's go, Abby," Marco said. "She needs to be with her family now."

I held Marco's hand all the way to the car. "Poor Rosa. She'll have to raise and support her son alone now."

"She's fortunate she has family close by."

"But who will she turn to in the night when she's frightened or sick?"

Marco was silent as he opened the door for me.

Before I got into the car, I wrapped my arms around his chest and hugged him hard. Gazing up into the face I loved so much, I said, "Don't ever leave me, okay?"

He smiled tenderly. "I don't plan to, sweetheart."

I mulled over the bruise as we drove home. "I still think it's too coincidental that Sam saw Sergio put his hand over the spot where Rosa found the bruise a second before he fell."

"The simple explanation might be that the bruise hurt and he was rubbing it. Maybe that motion threw him off balance."

I couldn't help but think that there was more to it than that. Yet for the life of me, I didn't know what.

Thursday

At the end of a very busy morning, while I was in the workroom putting together my twenty-fifth arrangement, the curtain parted and Rosa entered. She was wearing a black coat and high heels and carried a black purse. She wore little makeup and her eyes registered deep sorrow, yet she still looked beautiful.

"Rosa, what are you doing here?"

"I just came from the funeral home," she said in a voice heavy with grief. "The funeral is set for Saturday at one o'clock. Now I need to order the arrangements. My mother is in the other room looking at the flower book with Lottie right now."

"Would you like my help, too?"

"Thank you for offering, but that is not why I have come." She took a folded piece of paper from her purse and handed it to me. "I found this in the chest pocket of Sergio's coveralls."

On the paper were two words printed with red marker: *Help me.*

She tapped the note. "You see? My husband knew someone was trying to kill him."

Chapter Eighteen

"Rosa found this in Sergio's chest pocket, Marco," I said, handing my husband the note sealed in a plastic bag. I wanted to preserve it as evidence—assuming I could convince Marco to continue the investigation. "She believes it proves that Sergio knew someone was out to get him."

Marco turned the bag over to see the back of the note, then flipped it to the front, frowning as he studied it. We were seated on a bench on the courthouse lawn eating our brown bag lunches while Seedy explored as far as her leash allowed.

"This was just now found in Sergio's coveralls?" he asked.

"His clothes were put in a bag when he was first brought in," I said. "Who would have thought to search them? Detectives weren't involved."

Marco had no comment.

"When Sam saw Sergio put his hand to his chest," I said, "maybe Sergio was actually reaching for the note."

Marco handed the bag to me. "It doesn't add up. All of our suspects remember hearing Sergio call for help, so why would he write out a help note beforehand? And which man would he have given it to anyway? He didn't get along with any of them."

"Then why did he have the note in his pocket?"

"Are you sure it's Sergio's note?"

"What are you saying? That Rosa wrote it?"

"Maybe she sensed that we were pulling out and wanted to make sure we stayed involved. In any case, first rule, Abby. Verify. If we *were* going to follow up on this, we'd need Rosa to show us something else that Sergio has written so we'd know whether it was normal for him to print rather than write."

"But if it *is* his printing, Marco, doesn't this note together with the bruise tell you that we should continue our investigation?"

"You're trying to connect two separate facts, babe."

"But it's too coincidental not to be connected."

"Coincidences do happen, Abby. And how would we follow up on it? Go back to the men and ask whether someone wrote it? Have them volunteer a handwriting sample? With Sergio dead, we'd never get their cooperation now."

"If they're innocent, why wouldn't they give us a handwriting sample? At least we'd be able to rule out who didn't write it."

Marco ate the last bite of his ham sandwich and wadded up the wrapper. "You've got two words written in block letters. Handwriting analysts like to have at least a paragraph, if not a page, to compare. And seriously, with the way they felt about Sergio, can you picture any of them giving *him* a note asking for their assistance? I know you want to help Rosa, but at this point the best we can do is convince her to turn over the note to the detectives and let them decide whether to pursue it."

I let out a huff and leaned against the bench back. "She just lost her husband, Marco. I don't have the heart to tell her that we're not going to continue the case."

"Then wait until after the funeral. She's probably in a state of shock anyway. Just assure her that we're doing all we can, and then, when her life has calmed down, we'll talk to her . . . And I need to get back." He rose abruptly. "See you at dinner."

"You're leaving now? You haven't even finished your coffee."

"Seems like a good time to go." He nodded toward Bloomers, where I saw my pregnant cousin waddling toward us. Seedy must have spotted her, too, because she crawled beneath the bench and hid behind my legs.

"You're both cowards," I said.

Marco gave me a kiss. "Some would call me a wise man. Good luck." He strode off, giving Jillian a wave.

"Dear God, could you be any further away?" Jillian called. She wore a violet swing coat that had no room to swing at all, with black tights and boots, and a patent leather purse in peony.

With some effort, she lowered herself onto the seat Marco had vacated and dabbed her forehead with a tissue. "If I don't have this baby soon, my womb is going to open like a ripe melon."

"I don't think that has ever happened before, Jillian."

"And once again, Abs, you know this because?"

"It would have made the news. Where's Princess?"

Jillian unscrewed the cap on a bottle of water. "With the dog sitter."

"You hired a dog sitter? How long do you plan to be out?"

"That depends on you. Besides, Princess hates spending time alone."

"Has she told you that or what?"

Jillian paused mid-swig. "Are you trying to make me crabbier?"

"Sorry. What brings you out here?"

Jillian sighed wearily. "This child hates me."

"This child? Is that what you're calling her now?"

"Actually I'm thinking of calling her Misery." She tapped my knee. "I found a house for you."

"Where?"

"Same neighborhood as the Victorian disaster." She stuffed the bottle in her purse and hoisted herself off the bench. "Come on. Let's go see it now."

"I can't. I've got a ton of orders waiting for me. I shouldn't have left for this long."

"Okay, five o'clock, then."

"I'm supposed to meet Marco for dinner at five."

She put her hands on her hips. "Do I have to remind you that civilized people don't dine that early? But whatever. We'll have dinner with Marco and then we'll see the house."

We? If I were to spring that on Marco, he *might* leave me. "What about Claymore? Don't you want to ask him to meet us at the bar?"

"He's working late tonight."

Imagining the look on Marco's face when I told him my cousin was joining us, I stood up. "On second thought, Jill, you're right about dinner. So let's see the house when I get off work instead." With any luck, I could wear my cousin out so she'd want to go home and nap.

* * *

The two-story brown cedar house Jillian wanted to show me was kitty-cornered from the Victorian, which now looked a hundred percent better than when I'd last seen it. I stood across the street from it, trying to remember exactly where Sergio's ladder had been in relation to where I'd seen the roofers.

"Are you coming?" Jillian called from the front porch.

"In a minute." I took out my cell phone and snapped a picture, then followed her inside. But this time we didn't make it beyond the small front entrance hall before she sank onto the staircase with a horrific groan.

"Jillian, please tell me this is not happening again."

Holding her belly with both hands, her face ashen, she made a guttural sound and clenched her teeth, then began to pant and blow.

"Come on," I said, taking her arm, "let's get you home."

"Time me— " She grunted, then made the animal-like sound again, her whole face clenching in pain.

I'd never seen her look like that, and it started to alarm me. "Time you? Are you really in labor?"

She opened her eyes and glared at me. "I'm having contractions. Time me!"

I pulled back my sleeve to see my watch, then sat down beside her on the steps. "How long does it have to be between contractions?"

Instead of answering, another horrific groan escaped her clenched lips, bringing to my mind the scene from *Gone with the Wind* when Melanie gave birth at home and nearly died.

I got up. "Forget that. I'm taking you to the hospital."

"It might be too soon," she managed to grind out.

"So do you want to wait here or there for the baby to come? Let's go."

For the second night in a row I was in a hospital waiting room, but the atmosphere in the maternity ward was completely different. People were excited, expectant, happy, and talkative as they waited for news.

And for the third time in a row, Jillian came out without a newborn in her arms. "False labor again."

"Seriously, Jillian?"

"It's not like I can control it. Come on. I want to show you how nice the new state-of-the-art nursery is." Pressing her hand into her back, she headed toward a set of double doors and hit a button to gain entrance, only to have a buzzer sound. A minute later a nurse came out and looked around. "Jillian, are you back again?"

"Yes." Jillian sighed. "I keep having Braxton Hicks contractions."

"You've got to time those contractions, sweetheart. That's how you'll know if they're real." The nurse, an older woman with short, curly gray hair, put her arm around Jillian's shoulders and said in jest, "How many times do we have to tell you that?"

Jillian shot me a glare. "I would have timed them but *someone* didn't want to wait. Is it okay if I show my cousin the nursery?"

"Well," the nurse said, glancing around, "we're not supposed to let in anyone other than family, but you're starting to feel like family. Come on—I'll give you a peek."

"Why do you need a buzzer on the door?" Jillian

asked as the nurse waved an ID tag over a monitor on the wall.

"Because we don't want anyone making off with our babies," the nurse said.

"Please don't tell me that's ever happened," Jillian said as we were taken to a glass-fronted room filled with baby cribs and beeping monitors.

"Not at this hospital." The nurse looked around, saw that no one was nearby, and said in a low voice, "But a baby was snatched from the hospital where I used to work." Resuming her normal voice, she said, "Now this is our full-term nursery. Next door we have a room just for preemies."

"Wait. Back up," Jillian said, clutching the nurse's arm before she could take us farther down the hallway. "Did this babynapping happen recently?" She was starting to look panicked.

"No, honey, that was ten years ago," the nurse said. "It happened at St. Christopher's in Maraville. That would never happen here, or there today, not with the security these hospitals have now." She held up the ID card hanging from a lanyard around her neck. "No one has access to this ward without one of these. And we have practice drills constantly, just in case."

"Did they ever find the baby?" Jillian asked, sniffling back tears.

The nurse shook her head. "I'm afraid not. What a sad case that was. I still remember the baby's name—Brody Dugan. That child had the thickest, blackest hair and the bluest eyes you could imagine. His mom said he was a throwback to their Irish relatives."

Jillian pulled out a tissue and blew her nose. "Those poor, poor parents."

"They were heartbroken, as you can well imagine. Detectives were almost positive that the kidnapper was a woman dressed in a nurse's uniform. They worked around the clock for months to find her, but none of their leads panned out. It was like the kidnapper vanished into thin air. A sketch artist drew a photo of what Brody would look like as he got older, but the last time I saw any mention of it in the newspaper was about five years ago. He'd be a big boy of ten now."

My mind snapped to attention. Ten years old?

The image of a ten-year-old boy with black hair and blue eyes flashed in my mind: Bud Jones, as I'd seen him standing in front of the Victorian.

Suddenly Ted Birchman's words echoed in my brain. *I only found out about Ed's son because one day, about ten years ago, my brother showed up at my door needing a place for Sandra, him, and the baby to stay until he found an apartment. According to Ed, he had been evicted from his home in Maraville right after Bud was born. But who knows what the real story is?*

My radar began to buzz. Was it too far-fetched to think that Bud Jones was Brody Dugan? Had I stumbled upon the reason for the Joneses' sudden departure?

I needed to see the sketch of that boy.

"Reilly, come on, answer," I said as I listened to his phone ring. I waited until I heard a beep, then left as detailed a message as I could squeeze into a minute's recording. I had been to see the house for sale with Jillian, which was just okay as far as houses went, but still too old for my taste. Now, as I drove to the bar to pick up Seedy, I had time to mull over the nurse's revelation, which had my mind spinning with possibilities, especially when I recalled Mrs. Welldon's words: *They were such nice neighbors, the Joneses, always willing to lend a hand. And whenever I took sick, Sandra would be right over to help. She was a nurse at one time, you know.*

Sandra would have been familiar with hospital routines. If she was clever and bold enough, she could have walked into the nursery without arousing anyone's suspicions and walked out with a baby tucked in a carryall. Naturally, she and Norm would have left town afterward. And where could they go to hide under their true identity? Bowling Green, Ohio.

But if my hunch about Bud Jones was correct, what about Daisy? Had she been snatched, too? Was there a reason that no one I'd spoken with knew about her birth or remembered that she was a part of the Jones family?

I'd have to do more Internet work when I got home to try to find out whether there had been another babynapping six years ago. Since I didn't know where the Joneses had lived at the time, I'd have to search databases for Bowling Green and Maraville and hope it had been one of the two. First, though, I had to pick up my dog.

"Any luck with Jillian's house?" Marco asked, pouring a beer for a customer.

If only I could tell him about my amazing stroke of luck *after* Jillian's house. "Well, first we made another hospital run—"

"False labor *again*?"

"Jillian is the modern version of an Aesop's fable, Marco—the woman who cried baby. Anyway, we did see the house, but it wasn't a place I could picture us living in. I'm seriously beginning to think that there's something wrong with me. The only house I've liked, out of all the homes we've seen, is the new one, and that's sold."

"Can you wait five months for one like it to be built?"

"No."

"So there's our dilemma."

My phone rang and I saw Reilly's name on the screen. "I'm going to take this in your office," I told Marco, and hurried through the bar as I answered. "Hey, Sarge, thanks for getting back to me."

"You want me to dig up a missing-child sketch?" Reilly asked.

I closed the door and turned to see Seedy curled up in Marco's chair. "Would you? It's really important."

"Does this have anything to do with the Jones family?"

"Are you sure you want to know?"

There was a pause; then he said, "Just give me the name on the file."

"Brody Dugan, kidnapped from St. Christopher's in Maraville about ten years ago."

"I remember that case. Don't tell me you think the Joneses have something to do with that."

"Right now all I have is a hunch, but it's a strong one. I'd be happy to fill you in if you have time."

"Let me see if I can find the file first. Then we'll talk."

"Great. Thanks, Reilly. And this is just between us, okay?"

"You keeping secrets from Marco again?"

"If this turns out to be what I think it is, I want to surprise and amaze him with my investigative prowess."

"Right."

I could've sworn I heard him rolling his eyes.

"If it turns out to be what *I* think it is," Reilly said, "you'll owe me one for wasting my time. If it turns out to be what *you* think it is, I'll owe you one—but first I want your solemn promise that if that happens, you'll call me."

"Right. Like you'd answer."

He heaved a sigh. "I'll answer, Abby. Give me a day and I'll get back to you."

Before I left Marco's office, I scrolled through my phone and pulled up the photo I'd taken of the Victorian, then e-mailed it to myself so I could enlarge it on the computer at home. Then I gathered my sleepy dog and went to tell Marco good-bye.

"Sergio was working right there"—I tapped the screen of Marco's laptop—"painting the gingerbread trim under the peak of the roof. See that?"

I was on the sofa with the small computer on my knees, Seedy lying beside me, and the image of the Victorian in front of me. "So why were you watching him, Seedy, and not the other men?"

She lifted her head and tilted it to the left, trying to understand what I was saying.

"What caught your eye? Was the sun reflecting off the attic window?"

She tilted her head the other way.

I pictured the Victorian again as I'd seen it from the front yard that morning. The sun had been shining, but the house faced west. The morning light wouldn't have hit that side at all. "Okay, it wasn't the sun. Did you see a bird sitting on the roof?"

Unable to decipher my words, she settled down for another nap.

I thought back to Seedy tugging at her leash, eager to meet the Jones children. Could she have seen one of them gazing out the attic window?

Then another thought struck me. If one of the kids had been looking out the attic window while Sergio was painting, he or she might have witnessed the accident.

Bingo! Now I had a legitimate reason to talk to the kids—if I could convince Sandra and Norm to allow it. But first, I'd have to track them down.

Friday

The shop was crazy busy all day and we sorely needed another hand, but no one expected Rosa to come in to work. My mother stopped by after school to see how Dad's ski bench and her fish sconces were doing and ended up working the cash register so Lottie could help me in the back room.

"Your mom thinks we priced the sconces too low," Lottie said as we worked.

"I don't think we could give them away," I whispered.

"She also wanted to know why the bench doesn't have a price on it."

"I'm waiting on Tara to give me a comparison, but I'll bet she forgot. I'll have to call her."

My phone dinged to let me know I had a text message, so I stopped to read it. The message was from Reilly: *Faxing over sketch now.*

The fax machine began to print, so I texted back: *Thanks. IOU.* Then I pulled the sheet out of the printer. Unmistakably, there was a younger version of Bud Jones staring back at me. I was so excited, I wanted to throw my arms around Lottie and cry, *I was right! I'm going to solve this case!* Only to hear Marco's words: *Verify, verify, verify.*

I had to find those kids.

I sat down at the computer, eager to get back to my investigation, when I heard Lottie say, "Oh, lordy. Less than an hour before we close and look at the orders waiting."

What was I thinking? I couldn't afford to take time away from work now. My Internet search would have to wait.

"Abigail, there's a customer up front who wants to see you," Mom said, poking her head through the curtain. "Her name is Edna St. Pierre and she doesn't look happy."

"It's the bride-to-be's mother," Lottie said. "Want me to talk to her, sweetie?"

"No, but thanks anyway," I said. "I'm sure Mrs. St. Pierre won't be satisfied until she tackles the person who caused the problem."

Chapter Nineteen

"I have a bone to pick with you, young lady," Edna St. Pierre scolded. She was standing by the cash register, where the other customers in the shop could hear her.

With short blond hair and big diamond earrings, Edna was dressed in a tailored linen coat, patent leather pumps in cream with gold heels, and a cream-and-brown purse with a big *D&G*, for Dolce & Gabbana, on the front. She was a woman who knew how to attract attention, and at that moment that kind of attention was the last thing I wanted.

"Let's discuss this over a cup of tea in the parlor," I said, and headed straight through the doorway before she could argue. "Grace, two cups of chamomile, please?"

Grace had obviously already deduced why Edna had come, because she had a small china teapot of hot water and two rose-patterned cups and saucers on the table moments after we'd sat down.

"How lovely you look today, Mrs. St. Pierre," Grace said, sounding both complimentary and royally condescending, as only Grace could. She had just come back to our table with a plate of scones and a small jar of clotted cream. "Won't you try my pecan scones? They are on the house, naturally."

Scones were never naturally on the house. But Grace knew exactly what she was doing because Edna's fierce scowl relaxed as she reached for one and set it on her plate.

"Thank you," Edna said with a gracious nod. "I haven't had a scone since my stay in London last fall."

She waited until Grace had poured our tea and left to say to me in a low voice, "I am furious with my daughter, and it's all your fault. You had no business advising her on her wedding plans. That is *my* duty."

"Isn't it also your duty to help your daughter have the wedding of her dreams?"

"Her *dreams*?" Scoffing, Edna said, "Darla's dreams range from eloping on a white charger to renting a castle in Milan. She doesn't know what she wants."

"She knows she wants aqua- and melon-colored flowers."

"Drab, dreary, dull. The girl has no sense of style."

"Darla wouldn't be designing the flowers. I would. And I do have a sense of style. I think you've been pleased with what I've done for you in the past."

Edna picked up her cup and glowered at me as she took a drink. "You did the arrangements? I thought Lottie did."

"Lottie trained me. I do most of them myself now."

"But aqua and melon? Please. They are the colors of last year, Miss Knight."

"It's Mrs. Salvare now, but please call me Abby. You want your daughter to be happy, don't you?"

"That's a silly question. Of course I do, but she keeps making the wrong choices."

"Just because they're not your choices doesn't make them wrong."

"I beg to differ. You should see the"—she rolled her eyes—"*man* she's marrying. Then you'd understand about wrong choices. I'm sorry, Abby, I simply cannot allow Darla to ruin her wedding."

"But that's just it. This is *her* wedding."

"That I'm paying for. And I will not pay for anything I dislike."

"In other words, forget about what Darla likes. This wedding is about you."

"I resent your tone."

"I hate to say this, Mrs. St. Pierre, but Darla is starting to resent you."

"How dare you talk that way to me!"

"Excuse me," my mom said, appearing suddenly at our side and pulling out a chair. "May I?"

I gazed at her in shock. What was she doing? "Mom, it's okay. I've got it."

"You're needed in the back, Abigail. This should be between mothers anyway. Mrs. St. Pierre?" Mom stuck out her hand. "I'm Maureen Knight, and I know something about stubborn daughters."

Fifteen minutes later, Lottie and I peeked around the doorway and saw the two women laughing together. Another fifteen minutes and Mom came into the workroom to tell me that Darla would be in on Monday to select her flowers, which would be in spring colors with melon and aqua worked in.

"Well, aren't you the little negotiator," Lottie said with a smile.

"Thank you," Mom said. "I've had quite a bit of practice mollifying parents, and I do know something about determined daughters."

I gave her a hug. "I really appreciate your talking to Mrs. St. Pierre. I couldn't seem to get through to her."

"That's why I stepped in, Abigail. I could tell you were frustrated."

"What did you say to get her to change her mind?" Lottie asked.

"I told her to stop worrying that her daughter was not going to need her anymore. That's all it was—a fear of not being needed. Edna wants that wedding to be perfect so she can prove to her daughter how much she needs her mother in her life."

"Thank goodness you weren't like that for my wedding," I said.

Mom gave me a kiss on the cheek. "I just didn't let it show."

"Thank you for that," I said. "Okay, everyone, let's get these orders finished. It's almost time to close." And I was so eager to get back to my investigation, I was practically wiggling.

"Hello?" I heard.

I turned to see Rosa come through the curtain. She had on a black jacket with black jeans and boots and, like yesterday, wore little makeup. But today she had a haunted look, with dark hollows beneath her eyes, like someone who hadn't slept in days.

"Rosa, I'm so sorry about Sergio," Mom said, giving her a hug.

"Thank you," she said sadly. "I still can't believe he is gone. My Sergio. My heart. My beloved husband. Gone! And my poor Petey, he keeps crying out for him, 'Papa, Papa, why would you leave me?' "

Lottie was ready with a tissue as Rosa began to sob, wrapping her solid arms around Rosa and rocking her as though she were a child. "We're here for you, sweetie."

"We are, most definitely," Grace added, placing her hand on Rosa's shoulder.

As was I, but only for the next fifteen minutes. Then I was out of there.

In a few moments Rosa calmed down enough to wipe her eyes and blow her nose. "I'm sorry. I did not mean to come here and make everyone sad."

"Nonsense," Grace said. "Isn't that, after all, what friends are for? As the fabled Roman philosopher Cicero wrote, 'Friendship makes prosperity more shining and lessens adversity by dividing and sharing it.' "

"Thank you, Grace," Rosa said, accepting a fresh tissue. "My heart aches for Sergio so much I cannot sleep at night." With a deep sigh, she said, "It would help so much if my husband would give me a sign to let me know he is okay, but I haven't seen anything. Not one thing."

"What kind of sign?" Mom asked.

Rosa shrugged. "I don't know how it will come, but I will recognize it when I see it." She glanced upward and shook her fist. "Hurry up, Sergio! Your little lightning bolt is not a patient woman."

That broke the tension in the room and made the women laugh.

"You didn't have to come in today, Rosa," I said, returning to the arrangement I'd started.

"I was going *loco* by myself at home," she said, sitting on a stool. "Too many memories there. Petey is with my mother, so I had to get out. This is the only place I could think of that makes me feel better. Can I do something to help?"

"You betcha," Lottie said, opening one of the walk-in coolers. "We have a bunch of orders still on the spindle."

"I can stay, too," Mom said. "I'm not in any rush."

But I was. All I could think about was that fax of Bud lying upside down on my desk. Of all the days to be swamped with orders, why was it today?

"Have you made any discoveries about Sergio's note?" Rosa asked me, her sad eyes lifting with hope.

"Not yet," I said. "But we can talk about this next week, after things settle down."

"How can things settle down until the man who caused it is caught?" she asked.

I studied Rosa for a moment. Despite her sorrow, there was a spark of determination in her eyes that I recognized. "Then I'll need to ask you a few questions."

"I am here, aren't I? What are you waiting for?"

I wasn't going anywhere until the orders were done, so what was the harm of talking to her? "First of all, are you sure the note was in Sergio's handwriting?"

"He did not write," she said. "He printed. He only went to school through fourth grade because he was needed to work on his family's farm. Anyway, why would someone else print 'Help me' on a piece of paper and put it in Sergio's pocket?"

"The only problem we're having," I said, smudging

the truth around the edges, "is that we don't know who Sergio would have intended to give the note to."

Rosa looked puzzled. "Why else would he have it?"

"Mr. Appleruth said the men usually carry pencils. I wondered if you'd ever seen him with a red marker."

"No, but that does not mean he didn't carry one in his tool belt. Why? What are you thinking?"

"That someone gave the note to him."

"Abby, that would not make sense. If someone handed my husband a note asking for help, Sergio would not stuff it in his pocket. He would do something about it." She patted my hand as though I were a child. "Keep trying."

"Here you go, Rosa," Lottie said, laying an armful of yellow roses on the table. "This is an order for a simple bouquet. You know what to do to roses, don't you?"

"I do," she said with a grateful smile.

"Abby, I'll be up front with your mom," Lottie said.

As Rosa and I worked, I could tell by the relaxing of her shoulders that she was so absorbed, her grief was not the first thing on her mind. Flowers were as much a balm to her soul as they were to mine.

She finished her bouquet, put it in the cooler, and sat down on the stool to watch me. "What is that arrangement for?"

"A table centerpiece."

"I recognize the peonies, but what are those flowers?"

"Snowballs."

"And those?"

"Dahlias."

"I like the pink and cream colors together. They're very romantic. What if you added lily of the valley? Wouldn't that be pretty?"

"I suppose it would."

"I'll get some for you."

I tried not to be annoyed—I knew she meant well—but would a painter want someone else telling her what colors to use?

Rosa returned from the cooler with her arms loaded down. "Here are the lilies and I brought some of these leafy things, too."

"Eucalyptus," I said, feeling my annoyance meter creeping upward. "I was going to use variegated euonymus—"

Rosa's face fell.

"—but these are good."

She smiled broadly. "See? I am a natural."

"How about putting your talent to work on an arrangement of red and yellow tulips?" I suggested.

"I would love to do that." She gave me an exuberant hug, then hurried to the cooler to gather her blossoms.

My cell phone rang and it was Marco calling from the bar, so I took the call in the kitchen. "Hey, Buttercup," he said. "What time will you be here for dinner?"

"I've still got work to do, so maybe six thirty?" I didn't tell him that work included the Jones case. I was so eager to get to it, I wasn't even hungry.

"I've got to meet with a client then, babe. Can you make it sooner?"

I stifled my frustrated sigh. It seemed that the universe was conspiring against me. "How about six?"

"See you then."

At five forty-five, as we put away supplies and cleaned off the table, Mom came in to say good-bye. "I enjoyed myself, Abigail. I can see why you like Bloomers so much. The shop is such a pleasant environment." She glanced over her shoulder toward the curtain and sighed. "I was hoping my sconces would have sold by now, but I guess it will take just the right buyer."

Lottie stuck her head through the curtain. "Don't forget the cheese you bought at the deli today, Maureen."

"Thanks for the reminder," Mom said. "Jeff would have been disappointed if I'd forgotten his favorite cheese."

When she went into the kitchen, Rosa gave me a discreet nudge and whispered, "I will talk to your mother now about the ugly fish."

I shook my head. "She had a nice day. Don't spoil it." Besides, if Rosa told my mother her art pieces were ugly, I'd have to stay and pick up the pieces of Mom's heart—and I didn't need any more delays.

Rosa planted her hands on her hips. "Is that what you think I would do?"

I was about to argue when Mom came out holding a small white paper bag. "If you need help tomorrow, honey, let me know." She gave me a kiss on the cheek, then turned to Rosa. "And if there's anything I can do for you, please call me."

I saw Rosa getting ready to speak, so I put my arm around Mom's back and ushered her rapidly through the curtain. "Okay, Mom. Hug Dad for me. Bye."

"Wait, Maureen," Rosa said, holding one side of the curtain back. "Before you leave, I need to talk to you."

Chapter Twenty

I paced for ten minutes, my anxiety rising with each step. Finally, I peeked through the curtain from the workroom to see what was taking so long.

"What's happening?" Lottie asked.

"Rosa's taking the sconces off the wall."

"Uh-oh. What's your mom doing?"

"I don't believe it. She's giving Rosa a hug."

"A hug? That Rosa is a wonder," Lottie said. "*La Mujer Maravilla.*"

"What about Maraville?"

"*La Mujer Maravilla* means Wonder Woman."

I turned to gaze at Lottie in astonishment. "You're speaking Spanish now?"

Lottie blushed all the way up to her brassy curls. "Rosa taught me that."

I stepped back as Wonder Woman came through the curtain and laid the sconces on the table. "It is done," she said solemnly, brushing her hands together.

"Was Maureen okay with painting the eyes?" Lottie asked.

"Of course." Rosa gave me a gentle poke. "As I told Abby she would be."

Woman with the swollen brain wins again. I wondered how that name would translate. "How did you convince her?"

"I told her that I was afraid she would be sued for copying another artist's work."

"What other artist?" I asked.

"An artist that I saw at an art fair last summer," Rosa said with a shrug, tearing off a piece of wrapping paper. She wouldn't meet my eye.

"Another artist made fish-shaped sconces with wiggly eyes?" I asked.

"Maybe not with the wiggly eyes." Rosa folded the paper around the sconces. "Maybe not in the fish shape." She taped the paper and put the sconces in a shopping bag. "But I saw many artists at the fair. That part is true."

I was not even going to think about how many times I'd used that same tactic on Marco.

Rosa set the shopping bag aside. "Your mother would like to paint them herself, so we are going to the hobby store now to buy the silver paint. And so you see? I told you she would be okay with it, and she is. Next time maybe you will trust me."

Lottie put her hand over her mouth to hide a smile.

"Hold on," I said. "Making up a story about imaginary sconces is just as dishonest as what I was going to tell her."

Lottie moved into my line of vision and dragged a finger across her throat, her way of telling me not to argue with Rosa.

"No, that's okay, Lottie," Rosa said, obviously having caught sight of her. "Abby, which is better? To let your mother believe that an artist who is good enough to show her work at a fair made the same sconces that she did, or to hide her sconces in the basement and have her think that they sold?"

"That's not my point," I said.

"Can't you just be happy that she is happy?" Rosa asked.

"Of course I can . . . and am . . . and will be. But what happened to that little speech you gave me about lying to my mom?"

Rosa put her hands on my shoulders and gazed into my eyes. "Abby, she is your mother, not mine."

"So my point was that Rosa lied, too," I said to Marco over dinner at the bar, "but the difference is that she came off looking like a hero. Now Lottie and Grace think Rosa is some kind of *Mujer Maravilla*. That means Wonder Woman, by the way."

Marco jabbed his French fry in ketchup and ate it. "You have to admit that Rosa's idea worked out well for everyone."

I scowled as I wound another forkful of spaghetti into my spoon. "We'll still have to sell them."

Marco slipped a French fry to Seedy under the table. "Why do I get the feeling you're jealous of Rosa?"

"I'm not jealous. I'm just . . ."

Just what, Abby? You like Rosa's spunk. You admire her creativity. You love the way flowers call to her. So just what?

Marco was waiting. I finally shrugged. "Maybe a little jealous."

"I thought so."

"I don't like feeling that way, Marco. Rosa is a sweet person, and she just lost her husband. How can I be so hateful?"

"Here's how I see it." Marco picked up another fry. "You've been Lottie and Grace's wonder child for almost two years, and suddenly another wonder child enters the picture. Now you have to share your space as well as the spotlight, and that takes adjustment."

"First of all, please don't call me a *wonder* anything. Second, you make me sound like a jealous sibling."

Marco reached across the table and took my hand. "You and Rosa are a lot alike, Abby. You have to get used to having a sister in the house, that's all." When I didn't reply, he said, "What is it, Sunshine? Something's still bothering you about Rosa."

"Not Rosa. It's me, Marco. I'm feeling extremely petty right now. Rosa is sexy, beautiful, exotic, and clearly talented—and I don't want her to be better than I am at arranging flowers, too."

"That's what's bothering you?" Marco sat back with a smile. "Okay, and what if she is? Then the two of you would be a dynamic duo. The hottest florists in New Chapel."

I was having a hard time imagining Rosa and myself as a team. She'd no doubt come off looking as sexy as Catwoman and I'd be her funny little sidekick. I pictured us side by side in an advertisement and had to shake the image from my head.

"So," I asked, not looking at him, "you think I'm as hot as Rosa?"

"Hotter. Baby, there's a reason why I call you Fireball."

I smiled to myself as I sipped my wine.

"Think what the two of you could do, Abby. You could put your heads together and come up with some new arrangements that would knock the socks off your customers. *Muy caliente.*"

Did everyone speak Spanish but me? I thought about Marco's idea as I ate a fry. "I don't know. Rosa has a lot to learn about being a professional florist before that can happen."

"And you and Lottie will be there to teach her."

Not Lottie. She was *my* mentor. If anyone was going to teach Rosa, it would be me. "Thanks, Marco. It's so nice having someone to talk things out with."

"I'm always here for you, baby." Marco glanced around at the growing crowd. "And I'd better get back to work."

I wondered whether he'd caught the irony.

"Okay, but before you go, I did talk to Rosa about Sergio's note. She said Sergio printed everything because he'd never learned cursive. Despite the doubts I laid out, she's adamant that it was his note. She said if someone had given a help note to him, he wouldn't have put it in his pocket. She's assuming we're still working on the case. I didn't have the heart to tell her we weren't."

"That's okay. After the funeral, we'll sit down and explain it."

As soon as Seedy and I got home that evening, I logged on to the Internet and started searching through the *Bowling Green Sentinel-Tribune*'s newspaper archives from five and six years back. I was hoping to find a story about a baby girl stolen from a hospital, but nothing came up. I tried the same search with Maraville's newspaper, *The Courier*, with the same results. Was it possible Daisy was the Joneses' real child? But then why didn't Mrs. Welldon remember her?

I pulled up Ted Birchman's phone number and gave him another call.

"Mr. Birchman, this is Abby Salvare again. I'm sorry to bother you, but do you know where your brother moved to five or six years ago?"

"You're still checking references?"

"Yes."

He scoffed. "Come on, Mrs. Salvare. I wasn't born yesterday. No one goes to the extremes that you're going to for one potential renter. Level with me or I'm hanging up now. Is my brother in trouble again?"

"What would you say if I told you I was tracking a pair of kidnappers who took a baby boy from a Maraville hospital ten years ago?"

"If you're talking about Ed and Sandra, I'd like to say you're barking up the wrong tree. My brother has done some shady things in his life, but kidnapping a baby?"

"I hope I'm mistaken, Mr. Birchman, but I'm following a trail that is leading to a man by the name of Norm Jones, the alias your brother is using now."

"Dear God," I heard him mutter.

"Do you happen to know if Sandra was pregnant when they left Bowling Green?"

"I didn't see Sandra before they left. I only met my brother at a coffee shop to say good-bye, and he didn't mention anything about her expecting another child. Why?"

"Because they have a six-year-old girl who might have been kidnapped, too."

"Oh, my God."

"As I said, I hope I'm mistaken."

"I hope you are, too." He paused, then said, "I just remembered something that Ed told me. He said that he and Sandra hoped to add to their little family. It never occurred to me that he'd snatch a baby to do it."

"Did he say where they were moving to?"

"Yes, they'd decided to move back to Maraville to be close to Sandra's family."

Then there should have been some record of Daisy being taken from a local hospital. Why hadn't I found it?

"Do you know Sandra's maiden name?" I asked, thinking I might be able to track her through her family.

"I'm sorry, no. Ed never mentioned it."

"That's all I need to know. Thank you for your help, Mr. Birchman. This must be difficult for you."

"Surprisingly, it's not as difficult as you might think."

I hung up, then began to plan my strategy.

Step one: Using Marco's first rule, I would have to get a look at the attic window in the Victorian to see whether it would have been possible for the kids to see Sergio on his ladder. To do that, I'd have to get back inside the house.

Step two: If that panned out, and once I'd found out where the Joneses lived, I'd have to approach Sandra about interviewing the kids at a time when Norm was gone so I wouldn't have to deal with both of them. That meant either waiting until Monday, when Norm was at work but I might be too busy to get away, or setting up surveillance on the house this Saturday, my day off, while

Marco was at the bar, in the hopes that Norm would leave on an errand.

I chose Saturday, with Monday as my backup. But first I needed to track down the Joneses, and the best way to do that was to follow Norm home from school. I glanced at my watch. He would be at the school late tonight. I could make it to Maraville in plenty of time to catch him.

Trying to be inconspicuous in a yellow Corvette was nearly impossible. I had been tempted to switch cars with Marco, but if he happened to leave early and found my 'Vette in place of his Prius, he'd want an explanation. So I parked down the block from the elementary school, pulled up my black hood, grabbed a flashlight, and walked as close to the school as I dared. Then, crouched down among a stand of trees alongside the school playground, I waited for Norm to come out.

While I waited, I texted Lorelei and asked her to set up another viewing of the Victorian as soon as possible. She texted back almost immediately to tell me I could see it at ten in the morning. Perfect. Marco would be at work. So far so good.

Shortly after nine, two men exited the rear school door, one of them Norm and the other Mr. Paisley, the janitor I'd talked to previously. I watched as Mr. Paisley drove off in a black-and-silver pickup truck with a Chicago Bears decal on the rear gate while Norm stood at the curb looking up the street. A few minutes later, their old blue van pulled up and he got into the passenger side.

Afraid I'd lose them, I darted among the trees and slid behind the wheel of my car just as the van drove past. I thought I was safe until I realized that my hood had slipped down. Before I could duck, Norm's head swiveled my way and I was certain he spotted me. But the van continued on, so I hoped I was wrong.

When they reached the end of the block, I waited until I saw the left turn signal on, then eased away from the curb and followed. Once the van had turned the corner, I sped up to make sure I didn't lose it, then pulled back and let a few cars go past before following. In this way I was able to keep track of the Joneses for the twelve blocks it took to reach their house.

When they pulled into a driveway alongside an old white-clapboard house, I backed up to the corner, then watched as Norm and Sandra exited the vehicle and entered the house through the front door. I was surprised that Sandra had left the kids home alone, but perhaps it would happen again tomorrow.

I waited until the porch light went off, then drove past, wrote down the address, and headed home, wishing I could share my elation with Marco. I was going to crack this case and possibly Sergio's as well. I was pumped.

Saturday

"What do you have on tap this morning, Buttercup?"

Sleeping until nine, if truth be known. But a husband landing on the bed beside me at eight a.m., bouncing me awake, had pretty much scotched that idea. "Nothing definite," I said, stretching like a cat.

"Seedy has been fed and walked, and my lady's coffee awaits." Marco gave me a playful pat on the hip. "Lucky you. It's a great time to be indoors."

"Because?"

"It's one of those rainy, dreary days that makes staying home a pleasure."

I threw back the covers and hopped out of bed. It was also a perfect day for surveillance, and I had already formulated my plan. The only glitch was that I had to leave Seedy behind, but I had a solution for that, too.

Then it hit me what day it was. "Marco, Sergio's funeral is at two o'clock."

"I'll be home by one," Marco said. "That'll give me time to shower and dress."

That meant I'd have to be back at the apartment with Seedy no later than twelve forty-five. I didn't have a minute to spare.

"Tara, how are you coming on that research I gave you?" I asked my niece on the phone as I gobbled down a piece of toast slathered in peanut butter and cinnamon.

She yawned. "Sorry, Aunt Abby. I forgot all about it. But I'm free this morning. I'll do it now."

"Good. And just to show how badly you feel for forgetting, would you watch Seedy for a few hours?"

"Sure. She can have a play date with Seedling. Want me to come over? I can be there in an hour."

"Better yet, I'll bring Seedy to you because I have to leave now." I was taking no chances of Marco finding Tara at the apartment and wanting to know where I was.

I dropped Seedy off, then headed downtown to pick up a bouquet of flowers for Sandra. I had to park a block away and then slip in through the alley door so Marco wouldn't spot me.

"What are you up to on your day off?" Lottie asked as I wrapped a bouquet of lavender, lilac phlox, blue wax flowers, and wisps of mountain grass.

"Nothing much, and you never saw me."

Lottie looked at me askance. "I don't like the sound of that."

"Nothing dangerous," I said.

"If it's not dangerous, why are you sneaking around?"

"How about if we call it undercover work instead?"

"A rose by any other name," Grace said, coming out of the parlor.

"Marco doesn't want to pursue Rosa's case," I said, "and I don't have the heart to tell her, so I'm trying to solve it on my own."

"You won't miss the funeral, will you?" Grace asked.

"Of course not. I'll see you both at the funeral parlor before two."

"Sweetie," Lottie called as I headed toward the curtain, "promise you'll be careful."

I paused to smile at her. "I promise."

"A fat lot of good that's ever done," Grace muttered.

Lorelei was waiting in her car in front of the Victorian when I pulled up. We both scurried to the front door with our umbrellas up, then left them on the porch as we stepped inside.

"I was really surprised to get your call," Lorelei said. "I didn't think you were interested in this house."

I started up the steps, calling back, "I'm not interested. I just need to see the attic."

"The attic?"

I waited until she had reached the landing at the top

to say, "I'm working on a private investigation. I really can't say more than that."

"Oh," she said in a whisper. "I see."

Hoping there weren't any spider assassins waiting to spring out at me, I opened the door to the attic staircase cautiously, then groped for a switch on the wall and turned on an overhead bulb. It was so dim I could barely see four steps in front of me.

"I have a flashlight if that will help," Lorelei said from behind, making me jump.

"Thanks. It would."

With her narrow beam as my guide, I made my way up the creaking staircase and stepped onto a wooden floor. With Lorelei sticking close—she hated spiders, too—I shined the light on the ceiling to see whether any webs lurked over my head, then on the floor in front of me. I swept it along the walls and into the corners, finding only an old wood-handled dust mop. Amazingly—and thankfully—I saw no spiders and let out a breath I hadn't realized I'd been holding.

"It's surprisingly clean," Lorelei said. "The last tenants must have been using it, though God knows for what."

There was only one window, white trimmed, narrow, and double hung, situated in a dormer at the front of the house. Sweeping the floor in front of me with the light, I made my way toward it. There, I inspected the area for spiders, then moved the beam around the entire window frame. I was taking no chances. I noticed colored flecks on the sill and touched my finger to them.

"Bugs?" Lorelei asked, peering over my shoulder. I jumped again. "Sorry," she whispered.

"Crayon shavings," I said, showing her. I found more on the floor, as though someone had sat there to sharpen crayons. There were also stray marks in a variety of primary colors, but they seemed to have soaked into the wood as crayon wax would not. From a child's paint set, perhaps?

"This must have been used as a playroom," Lorelei said.

Remembering that I'd seen only one twin bed downstairs, I said, "Or a third bedroom."

I noticed a long black hair snagged on the side of the window and pulled it free. Daisy was the only one with hair that length. If Sandra tried to argue that the children couldn't have witnessed the accident because they didn't use the attic, here was my proof to the contrary. I still had the plastic bag in my purse with Sergio's note in it, so I coiled the hair and tucked it inside.

I knelt on the floor to peer outside from a child's perspective, then pushed up on the frame to open the window for a better view. The window rose easily, as though the track had been oiled. With the window in the open position, I could see smudged fingerprints on the glass, as though small fingers had pressed up on it.

I poked my head out and looked up at the V of the roof, then down at the ground, glad the rain had stopped. If the top of Sergio's ladder had reached just below the windowsill, he would have stood several rungs below that, so the trunk of his body would have been about window height. Anyone could have opened the window and touched him . . . or pushed him.

I thought of the small round bruise Rosa had seen on Sergio's abdomen but I couldn't imagine Daisy's little fist hitting him with enough force to cause a mark like that, or even Bud's, although his fist would have left a mark larger than a quarter. Besides, why would either child have wanted to hit him?

I realized my knees were damp and stood up, blocking most of the light from the open window. "The floor's wet here. Be careful. The window must not have been shut all the way." I brushed my soggy jeans as though that would make the wetness disappear.

"Here," Lorelei said. "You can dry the floor with this."

When I turned around, she was holding the mop with the handle end toward me as though getting ready to joust. *Good thing you like me,* I almost said to her. One hard jab to my stomach and I'd fold in half, flying out the window like a—

Like a painter on a ladder.

I took the mop and examined the handle. It was round at the tip with a diameter the size of a quarter.

"Is something wrong with it?" Lorelei asked, peering over my shoulder.

"Hold the mop like you were before and pretend you're poking a hole through the window."

"What?"

"Use the mop handle like this." I demonstrated what I wanted her to do.

She gave me an odd look. "Why?"

"It's for my investigation."

"Oh, I see," she said again in a whisper. She took the mop and proceeded to make a jab.

"Now freeze," I said, pulling out my cell phone. "I need to take your picture."

It was only a hunch so far, but I had a strong feeling

that the mop handle, not Adrian's ring, had caused Sergio's bruise. The question was, who had been the jouster?

I parked down the street from the Joneses' residence, hoping no one would notice me. The rain had started up again and the sky was a dark gray, so lights were on in many of the houses on the block. I had a travel mug filled with coffee that I would have to drink slowly. The worst part of surveillance was not being able to consume liquids. Sitting for long periods didn't work with a full bladder.

I played a game on my cell phone for a while, then read a magazine. After more than two hours I was beginning to think that my plan was a bust, when the Joneses' blue van came into view, backing out of the driveway. I grabbed Marco's binoculars and focused on the windows. I saw Norm's large head in the driver's side, but the passenger side appeared to be empty. Sandra must have stayed behind.

I waited another five minutes after the van had turned the corner, then picked up the umbrella and my bouquet and got out of the car. I rang the doorbell and Sandra opened the door just a few inches to peer out. "Yes?"

"Hi, Sandra. Remember me? I'm Abby, the florist from Bloomers Flower Shop. I have a delivery for you."

I expected hesitancy. Wariness. Alarm. That wasn't what I got.

Chapter Twenty-One

Sandra opened the door wide, smiling as though we were old friends. "What an unexpected surprise."

She was wearing a brown-and-red-plaid button-down shirt, a pair of dingy brown pleated slacks, and brown shoes. Her dark hair was wound into a knot at the back of her neck, making her makeup-free face seem even rounder and plainer. I had a sudden image of her in a nurse's uniform, a plump, unremarkable woman able to slip into a nursery and out again with a baby in her bag.

"Please come in," she said in her cottony voice. "It's such a nasty day, isn't it?"

I stepped into the house and glanced around, trying to take everything in quickly. To my left was a tiny living room furnished with ugly gray carpeting, a heavy, old-fashioned television on a metal stand, and a shabby green sofa. To my right was a square kitchen furnished with golden brown linoleum, a red vinyl-topped card table, and brown folding chairs. There was a white plastic clock above the range, and white cotton café curtains on the windows, one over the sink and one looking out on the side of the house toward the driveway.

Straight in front of me, behind Sandra, was a steep staircase covered with a floral-patterned rug worn threadbare on the treads. I saw no sign of either child.

"To what do we owe this honor?" Sandra asked, eyeing the bouquet in my hand. "Has someone sent us flowers?"

"Yes, me." I handed them to her. "With my compliments."

She held them to her nose and inhaled, closing her eyes as though she'd found her bliss. "Oh, I do love the smell of lavender. How thoughtful of you. But what's the occasion?"

I heard giggling and glanced up the steps, catching sight of the top of a head and then two eyes peering over the edge at me. I waved, which caused more giggling. "Is that Daisy?"

"Yes, that's my Daisy," Sandra said. Then louder, "She and Bud are *supposed* to be cleaning their room."

"Would you let me visit with them?"

"Well, that's a rather surprising request." Still smiling, she darted a glance at her watch.

"Remember the accident that happened to the painter before you left New Chapel? I was hoping to talk to your kids in case one of them witnessed his fall—maybe while they were playing in the attic."

A look of surprise flitted across her face—was it because I'd guessed correctly about the attic's use? Then she nodded gravely. "I do remember the accident. Yes, of course I do. It was a tragedy. But my children were in the kitchen with me making cookies that morning."

"All morning?"

She blinked at me.

Before she could reply, I said, "If you don't mind, Sandra, I'd really like to talk to them about it."

I could see a battle being waged behind Sandra's small eyes. If, as she professed, her children had been with her the entire time, then where was the harm in letting me interview them? She couldn't refuse without being rude, and she seemed the type to find rudeness out of the question.

"Well, of course you may talk to them— But where are my manners? Let me make you a cup of tea." She glanced at her watch for a second time as she started into the kitchen, then paused to motion for me to follow. "Come sit down and talk to me while the water heats."

I pulled out a chair at the card table as Sandra filled an old black aluminum tea kettle with water from an even older faucet at the kitchen sink, the handle groaning as she turned on the cold-water tap. "This kitchen leaves something to be desired," she said over her shoulder. "Fortunately, it's only a temporary residence."

I was betting most of their residences had been temporary.

Next, she took a glass from a cabinet and filled it with water, then inserted the bouquet stems in it, taking her time to arrange the blossoms. Setting the makeshift vase in the middle of the table, she said, "Now, let's see what goodies we have to share today." She talked the way my mom did when speaking to her kindergarten class.

After opening a cabinet and searching inside for just the right vessel—and from the glimpse I got of the contents, she had no reason to search that long—Sandra placed a large orange plastic plate on the counter, then lifted the lid of a ceramic cookie jar painted to look like a fat friar and peered inside. "Do you like oatmeal cookies?"

"Love them, but please don't go to any trouble."

"Why would it be any trouble?" She pushed back the curtain over the sink and took a quick glance outside, then checked her watch for the third time before turning with a smile. "You're a guest in my home, and I always make guests feel comfortable."

Sandra's actions were beginning to make me feel anything but comfortable. "Am I keeping you from something?"

"Just chores," she said blithely, "and I certainly don't mind taking a break from them." She reached inside the ceramic jar and pulled out one small brown cookie at a time, humming softly as she made a neat mound on the plate. At the sound of a car door slamming outside, Sandra paused and lifted her head. Then she continued humming until she had filled the plate.

Now it was me glancing at my watch. Eleven thirty. I didn't have a lot of time to spare.

"Here we are," she said, setting the plate in the middle of the table. She sat down opposite me and smiled, resting her chin in her hand.

"I hope the kids will be down soon," I said. "It really won't take me long to talk to them, and I hate to eat up too much of your time." Or your cookies.

"Oh," she said suddenly, her eyes opening wide. "Napkins. Silly me."

Completely ignoring my request, Sandra went back to the counter, opened a drawer, and pulled out a handful of white paper napkins. After taking another quick look out the side window, she came back to the table and placed one in front of me and one in front of her. Then she sat down, folded her hands beneath her chin, and smiled at me across the table—only now the smile seemed more sinister than sweet. "Try one of my cookies."

Sandra was beginning to remind me of the witch from "Hansel and Gretel." My antennae were rising. What was going on here?

"Thank you," I said, reaching for the top treat. "Would it be possible to ask the kids to join us now?"

"Of course," she said. "I'll go get them as soon as I pour our tea. Tell me about your flower shop while we're waiting."

I rattled off some information about Bloomers, my eye on the clock, nervously waiting for the kettle to whistle. I saw steam coming from the spout for several minutes, but no whistle accompanied it. Since Sandra seemed to have forgotten it, I paused to say, "The water's hot."

She jerked around to look at the stove as though surprised to find it behind her. After scooting her chair back with infinite slowness, she went to the range to shut off the gas, then opened a cabinet and took out two mismatched mugs. After that she searched through a drawer for a hot pad to hold the kettle handle. Was she that unfamiliar with her own kitchen?

With her back to me, she filled the mugs, then paused to say in a voice that was almost brittle in its sweetness, "I spoke with my former neighbor yesterday. Mrs. Welldon?"

My breath caught in my throat.

"She loved the bouquet you brought her."

Oh, damn. This isn't good. Sandra knew I was investigating them—and she wanted me to know it.

My heart began to thump anxiously as she calmly replaced the kettle on the stove and began a hunt for tea, opening cabinet after cabinet until she found the right one. When she paused to glance out the window again, I knew she was expecting someone. It was obvious now that she was stalling me.

My antennae were waving frantically. I needed to get out of there.

"Here we go," she said, sounding almost giddy. She turned and held up two boxes, one in each hand. "Black or green? I may have chamomile somewhere, too. I'd be happy to look for it."

I stood up, the metal chair legs sliding back easily on the linoleum. "I really need to get going."

"You should try the green. Do you take milk? All I have is two percent."

At that moment, Daisy came skipping into the room and halted next to the table. She was dressed in blue jeans and an oversized navy T-shirt that had a motorcycle emblem on the front, clearly a boy's hand-me-down. Her black hair fell straight down around her freckled face, emphasizing her green eyes. "Hello," she said, twirling around.

Bud slouched into the kitchen as though bored and immediately spotted the plate of cookies. "Can we have some, Mommy?"

"Your tummy has been upset all morning, Bud," Sandra said, her voice soft but her eyes steely. "You don't want to upset it more, do you?"

"No," he said dejectedly.

"Hi," I said. "Remember me? I'm Abby, and I have a little dog named Seedy."

"I remember," Bud said. He seemed more interested in dessert.

"Me, too," Daisy said. "Your dog has three legs instead of four like my dog had."

"You didn't have a dog," Bud said.

"Did, too. His name was Buster."

"Daisy," Sandra said sharply. "Stop fibbing."

"It's not a fib," Daisy said, pouting. As she hung her head, I noticed the part in her hair, and a cold feeling ran through me. She had red roots. Daisy was a freckle-faced redhead just like me.

Sandra had dyed her hair.

My eyes met Sandra's. She knew I'd noticed.

"Children," Sandra said, clapping her hands, startling me, "we do not eat until we wash our hands. Go upstairs right now." She took a step toward me, pointing at my chair. "Abby, sit, please."

Her gesture was reminiscent of Lorelei handing the mop to me, prompting a shocking vision of Sandra thrusting the wooden handle through the open window and into Sergio's stomach. It would have been quick and punishing, and all Sam, the big wrestler, would have seen was Sergio reacting to the trauma. But what had Sergio done to deserve it?

Bud turned, his head down, his hands in his pockets, and started toward the staircase. "When will Daddy be back?"

"In a little while," Sandra answered.

I had to get out now.

At that moment Daisy, who had been chewing on

her thumb, pulled it out and said, "You look like my mommy."

I glanced at Sandra and saw the shock on her face. Pushing aside my anxiety, I crouched before the child. "How do I look like your mommy?"

Sandra immediately inserted herself between us and put her hands on Daisy's small shoulders, turning her around and ushering her from the kitchen. "Miss Abby hasn't finished the tea I made for her, and it would be rude of us to keep her from it."

"Why won't you let her answer, Sandra?"

Sandra stopped cold and turned to stare at me. In a voice tinged with ice, she said, "I beg your pardon?"

I stood up. "Why won't you let Daisy answer? What are you afraid of?"

Forcing the most disingenuous smile I'd ever witnessed, she said, "Well, that would be rude of me not to let Daisy answer. I was merely concerned that your tea would get cold."

"I don't have time to finish the tea."

"Sit down," she said, her upper lip curling back, her tiny eyes pinning me to the spot, as if I were a child she could order around. Had she poisoned my tea?

"Maybe another time." It felt as if my heart was going to beat through my chest as I strode past her and headed toward the front door. *Just let her try to stop me,* I thought. It wasn't until I was on the porch that I dared to glance back.

My last glimpse of Sandra before she slammed the door was of her glaring at Daisy.

I dashed up the street to my car and locked the doors as soon as I was inside, my heart still pounding. I took a few deep breaths, then started the engine, noticing that my hands were trembling. As I pulled away, a black-and-silver pickup with a Bears decal on it drove past and turned into their driveway. A shudder went through me as Norm got out of the vehicle. I'd left just in time. But why was he driving Mr. Paisley's truck?

More significantly, what was going to happen once Sandra told Norm about my visit? Remembering the fury in Sandra's expression, I prayed Daisy wouldn't be punished. With every fiber of my being, I knew I had to get those children away from the Joneses before they took off again. It was time to bring the police in on the case.

I called Reilly's cell phone, but as usual he didn't pick up. Frustrated, I kept my message brief. "The Joneses are kidnappers—I have proof—but you'll have to act fast or you'll lose them."

I turned on my navigating system and followed the directions to get back to the highway, my mind racing as fast as my Corvette. I kept going over every snippet of my conversation with Sandra and Daisy, wanting to hold it all in my memory so I could repeat it to Reilly. When he finally returned my call, I heaved a sigh of relief.

"Thank God," I said.

"You have proof that the Joneses kidnapped their children?"

"Yes. I was just at their house in Maraville. Let me tell you what transpired."

I repeated almost verbatim my conversation, told him about Daisy's red roots and her startling comment about me, and ended with what I'd learned about the Joneses from Mrs. Welldon and Norm's brother Ted.

"Do you see why you have to act fast? Sandra knows that I know that Daisy isn't hers, and once she tells Norm about my visit, he'll pull another disappearing act and those kids might be gone forever."

"I hate to burst your bubble, Abby, but all I've heard so far is conjecture. Where's this proof you mentioned?"

"Well, I have the sketch you faxed to me that you could compare with the actual child."

"That's it?"

"Wait. I have a hair from Daisy's head that I found at their former residence. Long black hair with a red root."

"And how do we prove it belongs to the girl without DNA testing?"

"Hold it up to her head, Reilly. The red roots and the rest of the length that was dyed black will be a perfect match."

"Abby, seriously, do you think we could get a search warrant based on that?"

"Don't you care about these kids, Reilly? They were taken from their parents. You have kids. Imagine what that would feel like. We can't let the Joneses abscond with them again."

"I understand your concern, Abby. I feel for their parents, too, but my hands are tied by the law. I can't knock on their door and demand they hand over the kids. An investigation will have to be made based on more than a strand of hair and a five-year-old sketch."

"So get it started, then." I was boiling over with frustration. "Look, Reilly, at least find out if a little girl matching Daisy's description was kidnapped about two years ago."

"How do you know it was two years?"

"I don't know for sure. It's a hunch. Daisy is six and has vague memories of her mom and her dog, which would be consistent with a four-year-old's memories. Don't memories start at around the age of four? So do the math." I had a sudden thought and said, "She might have been taken from a Maraville preschool. Norm Jones has been working as a janitor within the school system, and maybe that's by design."

Reilly let out a deep sigh. "Let me run it past the detectives. I'll get back to you."

"When? We might have only a day, Reilly."

"I'll try to talk to someone today. But even if I get them interested, nothing's going to happen overnight."

And overnight would be all it took to lose the kidnappers. It looked as though it would be up to Marco and me to stop them.

Chapter Twenty-Two

Back at my brother's house, I had to stifle my impatience when Tara wanted to show me the results of her Internet search. I had only an hour until Marco was due home, and I wanted to do a search of my own that was much more important than pricing a bench.

"I couldn't find anything like what Grandpa made, Auntie A," my niece said, sitting on the sofa in their family room, her laptop on her knees, "so I took the closest things to it and made a list of links to them with their prices. Here, I'll show you."

"Could you put it in an e-mail and send it to me?" I asked, trying to snap Seedy's leash onto her collar. It was proving difficult because she and Seedling were romping on the living room rug. "I have to get home. Seedy, come on! Hold still."

"Sure, but what's your rush?" Tara asked. "It's your day off."

"Unfortunately, Uncle Marco and I have to go to a funeral. Seedling, let go of the leash. Seedy, let go of Seedling's stuffed dinosaur. Tara, would you help me, please?"

"Chill out, Aunt Abby," Tara said as she picked up her puppy. "Nothing's that important."

She had no idea.

I finally got Seedy home and was relieved when she hobbled straight to her bed and curled up for a nap. I took a quick shower, then dressed in a tan silk shirt, black skirt, and black dress boots, made myself a sandwich, and fired up the laptop. I got into Marco's favorite database and began a hunt for a four- or five-year-old kidnap victim in the Maraville area.

I'd barely begun when I heard the key in the lock.

"Hey," Marco said with a smile, appearing in the doorway. "How's my bird-of-paradise today?" He stopped to glance through the mail lying on a table by the door.

Setting aside the computer, I said, "You won't believe what happened today."

Without looking up, he said, "Let me shower and then you can tell me while I'm dressing."

He'd obviously missed the urgency in my voice. I glanced at my watch, the gesture reminding me of Sandra. "We've got plenty of time. I'd rather tell you while everything is still fresh in my mind."

Finally he looked at me. "This sounds serious."

"It is serious. Children's lives are at stake."

Marco sat on the sofa beside me. "Tell me."

I pulled out my cell phone and found the photos of Lorelei at the attic window. "First I need to start with what I discovered at the Victorian this morning."

"You went back to see the house?"

"Just wait." I showed him the photos and explained what I'd deduced about Sergio's fall.

Marco took my phone and scrolled through the photos a second time, his forehead furrowed. "What reason would Sandra have for pushing Sergio?"

"I don't know yet, but I do know that Sandra and Norm are kidnappers."

"Wait a minute, Abby. You're confusing me. Let's take one case at a time."

"No, Marco, they're not separate cases. Sergio did or saw something that morning that alarmed Sandra. She grabbed the mop and pushed him. Remember when I first spoke with her in front of the Victorian? The only thing she wanted to know was whether Sergio was dead. And when he didn't die, they left town.

"We've been looking at the wrong suspects, Marco. And now that Sandra knows I'm onto them, they'll leave again. I tried to get Reilly interested, but he gave me the usual blah-blah about the law and how his hands are tied."

"Back up." Marco sat back and folded his arms. "How does Sandra know you're onto them?"

We really didn't have much time, so I gave Marco the details of my visit as succinctly as possible.

"Okay, don't scowl, Marco—I know I should have taken you with me. But here's the kicker. Almost right after I noticed her red roots, Daisy said to me, 'You look like my mommy.' Now seriously, you remember Sandra. There's no way I could have reminded Daisy of her. Daisy was talking about her real mother, who must have had red hair like mine. That's why she gave me that odd look the first time we met.

"And here's another thing. Twice now Daisy has insisted that she had a dog. The first time, Sandra brushed it off as an imaginary playmate. Today, though, Daisy got a sharp rebuke. But she said back to Sandra almost defiantly, 'I'm not telling a fib.'

"I believe her, Marco. And if she remembers having a dog, and her mom being a redhead, then she wasn't taken as a baby like Bud was. She would've been at least four years old to remember things from her past."

"You're jumping all over the place, Sunshine. How do you know Bud was taken as an infant?"

I backed up once again and told him, wishing I'd thought to start at the beginning in the first place. But I was so agitated that I was in a rush to get him to help.

"Reilly said he'd talk to one of the detectives, but something needs to be done right away, like after the funeral, because the Joneses will move again—I can just feel it. You saw how fast they got out of New Chapel. I don't want that to happen again, because we might never find them."

"Other than what the nurse and Norm's brother and the former neighbor told you, do you have any actual proof that these children aren't the Joneses'?"

I jumped up and took the plastic bag out of my purse. "I have one of Daisy's hairs. Look. You can see the red root."

"Abby, you're savvy enough by now to know that to prove this hair came from Daisy's head, and not some previous tenant's, a DNA test would have to be done on it. And then they'd have to compare it to Daisy's DNA, which they'd have to have permission to take. Imagine getting Sandra's approval for that if she is a kidnapper. And I haven't even addressed your theory of how Sergio fell. If Sandra pushed him, what was her motive?"

"Like I said, I haven't figured that out yet. But do you see the urgency?"

"What would you have us do? Kidnap them back?"

"Now you're just being difficult. We'd have to set up a surveillance so we can follow them if they take off."

"And then what?"

"Then—I don't know. You're the expert. How about we figure out how to get a sample of Daisy's DNA for starters?"

Marco stood up. "Let's get through the funeral and then we can talk about it."

"But there's no time to talk about it. Don't you get it? If the cops won't do something, we have to."

Marco glanced at his watch. "Right now, I'm going to take a shower and get dressed. And then we are going to the funeral. And *then* we will talk about it."

"I hate it when you go all dictator on me, Marco."

"I'm not exactly loving it that you went rogue on this case, Abby. You put yourself in danger today, and I didn't even know where you were. Did anyone know?"

When I didn't answer, he said, "Not only that, but you lied several times about what you were doing in your free time."

"That's because you would have acted just like you are now."

Marco was about to argue back but must have realized he would have proved my point. Clamping his mouth shut, he strode off to take a shower, and I returned to my computer to search for kidnapped little girls.

We were still at odds with each other as we took seats in the small chapel of the Happy Dreams Funeral Home. I didn't like being angry at Marco—it was hard to be angry and in love at the same time—but I felt justified. There was no way I was going to let the Joneses get away with kidnapping those kids. Somewhere there were heartbroken parents who needed our help. If Marco wouldn't work with me, and if the cops wouldn't get involved until they had more proof, then I'd go rogue again.

That very night.

Marco and I sat in a row with my mom and dad and Lottie and Grace, but we didn't talk to each other. After the service, Rosa's family had organized a dinner in the nearby Mexican restaurant's upstairs banquet room, but I had made a unilateral decision not to attend the dinner, even though Lottie and Grace urged me to join them. I wasn't in any frame of mind to sit and make small talk. I had children to save.

We were standing in a huddle—Lottie, Grace, Mom, Dad, Marco, and me—arguing about my leaving when Rosa came over to thank us for coming.

"You will come to the dinner, won't you?" she asked, holding Lottie and Grace's hands. "I would be honored."

"Of course we will, love," Grace said.

"You betcha, sweetie," Lottie said. "We wouldn't miss it."

They gave me pointed looks.

"That helps more than I can say," Rosa said, glancing at us with tears in her eyes. "I had more bad news yesterday."

"Oh, no!" Grace said.

"What is it?" Lottie asked.

"My boss is having financial difficulties and cannot

even afford to buy his employees insurance now. He is cutting me back to part-time employment."

"Oh, Rosa," Mom said, stepping up to give her a hug. "I'm so sorry. But maybe this is your opportunity to find something even better."

"That's exactly what it is," Lottie said. "You have to think positive thoughts, Rosa, so positive things will happen. It's the law of attraction. You're gonna find something you like even better. Watch and see."

"Where?" Rosa asked with a shrug. "No one is hiring these days. It was only with Mr. Appleruth's help that I managed to get this job."

Lottie looked at me. Then Grace looked at me. Then Marco looked at me. Mom was still talking to Rosa, but Dad was looking at me, too. I knew they wanted me to offer Rosa a full-time job, but I couldn't afford that. And even if I could, Bloomers was my sanctuary. My paradise. I didn't want Rosa to claim it as hers, too. And why was it suddenly my responsibility to employ her?

I looked away. I felt awful, like the worst ogre there ever was.

"Well, I'd better wash my face and try to make myself presentable before I go over to the restaurant," Rosa said. "I'll see you all there, right?"

"Of course you will, love," Grace said.

"We'll be along in a jiffy," Mom said.

They waited until Rosa had left the room to pounce on me. "Hire her, Abigail," Mom said. "You'll be doing a wonderful thing."

"Do hire her, love," Grace said. "She'll appreciate it forever."

"We don't need another full-time person," I said.

"Then make her a full-time part-timer," Lottie said. "That way she can stay at her current position and work for us, too."

I folded my arms across my chest and let them make their cases: Rosa would be an asset and a great teammate (that from Marco); a great draw for the Hispanic community; another pair of hands in the workroom, a talent-in-the-making (way to rub a raw nerve, Grace); and on and on.

"So what's your problem with Rosa?" Marco asked. Marco, the man of my dreams–turned-dictator. "I thought we had this solved."

"Solved?" Had I become just another case for him to *solve*?

"Figured out," he corrected.

"Rosa has a temper," I said. "I'm not convinced we would work well together, spending that much time with each other."

"Well, there's the pot calling the kettle black," Grace said sotto voce.

"Oh, boy," Dad said. "She's got that stubborn look on her face. Pack it in, everyone. Our Abracadabra isn't going to be swayed today."

He had that right.

I stayed at the restaurant for one torturous hour, all the time imagining the furious packing that was no doubt happening at the Joneses' house. With my nerves ready to snap, I said quietly to Marco, "I'm leaving. If you want to stay, my parents will bring you home."

"Why would I stay without you?"

"Because you think I'm being a stubborn idiot."

He didn't argue, but he did come with me.

When we got home, Marco snapped the leash on Seedy's collar to take her for a walk, so I said, "I'll be gone when you get back. I'm heading to Maraville to stake out the Joneses' house."

"Did you think this through, Abby? What will you do if they take off?"

"Follow them. I'm not about to let those kids disappear."

"What if they're moving back to Bowling Green? Or fleeing to Canada?"

"Then I guess I'll follow them there."

He studied me, his eyes narrowed, so I calmly returned his gaze. Finally, he shook his head and muttered, "Stubborn woman." Leading Seedy to the door, he paused to say, "I'll be back in five minutes. Don't leave without me."

I turned away before he saw my elation. I had been hoping he'd say that.

After he and Seedy returned, we donned our black stakeout garb, packed some supplies in Marco's duffel bag, and headed out.

We sat in the Prius a few doors away from our target, not talking. Finally Marco said, "Can we call a truce?"

"As long as there's no pressure to hire Rosa."

"Hey, you're the boss at Bloomers. It's your call."

I turned toward him with a smile. "That's what I've been waiting for everyone to remember. I'll know when the time is right to hire more help."

"Truce?"

"Truce."

Marco held out his hand for me to shake. When I reached for it, he drew me into his arms instead. "I don't like it when we argue, Sunshine. It really does take the sunshine out of my life."

"I don't like it when we argue, either— *Ouch*. The console is digging into my ribs."

He released me and grabbed his binoculars. "I see movement."

I glanced toward the Joneses' house and saw a black-and-silver truck backing out of the driveway. "That's Mr. Paisley's truck. I recognize the Bears decal on the back."

"Who's Mr. Paisley?"

"The other janitor at the school where Norm works. I'll bet he asked to borrow the truck so they could move. I knew they were planning to leave tonight."

"Norm is driving, but I don't see anyone else in the truck." Marco put the binocs aside and started the car. "We'd better follow him."

We tailed Norm to a Walgreens drugstore and waited in an adjacent store's parking lot until he came out holding a small white bag. Marco adjusted his binoculars. "It's a prescription bag. He went for medicine."

"I'll bet it's for Bud. Sandra mentioned that he'd had a stomach upset. He must be worse."

"That should work in our favor. Hopefully they won't move while he's sick."

"I don't know, Marco. They have to be nervous."

"Nervous, yes, but don't think they don't know the law. They're not stupid, or they'd have been caught by now. They know that even if you'd reported them today, the cops wouldn't act that fast."

"Then why did they take off after Sergio's accident?"

"They weren't taking any chances of the cops figuring out what happened. What bothers me is the truck. Didn't you say that a black pickup truck nearly ran you down?"

"Yes, but I can't imagine Mr. Paisley being a part of that."

"You saw a small figure in a hooded jacket. Why couldn't that have been Sandra? Didn't you see her pick Norm up once before?"

"Oh, my God, Marco. It makes perfect sense. They wanted Sergio to die, so they went to the hospital to kill him. What could Sergio have seen that made him so dangerous?"

"We need to talk to those kids," Marco said.

We followed Norm home, then sat in our car until all the lights went out. Marco put on his black stocking cap and crept around their house trying to peer in the windows to make sure they weren't packing in the dark, but all the shades had been drawn.

"What do we do now?" I asked as Marco buckled his seat belt.

"Go home and figure out our next move."

CHAPTER TWENTY-THREE

Twelve a.m., Sunday

I sat on the sofa with Seedy on my lap, stroking her little head, as Marco checked everything in his duffel bag. He was wearing a light blue button-down shirt and black pants with his black leather jacket. He had with him a black baseball cap with the New Chapel Police emblem on it, a souvenir from his days on the force. I'd never seen him use it before, and he was only going to wear it now to intimidate one or both of the Joneses into talking to him later that day.

"Won't Sandra remember you from the day of the accident and know you're not a cop?" I asked.

"If she remembers me," Marco said, "she'll also remember that I was standing with Reilly the entire time. She'll assume I'm a plainclothes detective." He added two bottles of water and his revolver to the contents, then zipped up the duffel.

"Ready to go," he said. Like a panther, he was eager to track down his prey.

"I wish you'd let me come with you."

"There's no need for both of us to sit up all night, Buttercup. You get some sleep so at least one of us will be fully functioning tomorrow."

I'd never seen Marco not fully functioning, no matter how little rest he'd had. He'd trained for this type of action as a Ranger. I, on the other hand, was not a pleasant person to be around when I'd had less than seven hours of sleep. But this was *my* investigation, and even though I knew Marco was being considerate, I still wasn't happy about being left behind.

Our plan was for him to watch the Jones residence all night, and if they didn't attempt to flee, I'd meet him there in the morning. I would park on the next block in a church parking lot and join him in the Prius, where we'd wait for an opportunity to talk to Sandra alone. If that didn't happen by dusk, Marco was prepared to meet both of the Joneses head-on. Divide and conquer, basically. He'd keep Norm occupied while I worked on Sandra and the kids.

There were a lot of pieces of the plan that could go wrong, and for that reason I was already on edge as I kissed and hugged him good-bye. "Good luck. Text me if anything happens."

"I know the drill, babe. Go to bed. It's late."

I locked the door behind him and then stood at the front window watching as he drove away. My stomach gurgled uncomfortably, reminding me I'd eaten little that day.

"Okay, Seedy, let's hit the sack." I turned around and found her already asleep in her bed.

Tiptoeing past her, I put on my pajamas and crawled under the covers, then checked to be sure my phone wasn't on mute. I laid it on the nightstand, turned so I could grab it easily, and tried to fall asleep, but without Marco's steady breathing next to me, I didn't even get drowsy. I read my floral magazine until my eyelids drooped, then turned out the light and waited for sleep to overtake me. The only thing that overtook me were concerns that the plan would fail and the kids would disappear.

I did my relaxation exercise—deep, slow breaths like the tide coming in and going out—until I realized at some point I'd started counting the minutes since Marco had left. I switched to counting sheep, and when that got boring, I tried to name a flower that went with every letter of the alphabet. *X* was the toughest, but I eventually remembered the xanthorrhoea. And I was still wide awake, worries crowding out any chance of getting some shut-eye.

After two hours had passed. I texted Marco: *Everything ok?*

His reply came in immediately: *Ys. Go to slp.*

I was trying to *slp* but *slp* wasn't coming!

I dozed and woke, dozed and woke, looked at the clock and realized only two and a half more hours had passed.

Still ok? I texted.

No reply.

I stared at the small screen as if that would make him answer. I got out of bed, drank some water, and came back—and still no reply. Where was Marco? What if Norm had spotted him and now he was lying somewhere in the dark, mortally wounded? What if even now Norm had packed up Sandra and the kids and they were on their way to Canada?

I threw back the covers, ready to jump into my clothes and drive to their house, when my phone dinged. Whispering a prayer of thanks, I ran to grab it.

Still ok.

My thumbs were trembling as I typed in my reply: *Where were you?*

Reconnaissance. Why RU up? Slp!

If only.

At five in the morning, I gave up. Sleep was futile. I needed to be there with Marco.

After taking a shower and having a piece of toast with half a cup of coffee, I put on my black jeans and a black hooded sweatshirt. Underneath the sweatshirt was a yellow long-sleeved T-shirt with the Bloomers logo on the front and orange and pink daisies in a stripe down both sleeves. If our plan was successful and I had the opportunity to talk to the children, I would shed the sweatshirt. I needed to look as friendly as possible.

Originally, I had planned to take Seedy along, but Marco had dissuaded me. Even though she would act as a kid magnet, with only three legs, she might also be a liability if we had to leave fast. I wasn't about to take a chance with her safety.

As the sun came up, I parked the car in the church parking lot, then walked to the Joneses' street to find the Prius. It was at the far end of the block, kitty-cornered from their house. As I approached, I texted Marco so I didn't startle him.

I heard the doors unlock; then I slid into the passenger seat and put down my hood. "I couldn't sleep. I was too worried about you."

"Sorry, babe."

Even as bleary-eyed as I was, I couldn't help but notice his day's growth of beard—more of a twenty-four-hour shadow now. It made him look even sexier than usual.

He turned to gaze out the window. "There's been no activity whatsoever."

And that's the way it stayed until noon. By that time, my legs were stiff, my back hurt, and I was ravenous as well as thirsty. I couldn't imagine how Marco stood it. He had to be dehydrated from not drinking anything.

He pulled two energy bars out of the duffel bag and handed one to me. "I know it gets uncomfortable. This will help with the hunger."

We waited another hour, and then suddenly Mr. Paisley's pickup truck came backing down the driveway.

"It's Norm," Marco said, starting the engine. "He's by himself again. Let's see what he's up to this time."

"I'll stay here. I want to make sure Sandra doesn't leave with the kids."

"Then put your hood up. Don't draw attention to yourself."

"This isn't my first surveillance, Marco."

He looked at me askance. "I knew you should've slept. Just promise me you won't take any action until I get back unless it's to tail Sandra. I don't want to worry about you."

I sighed.

"I'll take that as a promise," he said, one corner of his mouth curving up in that devilish way of his. I couldn't help but smile.

"Nothing's going to happen to me, Marco. Don't worry."

We made sure no one was around and then I got out of the car and strolled in the opposite direction of the Joneses' house. I stopped at the corner to watch Marco drive away, then circled around the block and cut through the yard of the neighbors directly behind Sandra's until I reached the shabby picket fence that surrounded the yard. I heard a little girl singing and peered through the slats to see Daisy sitting at an old wooden picnic table in the backyard drawing.

It was eerily like my dream.

I wanted to climb the fence right then and talk to her, but I knew that would be unwise. Not only would I frighten her, but Sandra would undoubtedly intervene. I needed Marco to distract her.

Daisy in backyard, I texted. *Hurry.*

He texted back: *Gd news. Norm at bar wtchng Brs game. B there soon.*

I cut back through the neighbors' yard and walked around until Marco texted to meet him at the corner. He parked the car, put on his cap, stuck his revolver inside his jacket, and got out.

"Ready?"

I patted my pocket. "Swabs are right here, and I'll record with my phone. I'll wait around at the side of the house until you get inside. Then I'll slip through the back gate."

"Let's roll."

Because it was broad daylight, we couldn't sneak around the outside of the house to see where Sandra was, so Marco simply walked up to the front door, rapped on it hard, and called, "Mrs. Jones? Sandra Jones?" And rapped again, just like the cops did.

I was crouched behind a thick boxwood shrub at the side of the house, so I couldn't hear Sandra, but I knew she must have answered the door when Marco said, "I need to talk to you, ma'am. Please step outside."

He had the cop act down pat.

Then he said, "This is about the accident that happened at the New Chapel property you were renting. I'm going to need to ask you and your children a few questions."

Sandra must have argued that she didn't have to answer because Marco said, "No, I don't have a warrant. That will involve bringing back officers in uniform, and I don't think you want that kind of attention."

There was a long moment of silence and then I heard Marco say, "Thank you. This won't take long."

I sure hoped it wouldn't.

At the sound of the front door closing, I knew Marco had gone inside, so I scrambled out of the bushes, took off my sweatshirt, and peeked into the kitchen window on the side of the house. I didn't see anyone, and fortunately the neighbors' house didn't have a window on that side, so I was praying no one saw me. I opened the gate to the backyard and said in a friendly voice, "Hi, Daisy. Remember me? Abby?"

She looked up in surprise, then said excitedly as I approached, "Did you bring Seedy?"

"She's sleeping right now, but I brought photos of her. Where's Bud? I want to show him, too."

"He's in bed. He has a bad tummy ache."

That must have been the reason for Norm's trip to the pharmacy.

I sat down beside Daisy on the old wooden bench, feeling splinters catch the fabric of my jeans. I put my sweatshirt on the table and pulled out my phone. I wasn't sure how long Marco would be able to keep Sandra busy, so with little time to spare I scrolled to the photos I'd taken of Seedy playing with Seedling and let Daisy look at them.

That was when I noticed her picture—a stick figure drawing of a mom and dad, a boy and a smaller girl, and a dog. All of the people had black hair, so I assumed it was the Joneses. But was that the dog she claimed she had? The picture gave me an idea.

When she handed back my phone, I turned the camera on and placed it on the table to get an audio recording. I would've preferred a video recording, but I didn't want to frighten her by aiming the camera at her. Then I pointed to her picture. "Is this your dog?"

Daisy glanced up at the kitchen window, as though afraid Sandra was watching, which pulled my gaze up there, too. Seeing no one, she nodded.

"Would you remind me what your dog's name is?"

With another quick glance at the window, Daisy printed underneath the dog in green marker: *Buster*.

She was afraid to say it aloud. Sandra must have forbade her to talk about him. I needed to get her on tape, so I tried again, pointing to the boy. "Is this Bud?"

Daisy shook her head as she drew in blades of grass.

"Who is it, then?"

She looked at me with worried green eyes, nibbling her lip as though trying to decide whether to trust me.

"I won't tell anyone, Daisy. I promise."

With a look of determination, she printed underneath the figure: *Kevin*.

"Is Kevin your brother?"

She nodded.

"Where is Kevin now?"

She shrugged as she hunted through a box of colored markers, settling on brown.

I pointed to a figure with long hair. "Is this your mom?"

She nodded again. Had Daisy given her mother black hair to deceive Sandra? I checked my phone to make sure the app was still running. Somehow I needed to get her to talk.

"Daisy, yesterday you told me I looked like your mom. Would you tell me how I look like her?"

Wordlessly, she pointed to my hair and several freckles on my face, then continued to draw.

"But you drew your mom with black hair."

Still coloring, Daisy finally spoke. "I lost my red marker."

My heart missed a beat, then started to race as the puzzle pieces from both cases began to weave themselves together. "Where did you lose it, Daisy?"

Her gaze shifted to the window. Then she shrugged.

"Did you throw it out the window?"

She shook her head.

"Did Bud?"

With a scowl, Daisy pointed toward the kitchen window and said in an accusing voice, "*She* did."

I glanced up in alarm, but no one was there. "Your mom?"

Without looking this time, she said, "No. *Her*."

"Why did Sandra do that, Daisy?"

"Because I gave something to the man outside the window."

A chill ran through me as I pictured Sergio standing on the ladder in front of her. "What did you give him?"

She looked at me fearfully, her lower lip between her teeth.

"Draw it for me, Daisy."

She began to cry. "It was just a little one."

"It's okay. I won't tell anyone." I glanced at the window again. Time was growing short. "Draw it for me, please."

She turned her picture over and drew a five-inch square. Inside it she printed in block letters: *Help me.*

Oh, my God. Daisy had written the note in Sergio's pocket. He must not have known what to do with it, so he tucked it away, and Sam had mistaken his gesture for one of pain. "Why did you give the man that piece of paper, Daisy?"

She put her fists against her eyes and sobbed, "Because I want to go home."

As she rested her head on her arms and cried, I glanced at the window again, but thankfully no one was watching. Marco was doing a great job of keeping Sandra in the front of the house, but I knew he wouldn't be able to draw out his interview for much longer. I dug in my pocket for a folded tissue and pushed it into Daisy's hand. "I'll work very hard to make sure you get to your real home, Daisy. Dry your eyes now. You don't want Sandra to see you crying."

Gulping back the sobs that shook her little body, Daisy raised her head and gazed at me, her freckled face swollen and tear-streaked. "Will you take me home?"

"I'll see that you *get* home," I said.

"When?"

I was about to explain that the police would come for her when a big truck roared up the driveway and stopped near the gate.

Norm had returned.

I grabbed my phone and texted Marco: *Norm is here.*

His reply came seconds later: *Leave now.*

I stuffed the drawing and my phone in my pocket and rose, preparing to flee. Then I glanced up at the window and saw Sandra staring down at me with such a look of rage that I shuddered. I had to get out of there.

A terrifying thought stopped me. What would Sandra do to Daisy?

Leave now.

Unaware of Sandra, Daisy put her hand on my arm and gazed at me hopefully. "When?"

I shut my eyes to the image of Sandra glaring at me.

"When, Abby?"

The truck's door slammed.

It's now or never, Abby. Run!

I couldn't do it. I could not leave Daisy with the monsters inside that house. I wrapped my arms around her and scooped her up. *"Now."*

With the child clinging to my neck, I ran through the neighbors' yard to the other street and hurried to my car in the church parking lot, breathing so hard I thought my lungs would burst, realizing only belatedly that I'd left my sweatshirt behind. I buckled Daisy into the passenger seat and dashed around to the driver's side. Luckily, because the 'Vette sat low to the ground, Daisy would be invisible to anyone seeing my car drive past.

I texted Marco: *In the car.*

My phone rang instantly. I saw Marco's name on the screen, so I said, "Are you okay? Where are you?"

"Looking for you."

"I'm right around the corner at the church. Don't worry. I'm safe."

"No, Abby, you're not safe. Norm is looking for you, too."

Chapter Twenty-Four

"Stay where you are," Marco said. "I can't follow Norm too closely because he knows my car now, but I can tell you when the coast is clear. Then I want you to leave the area as fast as you can and get back to the highway. We can meet up at home. I'll alert Reilly about the situation."

I put my key in the ignition, then glanced into the rearview mirror, and my blood ran cold. "He's coming up the street toward the church, Marco. What should I do?"

"Duck."

I slid as far down as I could and leaned over the console. Fortunately, there were at least twenty cars parked in the lot. What were the odds Norm would look for me there?

"What are you doing?" Daisy asked in a frightened voice.

"I—dropped a pen on the floor by your feet. Would you help me find it?"

Marco continued to talk in my ear. "He doesn't know your car, so you should be okay as long as he doesn't spot your hair. Stay on the line while I phone Reilly."

Marco was gone before I could tell him that there was a high probability that Norm did know what kind of car I had. It hinged on whether he had recognized me Friday night outside the school. I raised my head and twisted around to see out the back window, then held my breath as the truck drove by.

He hadn't seen the 'Vette. I sagged against my seat, weak with relief.

Then I heard the screech of brakes. I twisted around again and saw the truck backing up.

With my heart thudding like a hammer, I started the engine, put my phone on speaker, dropped it into my lap, and threw the car in reverse. *Don't draw attention, Abby. Steady as she goes.* I glided around the side of the church to another parking lot in the rear, where I pulled up between two SUVs, the motor idling. I was shaking so hard my teeth were chattering.

"Abby?" I heard from my phone.

"I think he spotted me, Marco," I called. "I'm sitting behind the church. What should I do?"

"Don't panic. I'll distract him. Keep both hands on the wheel and get to the highway as fast as you can, then head to New Chapel. He won't follow you there. Pedal to the metal, sweetheart. You've got a race car, remember?"

Daisy was whimpering, cowering against her seat, hugging her little arms around herself. There was no way I could terrify her even more by speeding through town.

"I can't, Marco," I called. "I have a passenger."

"What are you talking about?"

"Daisy is with me."

The phone went silent. I could only imagine what Marco was thinking.

"Just get to the highway," Marco said at last. "I'll be right behind you."

I exited the church onto a side street and drove to the corner. When I didn't see Norm, I got back on the boulevard and headed south, then glanced in my mirror expecting to see Marco's Prius behind me. But it wasn't Marco. It was the black pickup coming up fast.

My heart skipped a beat. Had I been alone, I would've gunned the engine and left the truck in the dust, but I had Daisy to consider now. I had to go the speed limit, and that was making my tension worse. "Where are you, Marco?" I called.

"Right behind Norm. Just keep going the speed limit. He's trying to intimidate you. Turn left at the next corner."

Daisy began to cry softly. "I want my mommy."

"You're going to see her soon, Daisy. I promise."

With Norm nearly on my bumper, I made a left turn, drove to the next corner, and turned right, keeping my speed low, stopping at every stop sign, and clenching my jaw all the while. Under Marco's directions, I zigzagged through the city on unfamiliar roads, and still I couldn't shake the truck. The black behemoth filled my rearview mirror like an evil predator. Every time I glanced up, I could see Norm's big face, focused, furious, desperate to annihilate me.

My fingers tightened on the wheel. I was trying to stay calm, but Daisy's whimpers weren't helping. I had no idea where I was or how far the highway was. I glanced at the gas gauge and my stomach knotted. The tank was empty. I hadn't filled up the 'Vette in a week because I'd been so busy.

"Where are we?" Daisy whined.

"Heading to a safe place. Can you sing a song for me?"

"I can't. I'm too scared."

Me, too, I wanted to say.

After what seemed like hours, I finally caught sight of the highway ahead. Within minutes I veered into one of the double turning lanes so I could head east, then sat in the right lane behind a silver Taurus, my gaze fixed on my rearview mirror. I saw Norm swerve into the left-turn lane, and even though there was no one in front of him, he stopped right beside me. Then I saw Marco pull up behind me.

With white-knuckled intensity, I gripped the wheel and stared at the traffic light, willing it to change, too petrified to look over at Norm. What would I do if he tried to stop me? What was he planning? He had a clear view inside the 'Vette, so I knew he could see Daisy. Did he care? What if he had a gun and was even now taking aim?

I lifted my gaze to meet Marco's in the rearview mirror and said, "Marco, I don't have a good feeling about this."

"Listen to me, Sunshine," Marco said in a confident, calming voice. "Here's the plan. When the light turns green, I need you to stay in the right lane. I'm going to perform a police maneuver on Norm's vehicle that should stop him cold. When you see it happen, get into the left lane and take the cutoff onto the old country road that runs parallel with the highway. Do you know which road I'm talking about?"

"Yes."

"Good. That'll lead you straight into New Chapel."

I took a steadying breath. "Okay."

"Stay on the line while I alert Reilly to the change of plans. No matter what happens, follow the plan. Okay?"

"But what if something happens to you?"

"Abby," Marco said sharply, catching me off guard. When he called me by my first name, I knew he meant business. "No matter what happens, follow the plan. I can take care of myself. But I need to take care of you and Daisy first."

I looked down at Daisy, who had a grip on my knee over the center console.

"I'm going to call Reilly now," Marco said. "Stay on the line and follow the plan. You're doing a great job, sweetheart."

Tell that to my stomach.

The light changed, and I moved forward with traffic, turning behind the silver Taurus onto the three-lane highway. I glanced in my mirror and saw Marco's green car turn, then ease in behind the pickup. Surely Norm would give up now. He had to know I was heading out of Maraville.

The Taurus moved into the center lane in front of Norm, so I gave the 'Vette more gas and pulled ahead, finally able to increase my speed. Traffic was fairly heavy at first because I was approaching a big shopping mall, but at the next light most of the cars turned off, leaving only a few on the road. I glanced in the mirror and swore silently. The black pickup was back in my lane and gaining on me.

In my rearview mirror I saw Marco pull almost even with the pickup. The next time I glanced into the mirror,

I saw the Prius hit the truck's right rear side, causing it to spin around.

"Hold on to your seat," I told Daisy, stepping on the gas.

"Why? What's happening? I'm scared, Abby."

"Nothing to be scared about. I just need to go fast."

I saw the cutoff ahead, pushed my blinker down, and swerved left through two empty lanes. I was preparing to exit when my 'Vette suddenly choked and sputtered but thankfully continued on. I glanced at the fuel gauge. The needle hovered over empty. Thank God I wasn't too far from the New Chapel border now.

"We're almost there, Daisy."

I turned onto the narrow road that wound through a wooded section of the county, breathing freely for the first time. Any second now I would hear from my husband, letting me know I was in the clear.

But instead I heard the fuel indicator ding. I rounded a bend and saw a railroad crossing in the distance, its gates lowered and a train going by. I lifted my foot off the gas and coasted toward the tracks, praying the train would be gone by the time we reached the tracks.

But it wasn't. In fact, it seemed to be going slower. I stopped at the gates and shifted into neutral to save gas.

Suddenly the phone clicked, and I heard Marco. "My plan didn't work. He pushed me off the road and into a ditch. Did you take the cutoff?"

"Yes. Are you all right?"

"Fine. Don't worry. I alerted Reilly and he's on his way, so just keep going. Norm won't know where you are now."

"But is he still headed this way?"

There was silence for a moment. Then he said quietly, "Yes."

Damn.

"How close are you to New Chapel?" he asked.

"Not too far, but I'm stuck at a railroad crossing. Where are you?"

"Standing by my car."

I glanced up at my rearview mirror and saw a vehicle round the bend, still far behind me. It couldn't be Norm, I assured myself. There was no way he knew I'd turned off the highway. But as it drew closer, I could see that it was a dark color and too large to be a car.

"Marco, I think he's behind me again."

"Is there a house nearby you can go to?"

I glanced at my surroundings, survival instincts kicking in. To our left was an abandoned gas station and to the right miles of barren fields. With the train blocking my path, there was simply nowhere to go, nowhere to hide. "No. Nothing."

"Okay, stay in the car. Lock your doors."

My engine began to sputter and chug. I looked down at the fuel gauge just as the motor died. I tried to restart it, but it merely chugged some more. I checked the rearview mirror and saw the black monster coming up behind me. "Oh, God, Marco—it's him."

"The New Chapel Police are headed your way, Abby."

"They can't get through. The train's still there."

"Can you see the end of it?"

"No."

Daisy began to cry, her small body shaking in terror. "I want to go home."

"Can you make a three-point turn?" Marco called.

I watched in absolute dread as the pickup stopped behind me, so close we had to be touching. "He's getting out of the truck, Marco. Oh, God. He has a baseball bat."

Through my side-view mirror I saw Norm slam the truck door, his large face twisting into a grin. He walked up slowly, pounding the bat in his palm.

"Don't worry, Daisy," he called. "Daddy is here."

I was trapped in a nightmare that wouldn't end. "He's going to smash in my window."

"Get down! Cover your head!"

I grabbed Daisy over the center console and pulled her under me. I had promised her I would take her home. I had promised her I would keep her safe. Now I'd put both of our lives in jeopardy.

I held her and began to pray, expecting at any moment to hear the impact and feel the shards of glass on my back. Ten agonizing seconds passed . . . Then twenty, thirty . . .

Nothing happened. I stopped praying and listened.

Were those sirens? My heart was pounding so loudly and Daisy was crying so hard that I couldn't be sure.

I waited another interminable few seconds, then lifted my head just enough to see over my shoulder. Norm was standing next to my window, baseball bat in hand, staring straight ahead. I looked forward as he did, and through the train cars caught glimpses of flashing red and blue lights. The police were on the other side of the tracks.

Norm turned to me and we locked eyes.

He bent down, his body filling my entire window, his gaze now upon Daisy. "Don't you want to come home with Daddy?" he asked in a sickeningly sweet voice.

"Come on, honey. Hurry now so no one gets hurt. Open the door and come with Daddy."

Daisy lifted her head and with a determination and cheekiness that astounded even me, she said, "You're not my daddy."

"But you *are* out of luck." I pointed toward the train just as the last car rolled past.

Norm glanced toward the crossing and, with a curse, ran back to his truck and started the engine. I sat up and twisted around, still holding Daisy, and watched as he backed up. My relief was so overwhelming, I began to laugh and cry at the same time. I found my phone on the floor and grabbed it with trembling hands. "Marco, he's leaving. He saw the cops across the tracks and it scared him off."

"Thank God you're safe," Marco said.

"Tell Reilly to stop him!" I called.

Daisy shouted, "And her car is broken, too."

"Your car is broken?" Marco called.

I let out a shaky breath. "No, it's just . . . could you ask Reilly to bring me some gas?"

Chapter Twenty-Five

Marco and I stood on the other side of a one-way glass window, watching as a female psychologist questioned Daisy. They were seated at a table in the police station's interview room. Daisy was drawing with crayons.

Once I'd gotten a few gallons of gas in my car, the police had escorted us back to the station, where I was given a cup of strong coffee for my nerves and Daisy was given a bottle of flavored water that one of the officers had stashed in the refrigerator. It hadn't been easy to get Daisy to let go of my hand, but she had finally agreed to sit with the psychologist as long as I promised to stay just outside.

Reilly came to give us an update. "Norman Jones is being booked into our jail even as we speak, and Maraville PD has already brought in Sandra and the boy. I faxed over our file on Brody Dugan, and they're in the process of locating his parents."

"That's going to be rough on Bud," I said. "The only parents he's ever known are Sandra and Norm. His real parents will be strangers to him."

"It *will* be rough," Reilly said, "for him and his parents. But they'll have a psychologist working with both sides before they're reunited, so don't worry."

"What about Daisy's parents?" I asked.

"I haven't heard whether they were located," Reilly said.

"What will happen if they aren't found?" I asked.

"The Department of Child and Family Services will place her in a foster home," Reilly said. "I'll check back with you in a while to see how she's doing."

After he was gone, I said, "I wouldn't do that to Daisy, Marco. She's traumatized enough as it is."

"It wouldn't be up to us, Abby."

"I don't care. I will not let her go to a strange home. She can come home with us."

"We'd have to get special permission from a judge and—"

"Then we'll do it."

"It's not that easy, babe."

The psychologist came outside. "I'm sorry to interrupt, but I'm not getting anywhere with Daisy. She refuses to talk to me. She wants Abby."

I looked at Marco and raised my eyebrows as though to say, *See?*

I opened the door and Daisy looked around in alarm. Seeing me, she scooted back her chair and ran to throw her arms around my waist, pressing herself as close to me as she could.

"It's okay," I said. "I'm here now."

We sat down again, and Daisy slid a blank piece of typing paper in front of me, placing the box of crayons between us. "Now you can draw, too."

I began to draw flowers, watching out of the corner of my eye as she made her familiar stick drawings, but this time her mother figure had red hair. Sandra was literally out of the picture. We continued drawing in silence for a good fifteen minutes. I hadn't felt so relaxed in weeks, and I understood a little better why my mom valued her art time.

As I put the finishing touches on a bouquet, I noticed I had an audience.

"Are those flowers from your flower shop?" Daisy asked.

"Yep. They're daisies. I made them for you."

"They're pretty." She reached for a different color crayon. "That's not my real name."

"What's your real name?"

Beneath the smallest stick figure she printed: DAPHNE

"Daphne," I read aloud. "I like it."

"Daphne?" I heard someone say behind me.

We both turned in surprise. A redheaded woman stood in the doorway. A redheaded man stood just behind her.

Daisy stared at them for a long moment. Then she whispered, *"Mommy,"* as though she couldn't believe what she was seeing.

"It's her!" the woman cried with a sob, turning toward the man. "It's our baby."

And then Daisy shoved back her chair, crying, "Mommy! Daddy!" Clutching her drawing in her hand, she ran toward them, propelling herself into both their arms at once.

Amid tears of joy and relief, they hugged and kissed her, stroking her hair and gazing at her as though they couldn't absorb their great fortune. I felt I was witnessing a miracle. They had their daughter back at last.

Holding Daisy as though afraid of losing her again, her parents thanked me profusely and then asked to thank Marco, too, so I called him into the room. When one of the detectives came to take them to see the psychologist, I followed them into the hallway, wiping tears off my face as I watched them walk away, each holding one of Daisy's hands, one of which still clutched her drawing. Halfway up the hall, Daisy tugged her parents to a halt, released their hands, and ran toward me.

"This is for you," she said breathlessly, handing me her picture. Then she spun around and ran back to her mom and dad. Just before they turned the corner, Daisy paused to wave good-bye to me. And then she was gone, just like her phony name.

I could barely see the image she'd drawn for all the tears in my eyes, but there on the paper were her four stick figures—a man with black hair, a woman with red hair, a girl with red hair, and a dog . . . with three legs! Beneath each figure she'd printed a name: *Marco. Abby. Daphne. Seedy*. They were all enclosed in a big red heart.

I couldn't speak.

Marco put his arms around me and said quietly in my ear, "You're *my* hero today, Sunshine."

Chapter Twenty-Six

Monday

The start of the week and the end of a nightmare.

Mondays were always special in my book, and today was extra special because Lottie had decided to throw a celebration breakfast in my honor. She'd arranged to have it at Down the Hatch and set the time bright and early so that my mom could attend before she headed off to school. It was definitely early but not at all bright. A nasty thunderstorm had rolled in overnight and continued with a constant downpour. Yet not even that could bring me down today.

I looked around the bar, watching as my family and friends filled the booths. Besides Lottie, Grace, Marco, and me, both of my parents were there, along with Marco's brother Rafe and, running in on the highest of heels with a newspaper over her head, the knockout Rosa. Marco's mom had to decline because of her babysitting duties and Sergeant Reilly was still a no-show, but my niece Tara was there, standing at my side, still half asleep but asking why she hadn't been invited to my stakeout.

"After what happened the last time you got involved," I said quietly, recalling with a shudder how we'd been trapped in a garage attic while killers plotted below us, "I'm surprised you're allowed within one hundred feet of me."

She waved the concern away like a pesky fly. "My parents are so over that now."

"Yeah, right." I sat on the first stool at the bar, my mouth watering at the spread in front of me. There was an egg-and-sausage casserole, a pile of thick cinnamon French toast with a pitcher of warm maple syrup beside it, a platter of crispy bacon, a basket of Grace's blueberry scones, a bowl of fresh strawberries, a dish of clotted cream, and plenty of coffee and tea. My stomach growled in anticipation. I hadn't had a decent meal in days.

But first Marco wanted to speak. "Of course you all know why we're here. We're celebrating my little hero." He put his arm around me.

"I believe he means *heroine*," Grace whispered, loud enough to be heard by all.

"My little heroine," Marco amended, "for solving not only one, but two cases." He glanced around the room. "I was hoping Sean Reilly would be here for this. He saved Abby and deserves to be honored, too."

Continuing, he said, "My wife's determination and courage not only pinpointed Sergio Marin's killer but also successfully reunited two missing children with their parents."

With that announcement came a round of joyful applause. I gave everyone a grateful smile and soaked in that wonderfully satisfying feeling of accomplishment. I couldn't help but think of Daisy and Bud—or rather

Daphne and Brody—those two little troupers who deserved more applause than anyone.

"I'm still in shock that the children were discovered living so close to their real parents," Mom said.

"It happens more often than you'd think," Marco said. "They're very fortunate that Abby sensed something was wrong right from the start."

"Hear, hear," Dad called, starting more applause. "That's my Abracadabra."

Basking in their admiration, I was about to stand and thank everyone for coming—and suggest we eat—when Grace came up and patted the stool next to mine. "Rosa, come sit beside our Abby. This breakfast is for you, too, dear."

What?

When she was seated, Marco said, "Sergeant Reilly wanted to share some news with you, Rosa, but"—he checked his watch—"since he's apparently otherwise occupied, I'll stand in for him.

"As many of you already know," he began, "the Maraville Police have Sandra Jones in custody. We've just received word that she will be brought to the county jail in New Chapel tomorrow and will be arraigned later this week. The DA told Reilly that she will most likely be charged with manslaughter."

Rosa's eyes welled with tears as she made the sign of the cross. Then, fingering the lightning bolt pendant as though drawing strength from it, she said in a choked voice, "Thank you for letting me know."

Grace put her hand on Rosa's shoulder. "We are here for you, love, and will support you through any upcoming ordeal in whatever way we can."

With a wavering smile, Rosa said, "I am very grateful, Grace. And thank you again, Abby. You have helped me more than you will ever know." She put her arms around me and gave me a long hug. Then she reached for Marco and hugged him, too.

Looking at everyone, she pressed her hands against her heart and said, "I know my Sergio thanks you, too. I only wish he would give me a sign."

"Perhaps he's waiting for just the right time, dear," Grace said.

She sighed. "I hope so."

At that, the front door blew open with a great gust of wind. Everyone gasped until Jillian lumbered in, her flawless hair and outfit protected by an oversized clear vinyl bubble umbrella carried by her dutiful husband, Claymore.

I was guessing *that* wasn't the sign Rosa was waiting for.

"Here we are, here we are!" Jillian cried, coming into the bar while Claymore shook the umbrella out outside, his fastidious brown suit soaking up the rain. "I hope you didn't start without us."

I glanced at Marco in surprise. "You invited Jillian?"

"I didn't invite her. She asked to come."

"We're just about to dig in," Lottie told her. "Grab plates, you two."

"I have an announcement to make first," Jillian said. She went to the front of the bar and rapped on the counter with an empty coffee cup to get everyone's attention. As if she needed more attention.

"As everyone knows," Jillian began, "Abby and Marco have been on an unsuccessful house hunt ever since they got married—" She put her hand to the side of her mouth to add, "Until I came into the picture." Then she resumed in a normal voice, "There was only one house that they really loved, but it sold before they could put in their bid. So . . ." She turned to Marco.

"So," he said, looking at me with a smile, "I bought a lot in the same neighborhood."

My mouth fell open. "We're going to build?"

"Yes, you are," Jillian said, hands supporting her huge belly. "And I am the magic that made it happen."

"We've got the best site in the development, babe," Marco said. "It has a southern exposure and backs up to the park, and the house will have all the features that you liked in the model."

I was overcome with happiness. My dream house! I was going to get my dream house after all. Despite the storm raging outside, it was suddenly sunny and warm in my heart. I could've sworn I even heard the happy twittering of birds. "Can we get granite countertops? And stainless steel appliances? And wood floors?"

"Whatever my Sunshine wants," Marco said. But upon seeing the twinkle in my eye, he added, "Within our budget."

I threw my arms around him. "Marco, I can't express how happy this makes me."

"And in just five short months, you can move in," Jillian said.

The sun sank. The birds fled. Five months! In my excitement, I'd totally forgotten that part. "Where will we live in the meantime, Marco?"

"We've got it all arranged, Abigail," Mom called.

"You're going to move in with us! You can even have your old bedroom back. Just think of the fun we'll have cooking together, buying groceries together, cleaning the house on the weekends . . . It'll be just like when you were growing up. And you can even help me with my art projects."

"All thanks to me," Jillian said.

I was speechless. I was aghast. I was going to kill Jillian.

"Aren't you excited?" Marco asked.

"Oh, yes," was all I could manage.

"Oh, no," Jillian said.

Everyone turned her way.

"Oh, no," she said again, and this time it was followed by a grimace and a moan.

"Oh, damn," Claymore said.

"Seriously, Jillian?" I said. "Again?"

"How many times have I told you I can't control it?" Jillian said, grabbing on to her husband's arm as another contraction hit. Through gritted teeth she said, "It's only been two minutes since the last one."

"Two minutes?" Lottie cried. "Bring the car around, Claymore. Hurry."

"No rush. It's false labor again," I said, but no one was listening.

While Claymore dashed across the street in the pouring rain, Marco and Rafe helped Jillian move slowly to the door. "I still haven't decided on a name," she moaned.

"Trust me, everyone," I said, walking toward her, "she'll have plenty of time for that. She's not having her baby."

Jillian paused at the door to snap, "And you know this because?"

"Because your water hasn't broken."

And right on cue, there was a gush that made a puddle between her shoes.

"Ew!" Tara cried, turning away. "I woke up early for this?"

"Let's get you into the car, Jillian," Marco said.

"Wait! Hand me my umbrella! I don't want to get my hair wet."

As the brothers took her by her elbows and practically carried her to the car, Lottie said, "Poor thing doesn't have a clue as to what's about to happen to her, does she, Maureen?"

"Oh, heavens no," Mom said. "My firstborn had such a big head that—"

"Grandma, stop!" Tara cried, putting her fingers in her ears. "Don't gross me out even more!"

"Everyone, make sure your cell phones are on," Dad called. "We don't want to miss Claymore's call."

"Here's to a safe delivery," Lottie said, raising her coffee cup, prompting everyone to do the same, "and to a healthy mom and baby."

Once everything had settled down, Grace stood up at the front and said, "Our lovely food is growing cold. Shall we eat?"

It was about time. My stomach was starting to eat itself.

Rosa, who was nearby, turned to us and said, "I would love to stay and have breakfast with you, but I have an interview with the social service agency in half an hour, so I will just take time for a cup of coffee. But thank you again from my heart. I appreciate everything you have done for me."

"You're very welcome, love," Grace said. "Do take a scone with you for later, and perhaps one for Petey as well."

"Thank you," she said, and moved off to get some coffee.

As I began to pile food onto my plate, Grace tapped me on the shoulder and tilted her head toward the hallway. I followed her into Marco's office, where Lottie and my mom were waiting. Something was up.

Lottie spoke first. "We were wondering whether you'd thought any more about hiring Rosa."

"Actually," I said, "I ruled it out."

"Why?" Mom asked.

"I just don't think she'd be a good fit."

All three women objected at once, talking over one another until Marco appeared in the doorway behind them. "Rosa's about to leave," he said, closing the door so we wouldn't be overheard. He nodded toward the women and said to me, "Why don't you tell them what you told me?"

They gazed at me expectantly. Marco gave me a nod of encouragement.

Now I had two choices: either dig in my heels and say no, end of story, or satisfy their curiosity as to why. If I wanted to fill the cavern in my stomach anytime soon, I knew what I had to do.

"Okay, fine. I'll tell you why, but I want you to know this isn't easy for me."

"Tell us, sweetie," Lottie said.

"Here's the thing." I drew in a steadying breath and let it out. Enumerating on my fingers, I said, "Rosa is drop-dead gorgeous, speaks two languages, has great people skills, and is smart, creative, and talented. Am I forgetting anything?"

"She sells my art," Mom supplied.

"Thank you," I said. "She can sell anything. And now you want to make her a florist, too."

"So?" Lottie asked.

"So—" I shrugged. "Then there's me. I'm a florist. Just—a florist."

"Ah," Grace said. "I believe I understand." She moved into lecture pose, hands in front of her, fingers interlaced, shoulders back. "As that most brilliant bard William Shakespeare quipped in *The Merchant of Venice*, 'As doubtful thoughts, and rash-embraced despair, and shuddering fear, and green-eyed jealousy!' "

Mom opened her arms and embraced me. "Honey, you're not jealous of poor Rosa, are you?"

"A little bit," I said, not wanting to meet her gaze.

"Oh, sweetie, why?" Lottie asked.

"For the reasons I just named. Rosa makes me feel"—I let out a breath—"inadequate."

"Inadequate?" Mom asked.

"You say that like you've forgotten I flunked out of law school," I said dryly.

Mom gave Marco a quizzical look. He responded with a shrug and a look that said, *I tried to tell her.*

"Sweetie," Lottie said, "you're letting negative thoughts control you. Remember what I said about thinking positive? Okay, just look at all the blessings in your life.

Look at that handsome man behind you. Look around at everyone who cares about you. Look down the street at the pretty little flower shop with the bright yellow door. And think about that sweet little three-legged mutt who is waiting eagerly for you. See what I mean? You don't need to be jealous of Rosa."

Now I felt ridiculous and small-minded. But everything Lottie had said hit home. Sometimes I simply needed a good kick in the pants to remind me of how blessed I was. I'd just have to get over my feelings of inadequacy.

I drew another deep breath and let it out. "Okay, I'll do it."

"That's my Fireball," Marco said.

"We're proud of you, Abigail," Mom said. "You're doing the right thing."

But I was doing it reluctantly. Did that still count toward goodness?

"Let's go finish breakfast now," I said, standing up. "I'm starving. Lottie, will you inform Rosa before she leaves?"

"Why don't we send Rosa in now and let you talk to her?" Grace asked.

I whispered to Marco, "Isn't it enough that I've agreed to hire her?"

Marco tweaked my hair. "Just do it. You'll feel better for it."

I wasn't so sure. I simply couldn't imagine Rosa as part of the Bloomers team.

They filed out and in a minute Rosa peered around the door. "You wanted to see me?"

"Please come in." I indicated Marco's leather sling-backed chairs in front of his desk. "Let's sit."

She sat down and leaned forward eagerly. "Do you have more news for me?"

"Rosa, how would you like to become a florist?"

"Perdón?"

"How would you like to work at Bloomers and learn the floral business?"

She stared at me, wide-eyed. "You want me to work with you every day?"

"Well, it would still be part-time, but yes, every day. You can't really learn much working a few hours twice a week, and you said you need the income. So you can start whenever you'd like, but as you know, we're short-handed, so the sooner the better."

She fingered her pendant nervously. "You are certain that you want me to work with *you*?"

I had to take another deep breath. "Yes."

She stood up and began to pace, clasping her fingers together and muttering something in Spanish that sounded like a prayer, obviously overwhelmed by her great fortune. When she reached the door on her second round, she turned to face me.

"No."

I was so stunned, all I could say was, "What?"

"Look at you," she said with a sweeping gesture. "How could I work for you? You are talented and beautiful and smart. You understand how to run a business. You catch *los criminales* and find missing children. You create the most beautiful floral arrangements I have ever seen. Next to you, I feel so . . . *estúpida*. How can I ever hope to live up to you?"

Rosa felt stupid next to me?

"Come." She took my arm and led me up the hallway until we were standing just inside the bar area. "Now look around. Do you see? Your family is here to celebrate all that you have accomplished. And what have I accomplished?"

"But, Rosa, you can learn. Think . . . positive."

"You say that now. But what if I can't?" She clasped her necklace again and said with a heavy sigh, "If only my Sergio were here, he would tell me what to do. He would give me the strength I need to make this decision. But for now I just don't know." Taking my hands in hers, she said, "Thank you for the offer. I will always treasure it."

Just then Reilly pushed his way through the bar's front door. "Sorry I'm late, but we had a little mishap out in the county because of the storm." He took off his soaking overcoat and brushed his hair back. "Not to worry, though. No one was hurt. Just a lone trailer that burned down."

I met Marco's gaze. We both glanced at Rosa and almost in unison asked, "Whose trailer?"

"Guy by the name of Jericho. I think you know him, Marco," Reilly said. "Very weird, though. Lightning struck his trailer and burned it to cinders. Even with all this rain."

"My sign!" Rosa cried, clutching her necklace. "*El relámpago.* My Sergio is here!" She began to cry big tears of joy. "Didn't I tell you that he would burn Jericho's house to the ground?"

She turned and wrapped her arms around me. "This was my sign. Now I know this is what my husband wants for me. I would love to work with you, Abby Knight Salvare."

My heart swelled with affection for this woman who really was like me. I held her close and whispered in her ear, "Welcome to Bloomers, Rosa."

AVAILABLE NOVEMBER 2015 FROM OBSIDIAN

FLORIST GRUMP

A Flower Shop Mystery

By *New York Times* bestselling author

Kate Collins

Flower shop owner Abby Knight wishes she had time to stop and smell the roses, but stress has turned her into a major grump. She and her new husband, Marco, are living with her parents, who drive her nuts. Her cousin, Jillian, just had a baby—who is the subject of every conversation—and Marco's mom keeps dropping hints that she wants a grandbaby of her own—now.

But life gets even thornier when a flashy former banker pushes up daisies. After a beloved window washer becomes the prime suspect in the murder, other New Chapel shop owners rally around Abby and Marco to prove his innocence. With Abby's energy wilting, she has to be alert as ever—or she and Marco may never make it out of her parents' house alive.

Available wherever books and ebooks are sold or at penguin.com

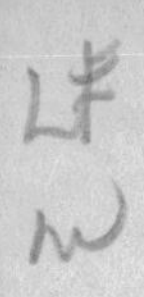

Mum's the Word
Slay It with Flowers
Dearly Depotted
Snipp
Ac
A Rose
Sh
Evil
Sleepin
Dirty
Night of th
To
Nightsh
Seed No Evil
Throw in the Trowel

"A sharp and funny heroine."
—Maggie Sefton

Available wherever books are sold or at
penguin.com

S914